HAWK OF THE WEST

PALACE OF THE ORNAMENTS
BOOK SIX

KYLIE QUILLINAN

First published in Australia in 2024.

ABN 34 112 708 734

kyliequillinan.com

A catalogue record for this book is available from the National Library of Australia.

Ebook ISBN: 9781922852403

Paperback ISBN: 9781922852410

Large print ISBN: 9781922852793

Hardback ISBN: 9781922852427

Audiobook ISBN: 9781922852496

This is a work of fiction. Any similarity between the characters and situations within its pages and places or persons, living or dead, is unintentional and coincidental.

Cover art by 100 Covers

Edited by MS Novak

This work uses Australian spelling and grammar.

LP09122024

CHAPTER 1

*W*hen Pharaoh summoned me to dine with him, it was in the same chamber as he always used when he visited the Palace of the Ornaments. It was just the two of us this time, plus the serving women, and Sehener who had accompanied me. He had barely spoken since his arrival and I was relieved when dinner was served because he would be too busy eating to wonder why I wasn't making conversation.

"Have you received any messages from Ishtar?" I asked Pharaoh after we had eaten in silence for some time.

I shouldn't have said it. I didn't even know why I did, except perhaps I wanted him to tell me she was well and to see in my face that I knew he lied.

"Who?" He glanced at me briefly before he returned to shovelling food into his mouth.

"My sister," I said.

If he remembered her, he gave no sign of it.

I forced myself to maintain my silence after that. It was clear his Favourites were only such for as long as it suited him. Then they became nobody. Just another woman whose name he had forgotten, even if he hadn't quite forgotten her face or her body. After all, how could any man forget my beautiful sister's face quite so easily as he might forget her name?

We passed the rest of the meal in silence, which seemed strained, to me, at least. Pharaoh probably didn't notice, too intent as usual on filling his belly. I picked at my meal, eating a bite here and there, but mostly only pretending to eat. My back ached, and I long to stand and stretch, but didn't dare rise while Pharaoh still ate. A serving woman refilled his goblet three times. She glanced at mine, but made no move towards it since I had taken only a sip or two.

At last, Pharaoh grunted and pushed away his plate. Goblet in hand, he lumbered back to the couch. I restrained my sigh. It seemed the rest of the evening would pass the way it had begun: with Pharaoh's hand latched firmly to my thigh. At least the advanced state of my pregnancy should mean he had little desire to bed me tonight.

As I sat beside him and tried to pretend his fingers weren't wandering my leg, my mind filled with thoughts I definitely shouldn't have in his presence if I wanted to avoid saying the wrong thing. Thoughts of women he had killed: my sister, the Ornament Nebtu, Khaemmalu's wife Tabiry. Others who had suffered at his hands even if they lived past the encounter: Hilde, Tiye, and, I suspected, Henutmire. Fury stirred within me and I pushed the thoughts away. No good could come of thinking such things in Pharaoh's presence.

"Your father is being most unreasonable," he said suddenly. "Some nonsense about a new trade deal."

I froze. My mind was blank and I had no idea how to

respond. How could he be thinking of something so mundane while I thought about my dead sister?

"Well?" he demanded. "Do you have nothing to say to that?"

I stammered, still searching for a response. Anything. You murdered my sister. Not that. Anything but that.

"My lord." It was all I could think of. Words. I needed other words.

Warmth pulsing at my wrist burst through my tangled thoughts. The Eye of Horus pendant. It lay flat against my skin and an unusual heat emanated from it. The warmth calmed me, stilling my mind, and suddenly words — appropriate words — came to me.

"I am sure whatever my father has requested is to the benefit of both Egypt and Babylon," I said. "Father does nothing without much consideration and good reason."

Pharaoh grunted and gulped the last of his wine. He held up his goblet and a serving woman swiftly appeared with a bottle. She refilled the goblet and backed away, careful to keep her behind out of his reach. Pharaoh took another swallow, then rested the goblet on his knee. He lapsed into silence.

I focussed my attention on the pendant at my wrist, trying to notice nothing but its warmth. Not the unbearable oaf of a man who sat beside me. Not the way his fingers pinched and prodded. Not the indecently loud slurps when he drank, nor the way he gasped for breath even when he did nothing other than sit and grope my thigh.

The pendant had protected me, just like Neferu said it would. It calmed me enough to formulate a reply before Pharaoh became angered at my lack of response. Tonight would not end the way our game of *senet* had, with me fleeing the chamber, convinced he was either chasing after me or sending guards to haul me back for punishment.

The remainder of the evening passed in a predictable way. Pharaoh drank and grunted, burped and farted. I sat beside him, forcing myself to maintain my silence, and trying to pretend I didn't feel his fingers digging into my leg. I kept my attention on the pendant and, sometimes, the ache in my back. At least it gave me something else to think about. Eventually, after what seemed like an interminable length of time, he gave one last grunt, set his goblet down beside him on the bench, and got to his feet.

He strode across the chamber without even so much as a farewell to me. His goblet toppled over to land on its side. A few drops of wine flowed out and seeped into the golden fabric of the cushion. Just one more thing Pharaoh discarded without thought when he tired of it.

CHAPTER 2

I waited until the door closed behind Pharaoh before I rose from the bench. It seemed I had managed to avoid angering him this time. I had also yet again avoided him bedding me, a situation which would likely change as soon as my son was born. Pharaoh would, of course, want to get another child on me as soon as possible.

My cheeks heated and I pushed the thought from my mind. How I would tolerate his hands on me again, I didn't know. Not now I had experienced what it was like to be with a man who actually cared for me. A memory of Khaemmalu came to me: his body on mine, the warmth of his skin seeping into me. The gentleness of his hands as he caressed me. My cheeks burned furiously and must surely be visible to anyone who cared to notice.

As I crossed the chamber, I met Sehener's eyes. She stood with her back against the wall while she waited for me. She raised her eyebrows, presumably asking whether I was ready to leave. I tipped my head towards the door and kept walking. There was no need to wait for her. She would follow me, and at least if she was behind me, she wouldn't see my heated cheeks.

The door opened as I reached it and it was Bebi who waited there. He gave me a nod, nothing but cool professionalism.

"Good evening, my lady," he said.

I nodded back. Nobody would think it odd if I made no reply to a servant and it was better I did nothing to make someone wonder just how well I knew him. If anyone spent too long thinking about Bebi, they might remember his friendship with Khaemmalu, which was surely no secret amongst the guards, and that might lead them to wonder if I knew Khaemmalu as well as I knew Bebi.

Unlikely, perhaps, but I would do nothing to risk my affair with Khaemmalu being uncovered. Especially now, when the memory of Hydna's liaison with the butler Weren was so fresh in everyone's minds, and the sting of their supposed execution still painful. Panouk had hinted there was more to their fate than anyone realised, leading me to suspect he may have surreptitiously intervened.

Regardless, I wouldn't risk either my life or Khaemmalu's. Nor my son's, for that matter. Not now when he was no more than a few weeks from being birthed.

It wasn't until I emerged into the hallway that I realised the rest of Pharaoh's squad had already left, gone with him to wherever he went, back to his palace, presumably.

Since there was nobody nearby, I expected Bebi might say something else, but he only looked straight ahead as he closed the door behind me.

"Bebi, are you well?" I asked.

"Quite well, my lady."

His tone was courteous but offered no invitation for

continued conversation, leaving me confused. He had been kind to me when we met previously. Friendly, even. And Khaemmalu had asked him to watch out for me.

"Has something happened?" I kept my voice low, although few folk traversed the hallways this late and none were in sight.

Bebi didn't even look at me.

"I am sure you have heard the news," he said, rather stiffly. "Many folk in both palaces keep secrets, and it would be wise for all concerned to be entirely above suspicion."

He meant the discovery of Hydna and Weren's affair. Bebi knew about me and Khaemmalu.

"Of course." I tried, and probably failed, to make my voice sound natural in case someone overheard us. "It is truly terrible news. We are all shocked."

"Indeed," was Bebi's only reply.

As it seemed he intended to say nothing further, I didn't push him. Sehener followed me out of the chamber and offered Bebi a quiet thank you, presumably for holding the door open for her as well.

My lower back ached fiercely and I rubbed my fists against it. I would be pleased to get back to my chambers and sit down again. Sehener said nothing as we walked. She had been so excited to come with me, her first time accompanying me in Pharaoh's presence. I thought she might have some comment to make, even if it was only that she hadn't realised how unpleasant he was.

We were halfway to my chambers when my stomach spasmed. It felt like the cramps I usually had just before my monthly bleed. I cradled my belly and tried not to panic. I hadn't bled since Pharaoh lay with me. I shouldn't bleed again until after my son was born. That wouldn't be for a few weeks, though.

"My lady?" Sehener asked. "Is something wrong?"

I shook my head, too busy trying to breathe through the pain to have anything left in me to reply.

The knowledge that my son would be born in no more than a month or so filled me with both fear and longing. I feared the act of childbirth, and for the survival of both me and my son, but who or what I longed for was less clear to me. Ahmose and her wisdom, perhaps. My mother, or maybe even my sister, although she had never borne a child and probably knew no more than me about such things. I wished I had a woman experienced in childbirth to guide me through these last few weeks before my son's arrival. I would be less afraid if I had such counsel.

CHAPTER 3

As we reached my chambers, the pain in my belly eased and my aching back subsided. The babe was still restless, but perhaps he felt my discomfort. I patted my stomach, hoping to soothe him, but another cramp, even more excruciating than the last, enveloped my belly.

"My lady, are you well?" Sehener's alarm at my groan was evident.

I nodded, too breathless to reply as I doubled over, clutching my belly.

"Should I send for a healer?" she asked.

"No, no." My voice was little more than a gasp. "I am—"

Before I could finish, warmth trickled down between my legs and splashed onto the tiles. I froze. It was too soon.

Sehener ran the last few steps and pounded on the door. It promptly opened a crack and Ettu peered out at us.

"Marduk!" she gasped and flung the door wide open.

She and Sehener took hold of my arms and led me across the chamber. They helped me lie on a couch just as another cramp gripped my belly. I groaned.

"What in Marduk's name has happened?" Ettu asked.

Faces peered down at me, but they blurred together and I couldn't quite make out who they were. The edges of the chamber dimmed and I knew nothing other than the pain. Something was wrong. It was too early.

"Send for a healer," someone said. "And the royal physician."

"Quickly," someone else said. "You must go."

Some of the faces disappeared.

A door slammed, voices whispered, someone's hand on my forehead.

"Is it the babe?" someone asked.

"How early is it?"

"A few weeks. A month at most."

"Early, but not so early…" The rest of whatever they meant to say went unsaid.

"All will be well." The voice was calm and confident.

A knock at the door.

"Some space please." A new voice. "How far along is she?"

Voices murmured. Opinions were offered. Their words flowed over me. I was a rock in the middle of a stream. The current passed by me, over me, around me, but it never affected me. I understood the individual words, but their collective meaning eluded me. It didn't matter. I was a rock.

"Did you say something, my lady?"

More words that meant nothing. A hand touched my arm. Cold fingers. They trembled.

"My lady? What did you say about a rock?"

I hadn't realised I said anything out loud.

"It's nothing," I said, or I tried to. The words stuck in my throat as another cramp grasped my belly. I groaned.

"Hot water, if you please." The new voice again. The healer. "And plenty of linens. Help me undress her."

My gown was removed with remarkable speed. My wig was already gone. Someone fumbled with the cord around my wrist. That cord fastened the Eye of Horus to me. The pendant was supposed to protect me.

"Not that," I managed to say. "I need it."

Then I was lost to the pain. Somewhere, above the current, or maybe behind it, a voice issued directions. Push now. Don't push. Breathe. I did what the voice said when I could, and when the time came that I could no longer do it, I stopped.

"My lady, you must push."

A firm hand on my shoulder. A cloth across my sweaty forehead, cool and damp.

"I cannot," I said. "I'm too tired."

"You must. There is no choice."

"Leave me be," I said.

"Push," the voice directed. "Else both you and your babe travel to the West this very night."

I pushed. And pushed. Then the cry of a babe.

"Congratulations, my lady. You have a daughter."

CHAPTER 4

Someone thrust a babe into my arms. A warm, wriggling, squawking babe. I clutched the tiny body, my hands somehow knowing what to do even as my brain stuttered. The words echoed in my mind. A daughter.

"A son," I said. "He is a son."

"I'm afraid not." An unfamiliar woman positioned between my feet shot me a sympathetic look. "The babe is a girl."

"But…" Desperation rose within me. Pharaoh expected a son. "The barley."

"Such tests are not always reliable."

She was in constant motion as she spoke, although with both the babe and my belly in the way, I couldn't tell what she did. Noticing my bare belly, I finally realised I was naked. I had forgotten they removed my gown. They had intended to take the Eye of Horus from me too, but the cord was secure around my wrist. I was still protected.

"Ettu," I said. "Where is Ettu?"

"Right here," came her voice.

"She says the babe is a girl." I didn't even know what I

expected her to do. Fix it somehow. Ettu always knew how to fix things.

"It's true," she said. "Shall I unwrap her so you can see for yourself?"

Tears welled and a sob choked my throat. I had failed to give Pharaoh the one thing he required of me. I had failed my father. My country, my people. The alliance.

"She is beautiful, my lady." Sehener's voice held an eagerness I didn't understand. "You must be so proud."

I stared down at the babe in my arms, searching her face for… something. She had my chin. My nose. Thank Marduk there was nothing of Pharaoh in her features. Maybe she had his eyes, though. When she stopped crying and opened her eyes properly, perhaps I would see him there.

She waved one hand as if to attract my attention. I took the tiny hand, felt the warmth of her skin, counted her fingers. She was so little. Much smaller than I expected. Something inside me stirred. This was my own babe, born from my body.

"Is there… anything wrong?" I asked. "She is…"

"She is early from what I understand." The healer's tone was brisk and matter-of-fact. "But not so early as to cause problems. She appears to be perfectly healthy, just a little smaller than usual. But now, my lady, you need to push again. There is more to be expelled from your womb. Pass the child to one of your ladies."

It was Sehener's hands who reached for the babe. Then I was occupied with following the healer's instructions. In the background, the babe cried.

My babe.

My daughter.

"Good," the healer said at last. "Well done, my lady."

"Is it over?" My limbs were weak and I couldn't have gotten up if the chamber was on fire.

"It is done," she said. "You can relax now."

A knock came and Ettu hurried to open the door while Sehener and Merytre cooed over the babe. The royal physician bustled in, followed by Amankhau. Of course it would be him. Panouk would be off duty for the night.

"You took your time," the healer said cooly to the physician.

It took me a few moments to remember his name, even though he had come to examine me numerous times during my pregnancy. Iyroy, Pharaoh's personal physician.

"I came as soon as I received the message." His gaze went from me to the babe.

"A girl," the healer said.

The babe let out a squawk.

"She is hungry," I said. "She needs to be fed."

"A wet nurse is waiting to do that." The physician nodded to the woman who had followed him into the chamber. I hadn't even noticed her. "You may take the child."

The woman went to Sehener and took my babe from her arms. Sehener released her reluctantly, her hands lingering on the babe.

"Wait," I said. "Let me feed her. She doesn't need a wet nurse."

"There is no need for you to be concerned with such things." The physician's tone was cool and he never even looked at me as he replied. "Everything has been arranged."

"But I want to nurse her myself."

The woman was already at the door, my babe in her arms. I somehow summoned the strength to try to get up, but swiftly found myself pushed back onto the couch.

"It is an honour for her to take care of a child of Pharaoh."
The healer's voice was far kinder than the physician's, even if
the hands with which she held me down were firm. "You need
not fret for your babe. She will be well cared for."

"Please." A sob burst out of my throat. "Let me have a little
longer with her."

But the door to my chambers opened and then they closed.
The woman was gone, and with her, my babe.

I had known she would be taken from me once she was
born. My babe was sired by Pharaoh, after all. She would live
in his palace, surrounded by her half-siblings and looked after
by a veritable army of staff. But I hadn't expected they would
take her from me so soon. I had thought I would have more
than a few moments with her.

I hadn't had time to look at her properly. To examine her
features. To memorise her face. It might be a long time before
I saw her again. Years, even. Tiye said she received a letter
from her son every month. Would I have to wait until my
daughter could write before I received regular news of her?

"Her name is Ishtar," I said to the physician. "Make sure
they know it."

He gave me a cursory nod, although it felt like too little
acknowledgement for such a significant fact. Perhaps my babe
would be given a new name. An Egyptian name, suitable for
an Egyptian princess. She might never know what I had
named her. Regardless of what they told my daughter, she
would always be Ishtar to me.

CHAPTER 5

After the wet nurse left with my babe, images of a life I would never know filled my mind. My sister, who should have been with me for the birth. She should have had children who would grow up with mine. They would have played together, taken their lessons together, been as close as Ishtar and I were when we were young. Before she understood what it was to be the oldest daughter of Marduk-apla-iddina. Or, perhaps, before I comprehended what it was to be the one who wasn't the oldest.

"My lady?" Sehener's voice brought me back to reality and I pushed away the images. That life was forever denied to me. "Are you well? Do you need anything?"

I shook my head as tears welled. She couldn't fetch me the one thing I needed and everything else was too trivial to bother with.

"She is perfect," Merytre said. "That must—"

She stopped abruptly as Ettu gave her a sharp look.

"Must what?" I asked, not that I cared. I was too heart sick and weary and sore from the babe's birth to care about anything but her absence.

"It must be a relief," Merytre said, somewhat reluctantly, and I suspected it wasn't what she meant to say. "Since she was born so early."

"But only by a few weeks." Ettu's tone was crisp as she busied herself with helping the healer clean up. She dropped soiled linens in a basket and set it by the door.

Sehener brought me a clean gown, and she and Merytre helped me into it.

"Why was she born early?" Sehener asked the healer.

The woman shrugged.

"The gods alone know the answer to that," she said. "From what I understand, my lady has recently endured the shock of losing a beloved companion. Such trauma might well bring on early childbirth."

For a moment I thought she meant my sister, but then I realised she must mean Ahmose. After all, it had been some months since my sister disappeared. There were probably few folk who still thought about her, other than those who lived here in my chambers.

"And, of course, even more recently was the very disturbing news about Lady Hydna." Ettu shook out an unused cloth and refolded it, studiously keeping her gaze on the linen. "That, too, was a great shock to all of us."

Ettu knew about Khaemmalu, of course. Not that we had ever discussed my affair with him, but she couldn't not know. She was too observant to miss something like that. Others of my companions might not have guessed, but Ettu would have.

"Well, then." The healer gave me a careful look. "You should rest for the next few days, at the very least, or longer if you can. Stay in bed until the fatigue passes. If you feel fevered or at all unwell, send for me immediately."

I nodded, suddenly too exhausted to speak. She made her way to the door, then with one last look at me, departed.

"You must be famished," Merytre said. "I know I am, and all I did was sit and watch."

"It's nearly dawn," Ettu said. "Breakfast won't be far away, or if you are too hungry to wait" — this she directed at me — "we could ask for something to be brought early."

"I think we should send for food." Sehener was already on her way to let the men out. I couldn't begin to guess how long the labour had taken — hours, at least. They had been locked away for a very long time. "My lady should eat something nourishing as soon as possible."

"Some soup perhaps?" Merytre suggested. "I will go find a runner."

"Onion soup," Sehener called from the hallway. "It's most nutritious. Some bread also, and maybe some fruit."

Merytre slipped out and Sehener soon returned with Tall and Half at her heels. Half went straight to his usual couch and climbed up using the stool we kept there for him. Tall hesitated in the doorway, his gaze seemingly fixed on a wall behind me.

Would Sutem still be waiting to walk Merytre home, or had she sent him a message at some point?

Ettu came to sit beside Half, and Sehener patted the cushion beside her as she gave Tall a questioning look. His face was pained and he still hesitated in the doorway, shuffling from foot to foot.

"Come sit with us, love," Sehener said.

Tall's gaze darted down to me, ever so briefly. So whatever

his problem was, it was something to do with me. Sehener followed his gaze.

"Oh, my lady," she said, jumping up. "You should have said something. I will fetch you a dry cloth."

I finally noticed the wetness soaking the front of my gown. I touched it, wondering where it came from. My breasts ached. No, it was more than an ache. They throbbed. The wetness came from them.

Sehener draped a cloth over my chest.

"That will help soak it up," she said. "We should change your gown, too, when you are ready to get up. There is no hurry, though. Sit for as long as you need to."

"We can leave the chamber if my lady needs to change." Half was already scooting forward to reach the stool.

I waved at him to stay. Speaking took too much effort and I needed to reserve my words for only the most necessary utterances right now.

"What…" I gestured to my chest.

"It's very common," Sehener said quickly. "I have seen it before with women…"

Her voice trailed away. When I gave her a questioning look, wondering why she didn't continue, Sehener's gaze went to Ettu, clearly requesting her assistance.

"Your breasts are ready for nursing." Ettu's tone was the crisp one she always used when she had unpleasant news to deliver. Tears already welled in my eyes, even before I comprehended her meaning. "Your milk has come in because your body doesn't understand it will not need to nurse."

"I wanted to feed her."

My voice broke and the tears spilled down my cheeks. I was too tired to even try to control them. Instead, I buried my face in the cloth Sehener had brought for my chest, and sobbed. Someone patted my shoulder, but nobody spoke until my tears slowed. I wiped my face and fixed my gaze on the floor. I couldn't meet their eyes. Any sign of sympathy would probably make me cry again. Sehener took the wet linen from my hands.

"I shall fetch you a clean cloth," she said brightly. "And a bowl of water so you can wash your face."

I could only imagine how I looked by now. My make up would be irreparably smudged and my cheeks probably streaked with kohl.

"I will take your wig." Merytre was already lifting it from my head as she spoke. I never even noticed her come back from finding a runner.

"You must be very tired," Ettu added. "Perhaps you would like to retire to your bedchamber? You will be more comfortable in a nightgown. We will clean your face and get you ready for bed."

"Shall I send for hot water?" Merytre asked. "My lady might like a bath? Or maybe a brew? I can send another runner to the kitchens."

"Good idea," Ettu said before I could reject either suggestion. "A bath and a hot drink. Even if you don't think you can sleep, a change of clothes and a soothing drink will help. I will send a runner to tell your lady's maids you won't need them this morning. That way you can lie in bed for as long as you want."

I didn't want to lie in bed, alone in my chamber, with empty arms, my breasts throbbing with the need to nurse my babe. For once I would have welcomed the bustle of my maids, their mindless chatter and their constant attentions, even if it involved me being stripped naked. At least it would give me something else to think about.

CHAPTER 6

erytre was swift to procure water for bathing and I allowed Ettu to urge me down the hallway to my bedchamber. Although I tried to keep myself from looking at anyone on my way out, I accidentally caught sight of Tall. His hunched shoulders showed his unhappiness and I averted my gaze before I saw his face. I couldn't bear anyone's sympathy right now.

Sehener and Merytre followed us, and between them, the three women had me bathed and attired in a clean nightgown in remarkably short order. I sat on my bed while Merytre removed the last traces of kohl from my cheeks. Sehener rubbed lotion into my feet, which ached even though I had been lying down all night, and Ettu bustled around the chamber, seemingly tidying things she would never have allowed to be out of place to start with.

"That's everything then," Sehener said at last. She set a folded linen beside me on the bed. "That is for…"

She gestured towards my chest and a sob welled in my

throat. Sehener edged towards the door as I nodded a thank you at her.

"Do you need anything else?" Merytre hesitated in the doorway and it was clear she would rather be anywhere but here.

I shook my head and they disappeared down the hallway. Ettu kept her back to me as she straightened the row of cosmetics on my dresser.

"I could sit with you." Her voice was offhand, as if she spoke of nothing of any consequence. "Until you fall asleep."

It wasn't Ettu I wanted here with me, though. I wanted my babe. Or Khaemmalu. With a sudden, desperate pang, I wanted Khaemmalu. I wanted him to lie beside me in my narrow bed. To wrap his arms around me and hold me while I cried. I wanted to feel the warmth of his body beside me when I woke during the night. To hear him breathing, and know I wasn't alone in the dark.

"No," I said, finally realising I hadn't yet replied to Ettu. "I will be fine."

I could hardly ask her to send for Khaemmalu, although for one wild moment, I was tempted. We had smuggled Half and Tall inside, and more than once. Surely we could get Khaemmalu in. The pain of missing my babe would never end, but I could tolerate it if Khaemmalu was here with me. But once would never be enough. Every taste of him made me want him more. I would want him here tomorrow night, and then the next.

"Are you sure?"

I had forgotten Ettu until she spoke. She kept her back to me. Perhaps she knew me well enough to know I couldn't stand to see her sympathy right now.

"Yes." The word wobbled on my lips and didn't sound

nearly as decisive as I wanted, but it was enough for Ettu. With one last twitch of a kohl bottle, she left, giving me a nod as she departed, but still managing to avoid looking at me.

Alone in my chamber, I lay on my bed. I might have expected the tears to come in earnest now I had privacy, but my eyes were strangely dry. My breasts weren't, though. Milk already seeped through the front of my nightgown, leaving the fabric sticking to my chest, warm and wet. I draped the cloth over the wetness, unable to summon the energy to change my nightgown again. There was no point anyway. Not until my body realised there would be no babe to feed.

A heavy feeling of despair rolled over me. I sank down into it, letting it envelop me as I closed my eyes and waited for sleep. The peace of unconsciousness, however, was stubbornly elusive, despite my fatigue and my desperate need to lose myself in it.

I must have fallen asleep eventually, because at some point I found myself standing beside a bed of narcissus. A babe cried and I knew she was my own. I searched for her, but the voice echoed around me, and I couldn't tell where she was. She cried again and this time a lion's low purr followed her cry.

I froze, my heart beating so hard, I thought it might burst right through my chest. My legs went weak and I could hardly breathe.

Movement behind me. I turned, and there he was. Whether he was the same lion who had stalked my dreams for months, or another, I couldn't tell. He studied me, his expression almost quizzical and holding an intelligence I hadn't expected.

Ishtar cried again, and this time there was no echo. I knew exactly where she was: amongst the narcissus.

The lion's head turned as he searched for the source of the sound. Horror welled within me.

"No." I edged closer to the lion, fearful of being near him but desperate to divert his attention from my babe. "It's me you want."

But if the lion understood, he gave no sign of it. He circled the flower bed, searching for the crying babe.

"Come back." I waved my arms at the beast, but he still paid me no attention.

I examined the narcissus, hoping to find my babe before the lion did. Could I beat him to her? I could race through the flowers, cover her tiny body with my own, keep her safe from the lion.

But even as I studied the place where my babe's cry came from, the narcissus seemed to grow taller. They leaned together, shielding my babe. The lion roared and paced around them. He reached out one paw to touch a flower, but pulled back quickly as if he had been stung.

My breath came a little easier. The narcissus would protect her, just as they had protected me.

Even as my body relaxed with the realisation the lion was no threat to my babe, the beast crouched. He gathered himself, then made one powerful leap into the middle of the narcissus. His paws barely touched the ground before he sprang up again, right over the flowers. Then he ran.

My babe's cry trailed behind him.

He had taken her.

CHAPTER 7

T woke sobbing and flung myself from my bed. Whether the dream was a premonition or a warning, it demanded to be heeded. I was halfway to the sitting chamber when Ettu appeared in her doorway. She must have said something I didn't hear, because she raised her voice.

"Whatever is the matter?" she asked.

By then, the others had emerged, probably drawn from their sleep as much by Ettu's loudness as my wild flight down the hallway.

"My lady, are you well?" Sehener asked.

I didn't stop. There was no time to explain. The lion was coming for my babe. I had to go to her. Protect her. I didn't let myself wonder why the beast wanted her. My dreams were clear about the safety the narcissus offered, but what if that wasn't enough? Whatever the lion wanted her for, it could be nothing good.

At the sitting chamber door, my shaking hands fumbled with the bar. Then Tall was beside me, his hands over mine. He hesitated, but slipped the bar back into place.

"No." My breath came in gasps. "Let me out."

"What you need to do," came Ettu's firm voice as she appeared beside me, "is come and sit down. You can explain what has happened and we will figure out what to do about it."

"There is no time," I wailed. "I must go to her."

"Who?" Ettu asked, although she surely knew. Who else would I mean?

"Please." I was sobbing now. Begging. But still Tall didn't open the door. "Let me go."

Ettu's hands on my shoulders firmly, but gently, turned me around. She led me back to the couch, while Tall stayed by the door, as if guarding it to be sure I wouldn't escape. Who would save my babe from the lion if they kept me locked in here?

"Tell us what the problem is," Ettu said, "and we will figure out how to deal with it."

Between sobs I told them about my dream. Despite the tears that obscured my vision, I didn't miss the look passing between Ettu and Half. They thought me deranged and I could hardly blame them. My tale about a lion snatching up my babe and how some flowers were supposed to keep her safe sounded like foolishness.

"Merytre, send for the healer," Ettu said when I ran out of ways to convince them of the danger. "Tell her my lady is hysterical."

Her words sent me into another round of tears. Why didn't they believe me? And why was Merytre even here this late? She should be at home with Sutem.

"I'm not hysterical," I wailed. "She's in danger. She needs me."

Tall, of course, made no move to stop Merytre as she left.

In fact, he raised the bar for her and stood behind the door so nobody would glimpse him while it was open. Half left the chamber and returned once the door was safely closed again.

"Come with me," I begged Ettu. "You will see the truth."

"And where exactly do you propose to go?" she asked.

"To the seer," I said, astounded she hadn't figured this much out on her own.

"Was the seer in your dream as well?" she asked. "You didn't mention her earlier."

"Of course not," I said. "But she will know where the lion has taken my babe and how to get her back."

The look on Ettu's face said quite clearly this new information had done nothing to convince her of the soundness of my mind.

"Perhaps you would care to lie down while we wait for the healer?" Sehener's tone was overly bright. "A short rest after such exertion will do you good."

I didn't know whether the exertion she meant was childbirth or my hysteria, as they considered it, but it didn't matter. She didn't understand. None of them did. I wasted time trying to reason with folk who couldn't possibly comprehend the situation. I was the only one who could save my babe and I wouldn't allow myself to be delayed another moment.

But as I got to my feet, determined to push my way past Tall, a knock came at the door.

"It's me," Merytre called. "With the healer."

"Quickly." Ettu gestured for Tall and Half to leave. Sehener followed to lock them in their bedchamber.

The healer came straight to me. She set down her basket and pulled out an assortment of clay jars. Merytre, it seemed, had told her enough for the woman to have already decided what I needed. Another knock came and Merytre slipped back out into the hallway. She returned with a jug, which she set on the floor beside the healer. Hot water, I assumed. They had, indeed, come prepared.

The healer worked swiftly as she mixed herbs with the water, clearly already knowing which herbs she needed and in what quantities. She covered the jug and set it aside to brew.

"Now, then." She cast an appraising gaze over me.

I met her stare, trying to look calm and composed, but all-too-aware of my swollen eyes and dishevelled appearance.

"My lady is to rest for the next week." Although she fixed her gaze on me, I had no doubt her words were intended for those who would be expected to enforce her instructions. "She should lie in a darkened chamber as much as possible. Keep the shutters closed, as fresh air will be too disruptive while she is in this state of mind. Do you have a brazier?"

She didn't wait for an answer, but set one jar apart from the others.

"Burn these herbs every day. They will deter any evil which might be lingering nearby. She must have onion soup every evening, and she should drink a full mug of this tonic three times a day." She uncovered the jug long enough to sniff the contents. "It needs a few more minutes to brew, but it will help dry her milk and calm her nerves. I will return tomorrow with more herbs for a fresh batch of tonic."

She studied me for a few moments longer.

"Is there anything else you need?" Her voice was kinder this time and I sensed a genuine concern for my wellbeing.

Her sympathy sent me into tears again and I could only shake my head.

"Well, then." She nodded towards the three women, making it clear her words were for them. "Send for me should she need anything else, or if her condition worsens. Otherwise, I will return in the morning."

Then she was gone. Merytre barred the door behind her.

"That was unnecessary," I muttered. "I did not need a healer."

"We thought you did," Ettu replied, "and she hardly seemed to think she was summoned unnecessarily. Now, we will do exactly as she says and I am sure you will feel much better by the time she returns."

What they didn't understand was that I didn't want to feel better. I wanted to know my daughter was safe, and how could I do that when I didn't even know where she was? But if I could do nothing for her, there was someone who could: Khaemmalu.

He knew guards in Pharaoh's palace, and my babe would have guards watching over her. Khaemmalu might even know the very men charged with keeping her safe. He could get a message to them. Warn them she was in danger, even if I didn't know what form the danger would take. It would hardly be an actual lion, although such beasts still roamed Egypt's southern territories.

Clarity hit me. I had taken the dreams too literally. The lion symbolised a person — a particular person who would be a danger to my daughter — and the narcissus symbolised those who worked to keep her safe. The guards, perhaps. Maybe even the palace as an entity. If I could figure out who the lion represented, I would know where the threat to my daughter came from.

And that realisation brought me back to the one person who would know the lion's identity: the seer.

CHAPTER 8

*T*he rest of the day passed with excruciating slowness as I feigned compliance with the healer's instructions. Ettu gave me a sharp look once or twice, as if suspicious about my lack of resistance, but I pretended not to notice. I lay in my bed and did everything they told me to. The closed shutters kept out the breeze and the brazier they brought in left my bedchamber stifling. I breathed the herby smoke and tried not to cough.

The healer's tonic was bitter and nobody made any attempt to sweeten it. I dutifully drank it when prompted and didn't complain or ask for honey, even though its foulness made me gag. Other than that, I closed my eyes and pretended to sleep. It left me free to plan how I would sneak out to find the seer.

Even after everyone had retired for the night, I waited a while longer before I got out of bed and retrieved a gown from my clothing chest. I dressed in the dark, not wanting the glimmer of light to bring anyone to check why I needed a lamp when I should be fast asleep in my bed.

I tiptoed along the hallway. To my relief, the sitting chamber was in darkness, so as long as I made no sound, I would escape without discovery. I would have to leave the door unbarred, but surely this late at night, nobody would come to my chambers. For a moment, I hesitated, wondering whether I should lock the men's door, just in case someone came in. But if there was a fire, or some other reason they needed to leave urgently, nobody would know I had locked them in.

I was halfway across the sitting chamber when somebody coughed. I froze.

"Me!" came Tall's quiet voice.

"What are you doing up?" I asked.

He could, of course, ask the same of me. I could feel him flapping his hands as he tried to find the words to reply.

"I have to do something." I peered through the darkness, trying to glean some clue as to his intention, but could see nothing other than a dark shape that loomed where he sat.

His reply took some time. I waited, knowing he painstakingly searched for the word he needed.

"Do!" he said at last.

"I have to find the seer," I said. "She is the only one who will understand."

"Me!"

The word sounded mournful, although without being able to see him, I couldn't tell whether he was saddened I thought he wouldn't understand, or if he tried to say he, too, knew the pain of being misunderstood.

"Will you bar the door behind me?" I asked.

A soft grunt, which I took as confirmation.

"Thank you, Tall." I slipped out before he could change his mind.

I hurried through the Palace, avoiding the eyes of anyone who passed. A runner boy, probably barely ten years old, stifled a yawn as he trotted by. A young man with a studious air about him. Some lady's tutor, perhaps. Modified, for certain. He would not be permitted to wander the Palace otherwise.

A maid whose face was somewhat familiar — perhaps she was one of those who brought our meals to my chambers — ducked her head as she passed me and seemed to wipe a tear from her cheek. I hurt, too, I wanted to say to her. I, too, feel like I must hide my pain. But I didn't stop and neither did she. We had nothing to say to each other. An Ornament and a servant. Just two strangers hurrying past each other in the deep of night.

As I exited the Palace, the air outside was so fresh and cool, it brought me to a halt. For a few moments, all I could do was breathe. Such a welcome relief after my stifling bedchamber, with its closed shutters and the brazier sending out its herb-filled smoke. A runner hurrying up the path gave me an odd look as he took a deep breath, perhaps preparing to ask if I needed assistance. I walked on before he could speak.

As I left the main path, which was lit by torches at regular intervals, and ventured onto darker, more shadowed paths, I let myself slow down. I avoided the place where Khaemmalu and I most commonly met. My body craved his touch, and I pined for his arms around me. His warm breath in my hair. The security of being safe in his embrace. But I wouldn't find the peace I wanted with him until I had spoken with the seer.

As I wandered the paths, I learnt the folly of venturing out alone so soon after childbirth. In a remarkably brief time, my legs trembled and my breath grew short. My head was dizzy and my thoughts became muddled. I was too fatigued for such exertion. I should return to the main path.

But my feet didn't listen when I told them to turn back and I found myself continuing on in the darkness. The trees around me wobbled and then they lay on their sides.

I realised it was me who lay on the ground at the same time as someone lifted me.

"It's all right," came a familiar voice. "I have you."

For a moment, I leaned into Khaemmalu's chest, then I remembered my purpose.

"No," I said. " I have to find her."

"Who?" he asked.

I was surprised he understood. My speech was probably barely comprehensible.

"The seer."

"Aah." He stopped walking, hitching me higher in his arms as he considered this. "Would you care to tell me why?"

"I cannot." He would think me a fool. I mightn't care if those who shared my chambers knew how much of a fool I was, but I cared deeply if Khaemmalu did.

"You can tell me, Kassaya." His voice was low and intimate. "Whatever it is. You know that."

"Please," I said. "Just take me to her."

"She is not the kind of woman who can be found. From what I understand, she will find you if she wishes to. Never the other way around."

"I have found her before."

"Then she allowed you to find her," he said. "That doesn't mean she will do so again."

"She has a message for me," I said.

He didn't need to say it. I knew him well enough to feel

when he had made his decision. He had resolved to take me back to the Palace.

"Put me down," I said. "I can walk."

He lowered me to the ground, although he kept a firm grip on my waist until I proved I was steady on my feet.

"Perhaps I could hold your arm," I said. "Just in case. But I think I can walk now."

When I set off again in the same direction, he didn't object, only walked beside me and allowed me to grasp his arm. I wanted to run my fingers along the length of it, to marvel at the softness of skin over hard muscle, but I didn't let my hand wander. It would be difficult to explain if anyone saw.

"I heard you delivered the babe," he said. "A girl."

"I was going to tell you. I needed to speak with the seer first, then I meant to find you."

"You were so sure the babe would be a boy," he said.

I shrugged, not knowing what he expected me to say.

"I was wrong," I said.

"You are dissatisfied with a girl?"

I hesitated as I sorted through my thoughts. I wanted to give him an honest answer, but I wasn't sure I even knew what that was.

"Not for myself," I said at last. "I care little whether my babe is a boy or a girl, only that she is healthy. But Pharaoh told me to take care the child would be a boy and I failed."

"That doesn't make you a failure."

When I glanced up at him, he was biting his lip.

"What are you not saying?" I asked.

Did he really think I had failed, despite what he said? I couldn't bear to know that. I didn't care if Pharaoh considered me a failure. Even my father, to some extent, was too far

HAWK OF THE WEST

removed from my life now for it to bother me if he thought such a thing. But not Khaemmalu.

He started to say something, but stopped.

"Tell me," I said. "What are you holding back?"

"You told me to stop asking you to leave," he said. "So I have, but that doesn't mean I have changed my mind."

"I cannot, especially now." Surely he wasn't asking me to flee without my babe? I would never leave her behind.

"You don't understand the situation here," he said.

"Then tell me. Help me comprehend it."

He shook his head and gave a heavy sigh.

"Have you heard anything from him?" he asked.

He meant Pharaoh, of course.

"Not yet." I was reluctant to voice my fear Pharaoh wouldn't acknowledge my babe's birth. That I had disappointed him by not delivering a son as he bid me to. "I named her for my sister. I don't know if he will give her a different name."

"It is a beautiful tribute," he said. "Lady Ishtar would be pleased to know the next generation bears her name."

My throat choked and I could only shrug. In truth, I wasn't sure what Ishtar would think of it. She might well have viewed it as my daughter encroaching on the name she herself already bore. Ishtar never liked competition.

We had meandered along the length of the path and reached the place where it circled back to re-join the main path.

"You should return to your chambers, my lady." His voice was overly loud and I wondered if he knew another guard was nearby, even if I saw no sign of anyone myself. "Do you require any further assistance?"

"No," I said. "Thank you for helping me."

My fingers left his arm reluctantly, but if I was to walk away, there was no longer any reason to hold onto him. It was only as he stepped back, preparing to return to the shadows, that I noticed a rip in his sleeve.

"What did you do?" I pointed.

He followed my gaze and his fingers inspected the tear as if he only just now noticed it.

"A branch," he said. "I saw you looking unsteady and was hurrying to you. Didn't notice the branch until my shirt caught on it, and I was in too much of a hurry to untangle it, so I pulled it and it tore."

"One of my maids can fix it for you," I said. "They are all quite handy with a needle."

"My sister can do it," he said. "Gautseshen."

It was she who stitched up Half after he was stabbed.

"I know," I said, "but it's my fault you tore it. There is no need to make work for her. Give me your shirt and I will bring it back to you tomorrow."

He shrugged again and seemed ill-inclined to argue any further. I tried not to stare as he pulled the shirt over his head. I knew his body by touch, but I hadn't seen him in torchlight before. We were always hidden away in the depths of the shrubbery where no more than the faintest glimmer of moonlight pierced the canopy. His chest was hairless and the muscles of his abdomen sharply defined. Three daggers secured in the waistband of his *shendyt* were evidence of why the guards who patrolled the Palace grounds wore shirts.

As he held the garment out to me, my gaze wandered his chest, despite how I tried not to look. A black marking caught my eye and my heart thudded to a stop.

"What is that?" I could barely breathe as I forced out the words.

He followed my gaze.

"Sekhmet," he said. "The Protectress."

"It's a lion?" I had to be certain. Perhaps I was wrong.

"A lioness, I suppose," he said with a shrug. "A deity most suitable to be worshipped by a guard."

My mouth went dry and my thoughts fled. I could only stare at the figure inked on his chest. It couldn't be a coincidence. Surely, this wasn't just another example of a lion in my life. This was significant. This was what the seer had meant for me to figure out.

Khaemmalu was the lion.

It was Khaemmalu my dreams warned me of.

Khaemmalu who the narcissus protected me from.

Khaemmalu who would take my babe.

CHAPTER 9

"*K*assaya?"

It was Khaemmalu's voice that brought me back to my senses. He must have been saying my name while I was lost in the maelstrom of horror that engulfed me.

"Can you hear me?" he asked.

"I have to go."

The realisation of fabric in my hand. White linen. A shirt. Khaemmalu's shirt. If it wasn't for the rip through his sleeve, I might never have understood the narcissus' warning.

I wanted to scrunch the shirt into a ball and throw it at him. I wanted to tear it apart, to hear its seams rip. But I did none of that. Instead, I forced my mouth into a smile and tried to pretend nothing had changed. But, in reality, everything was different now.

"Are you ill?" he asked.

I searched his gaze, looking for some sign of insincerity. An indication he meant to betray me and take my babe. But however hard I looked, his eyes showed nothing but concern and care. He was good at pretending. Too good.

"Kassaya?" he asked, and I realised I still hadn't answered him.

"No," I managed. "I am well enough."

"I will walk you back to the front door."

"There is no need," I said. "I will be quite fine. You surely have other things to do and it's best we don't draw attention."

After all, he was the one who said we shouldn't be seen together.

He studied me, frowning a little.

"Really." I mustered another smile. "Follow if you must, but let me walk alone."

I must have been convincing enough, because he nodded.

"I will be watching," he said. "Should you need me, I will be here."

I didn't know what else to say. Normally when he farewelled me, we were hidden in the shadows. He would kiss me. I would cling to him, wrapping my arms around his neck, and leaning into his body. Thank Marduk this place where we stood was too public for that. Since he wouldn't expect our usual farewell here, I could simply turn and walk away.

I didn't let myself look over my shoulder. It was not just Khaemmalu I left behind me, but any fantasy of a future in which we could be together, however unrealistic it might be. I left behind the possibility of ever loving a man again. Of ever being touched by a man other than Pharaoh. That anyone other than those who shared my chambers might ever care for me. Yes, I had developed friendships within the Palace, but nobody I could trust completely and unhesitatingly. Not like I had trusted Khaemmalu.

As I reached the main path, I finally let myself cast a single glance back over my shoulder. One last look at Khaemmalu and then I would stay away from him. But he was gone. He had already returned to the shadows.

He would be watching, though, so I didn't allow myself the luxury of tears at this shattering of the one thing I had treasured. Instead, I held my head high as I returned to the Palace. *Show Pharaoh what the women of Babylon are made of.* My mother's final words to me echoed in my mind.

It was only as I went back into the building that I remembered why I had gone out. But Khaemmalu would see me if I went again to find the seer. I couldn't risk encountering him right now. As much as my mind knew he was a threat to me and my babe, my body still craved his touch. For tonight, the only thing I could do was return to my chambers and try to pretend everything was normal.

I made my way through the Palace in a daze. If anyone gave me more than the most casual of glances, I didn't notice. At my chambers, I rapped on the door.

"Tall," I whispered. "It's me."

But when the door opened, it was Ettu, and not Tall. She gave me a hard look, then stood aside so I could enter. The door closed behind me and she slid the bar into place.

"I will not ask," she said, and her voice was gentler than I might have expected. "You know you should be resting, and you know we have agreed you will not go out alone. I assume your need was dire."

I swallowed hard and nodded. I couldn't tell her what I had learned.

"Go back to bed," she said. "It's still a couple of hours until dawn. I will send a message to tell your lady's maids you won't require them today."

"Thank you."

I hurried across the chamber, hoping to get away before she said anything else.

"I would have gone with you, had you woken me," she said. "I know you probably think I ask too many questions, but I do know how to hold my tongue when I must. Should you need to go out again unexpectedly in the middle of the night, wake me. I promise I will ask you nothing."

Tears welled and my throat choked. She was far kinder to me than I deserved. I should thank her. I owed her at least that much for her compassion, but I would burst into tears if I tried to say anything. Instead, I raised one hand in acknowledgement and slipped away to my bedchamber.

There, with the door closed, I stuffed Khaemmalu's shirt under my mattress, then tried to make sense of my thoughts. I had been surrounded by lions ever since I came to this country, and my dreams made it clear the lion was a threat to both me and my babe. Why was I so sure the marking inked on Khaemmalu's chest meant he was the lion? Couldn't this be just another of the lions that seemed to be everywhere around me?

But it wasn't just another warning. Something deep in my gut told me Khaemmalu was the lion my dreams warned of. It made perfect sense. He had the skills to be a threat, in whatever form he chose, and I had allowed him to get too close to me. No wonder the dreams came again and again. I had paid no heed to their warning. The seer must think me such a fool. *The answer you seek is behind you,* she had said to me. Could she have told me any more clearly? I knew Khaemmalu was there at the time, and yet even then I didn't comprehend what she meant.

I finally let myself cry. How could I have done such a thing as to fall in love with a man who was forbidden to me? And worse than that, a man who was a danger to me. I had trusted him, with my secrets, my body. I had believed myself safe with Khaemmalu, but I couldn't have been more wrong.

Some time ago, I had dreamed the narcissus spoke to me. By the time I woke, whatever they said had slipped away and I had never been able to remember it. Could they have been warning me about Khaemmalu? Had I made a terrible mistake in embarking on an affair with him? If I had remembered their message, I might have been able to stop myself before I fell in love with him.

It was too late to save my heart, but maybe I could still save my babe from him. It would mean taking her away from here, though. Even in the security of Pharaoh's palace, she wasn't out of Khaemmalu's reach. I had to get her away from Thebes and far away from Egypt.

But even if I could somehow get to her, and get us both out of the city, where could we go? I couldn't take her home to Babylon, not if I had broken the alliance and taken Pharaoh's child. Pharaoh was not a man who would tolerate someone taking something he considered to be his. He would hunt me to the ends of the earth to retrieve his child, and Babylon was the first place he would look.

I was trapped. Before, it had felt like my decision to stay, a choice I made for the sake of the alliance and to be near Khaemmalu, even if I didn't let myself admit how much he influenced my decision. But now I truly couldn't leave because I couldn't take my babe with me and I wouldn't leave her behind. Even when Pharaoh tired of me, I knew I would beg him to let me stay to be near my daughter.

I was truly trapped here, for the rest of my life.

CHAPTER 10

I hardly expected to sleep, but exhaustion won and I woke long after the bird that sang its dawn song outside my window had fallen silent.

Over the next couple of weeks, there was no possibility of venturing from my chamber in search of the seer. My maids kept close watch over me, and even when I got up during the night for a drink or to use the chamber pot, there would always be someone sitting up. Sometimes it was one of the women, at other times it was Tall or Half.

Despite the varying excuses they provided for why they weren't in bed — all of which were apparently nothing to do with me — it seemed obvious they colluded to ensure I didn't slip out alone again. I overheard enough of a conversation between Ettu and Tall to know she had reprimanded him for allowing me to leave, and I didn't dare ask him to do it again.

So I passed my days in a monotonous routine of lying on the couch, because apparently my condition required me to be prone as much as possible, interspersed with periods where I was permitted to sit up long enough to eat or to force down another of the healer's dreadful tonics. I ate so much onion soup that the very smell of it soon turned my stomach, and I spent so much time lying down that my head spun when I got up.

My eyes itched and my nose ran constantly from the brazier's smoke. Since I pleaded to be allowed to spend the daytime hours in the sitting chambers, an additional brazier was brought in so the other didn't have to be continually moved between chambers. Within a couple of days, we were all coughing and Ettu soon declared that as long as we kept the sitting chamber shutters closed during the day, the brazier burning at night in my bedchamber would be quite enough. I would have welcomed some fresh air, but knew better than to argue past the removal of the second brazier.

Ettu had told the rest of my maids I wouldn't need their services while I recovered, since I would neither be leaving my chambers nor accepting visitors. The forced confinement left me wishing for the presence of my maids for the first time. Enduring their attentions would have been a welcome reprieve from the monotony of my current situation.

The healer came every second day, an event which quickly became a high point since she was the only visitor I was permitted. She would check my heartbeat, sniff my breath, and squeeze my breasts to check for milk. As much as it grieved me that my body had ceased to produce the milk which should have nourished my babe, it was also a relief to no longer have heavy, aching breasts constantly reminding me of her absence.

With nothing else to do, I had far too much time to think. I missed Ahmose with an unexpected intensity. The old woman had become family, of a sort. Not quite a mother or a sister, but certainly something more than a friend. She would have understood the pain of giving up a babe, having been parted from her own daughter, Henuttawy, for many years.

They were reunited after our arrival here when Ahmose discovered her long-lost daughter was lady's maid to Tiye. It was Henuttawy's sudden and unexpected departure from the Palace, without even so much as a farewell for the mother she had been separated from for so many years, which shocked Ahmose so severely that her heart stopped beating and she died.

Another person I missed was my mother. She had never been particularly warm or loving to her children, too focussed instead on her role as queen and consort to our father, but she had survived childbirth seven times, a feat none of my companions could claim. Even though she had never suffered having a child taken from her, a mother would understand my grief in a way nobody else did, and I wished she was here with me.

My sister's absence was another source of agony, the pain of losing her sharply re-opened. Our children should have grown up together, and even though any babe she bore Pharaoh would be taken from her just as mine had, it would have eased my pain somewhat to know our babes were together.

I even missed Khaemmalu. I tried to hate him, because that would have been easier than loving him, but I couldn't. I ran through my memories of him over and over, searching for any sign he would betray me. A hint he meant to take my babe. Anything at all that might make sense of the narcissus's warning. But Khaemmalu was much cleverer than me, and I could find nothing in his actions or his words or his face that suggested he was anything other than the sincere and loving man I had thought him to be.

I asked several times to send a message to my father about the birth of my babe. At first, Ettu only frowned and pretended she didn't hear me. It seemed even the scribe was a visitor I was not permitted. But when I continued to ask every day, she finally pulled the healer aside on one of her visits and spoke to her quietly. They gave me assessing looks, making it perfectly clear they discussed me even if I couldn't hear their conversation. At last, the healer nodded. Ettu frowned and seemed displeased, but when I next asked her to send for the scribe, she agreed.

Pentau arrived late that afternoon. He had always been a slight man, with a belly that sank in beneath his ribs, but today he looked even smaller than usual. Perhaps he had been unwell. I considered asking, thinking that showing concern for his condition might make him more favourably disposed towards me, but he so completely ignored me as he set up his little wooden table, that I swallowed down the words.

"You may begin," he said when he was ready. Kneeling at his writing table, he dipped a reed in a pot of ink and straightened a sheet of papyrus. He didn't so much as glance in my direction.

"You will write to my father," I said. "His name is—"

"I know his name," Pentau said, cutting me off. "I have written to him before."

He shot me an irritated look, as if my intention to give my father's name suggested some failure on his behalf. I pretended not to notice.

"My dear father," I said instead, figuring I may as well get on with my message. "This letter brings to you the very happy news that I have safely delivered my babe. I have named her for my sister."

My voice broke and I paused to compose myself. The

scribe's only reaction was another irritated look when I took what he clearly considered to be too long.

"She has been taken—" I hesitated as I reconsidered my words. "No, don't write that. She will be brought up in Pharaoh's palace."

The scribe kept going and made no sign of crossing out what he had already written.

"Did you change it?" I asked.

"Continue." He waved his reed in my direction, but didn't look up.

There was no point arguing with him. He wouldn't tell me what he had written even if I demanded to know.

"She will have many friends her own age, as well as tutors, maids and guards," I said. "I pray to Marduk I will see her soon. I trust I have fulfilled your expectations in sending me here now I have borne Pharaoh a child."

I hesitated, wondering whether to ask if he might petition Pharaoh to let me see my babe, but the scribe was already frowning before I could decide. The way Pharaoh reacted to the messages from Henutmire's father suggested he mightn't respond well to such intervention anyway.

"Please give Mother my love and tell her I wish she could meet her granddaughter. I remain, as always, your dutiful daughter, Kassaya."

The words were barely out of my mouth before the scribe set down his reed and sprinkled sand on the papyrus. Surely he left off my final words. He must have already decided how my letter would conclude. He was equally swift to pack up his things and get to his feet. With a cursory bow in my direction, he went to the door. It closed behind him with a thud.

"Well, then," Ettu said. "You must be exhausted after that.

Best you return to your bed for a while. Merytre will prepare a dose of your tonic and bring it in presently."

She ushered me down the hallway and helped me into bed. Merytre brought the tonic and Ettu sat with me while I drank every last drop. Then she wished me a peaceful rest and departed.

I was alone in my smoky, darkened chamber, longing for both my babe and Khaemmalu, and knowing there was little prospect I would ever hold either of them again.

CHAPTER 11

J thought I had endured loneliness before — after all, when one is a princess and surrounded by servants and courtiers, life is always lonely to some extent — but those first weeks after my babe's birth were truly the loneliest of my life. My companions tried to lift my mood, but everything they did only reminded me of what I had lost.

When Sehener made cheery comments about how well my babe would be taken care of, it reminded me I would have no part in her upbringing and was not even permitted to feed her from my own body.

When Merytre relayed a funny story Sutem had told her, it reminded me she had what I never would: a husband who loved her, a home of her own, the possibility of a child she and Sutem would raise together.

Even when Ettu bustled around my chamber, tidying it but saying nothing, it reminded me of how a mother might position herself nearby in case she was needed. Not my mother, perhaps, but surely others did. That was the kind of mother I would want to be.

When Half expounded on some theory about the gods, it reminded me of Ahmose and the wisdom that died with her, wisdom which would have been most useful to me right now.

When Tall sat beside me and wordlessly patted my hand, it reminded me of my sister who should have been here. A sister who would understand what I felt without the need for words. Perhaps that wasn't what our relationship had been like, but it could have been, had we more time together once we were past the insults and injuries of childhood.

My mood grew darker with each passing day and it wasn't long before they encouraged me to spend my time in my bedchamber instead of the sitting chamber. Nobody came to sit with me, to tell me amusing stories, or even to keep me company while the women did needlework or Half perfected his latest woodcarving. They came to bring me food, or because it was time for the next dose of my tonic, or because I had to be bathed, even though I had done nothing but lie in bed all day. When I begged to be allowed to go out to the sitting chamber for a while, they only reminded me the healer had said I was to stay in my bed.

At least they stopped coming to stoke the brazier after I pried open the shutters and threw it out the window. I ruined a perfectly good gown because I needed something to wrap the hot brazier with in order to handle it, but I couldn't stand its dreary smokiness another moment.

I spent far too much time calculating how long it might take my letter to reach Babylon, and precisely what day I might first expect a reply from my father. Not that he was likely to reply. Given he had yet to respond to my letter telling him Ishtar had disappeared, my delivery of a girl child would hardly solicit an answer.

If Father's silence could be taken as expressing his disappointment, surely Pharaoh's could, too. I had heard nothing from him since her birth. Not a messenger to summon me to dine with him, or even a gift for delivering a child. Not that I wanted anything from him. I hated wearing his sapphire, but a gift would have signalled acknowledgement of my babe. His silence meant I didn't know whether he was unaware of her arrival, or whether the lack of a son had angered him.

After yet another day spent tossing and turning in the confines of my bedchamber, I could tolerate it no longer. I had lost count of the days since my babe was born, but it must be at least a month. Maybe more. They were practically keeping me imprisoned in my own chambers and I had allowed it for far too long. I was, after all, the Ornament. I would not obey my servant's whims.

The conversation in the sitting chamber died as I walked through and went straight to the door. I held my head high and reminded myself it was my decision when I went out, not theirs.

"I am taking a walk," I said. "Who will accompany me?"

Silence. I had expected a fierce argument, from Ettu at the least, but I got as far as putting my hand on the bar securing the door, before someone cleared their throat.

"Well, then," said Ettu. "I suppose it should be me."

"I will come too," Merytre said. "It's almost sunset and Sutem will be off duty soon. If my lady wishes to walk for a while, she might perhaps be pleased for me to leave with him when she is finished."

"Of course." I started to raise the bar, but stopped when Tall and Half got up. I had been secluded in my bedchamber for so long, I had almost forgotten the need to ensure they were safely out of sight before we opened the door.

"I will stay then," Sehener said.

I hurried out before anyone could raise an argument. In the hallway, I set a swift pace, but got no further than the first flight of stairs before I realised I couldn't sustain such speed after so long doing nothing but lying down. I slowed and prayed nobody would comment. Ettu would notice, of course, but perhaps she would keep her thoughts to herself for a change.

A small sound behind me was undoubtedly Ettu's way of letting me know she had indeed noticed. I gave no sign I heard her impertinence. At the main entrance, a guard held open the door for us. I gave him what I hoped was a cheery smile, although it probably looked more like a grimace. I felt unexpectedly weary already. My legs trembled, my muscles ached, and my heart pounded far too fast. It was shocking, really, how out of condition I was. I held my head high and tried to hide how heavily I breathed as I set off for the place where I had previously encountered the seer.

"Isn't this a lovely spot?" Ettu's voice was overly cheery as she pointed out a wooden bench positioned beside a garden bed. For once, there were no narcissus nearby. "Perhaps we could sit here for a short while? I find myself quite weary tonight."

I knew exactly what she was doing. I ignored her and marched on, although it felt like I waded through mud and every step became more difficult than the last. Ettu and Merytre dawdled behind me, and I caught the whisper of a conversation between them.

"Oh!" Merytre exclaimed. "My sandal just broke."

"Perhaps we should go back," Ettu said. "You can hardly walk with only one sandal."

I didn't bother to look, knowing they would have contrived a way to ensure Merytre's sandal really was broken in case I asked to see it. We weren't even halfway to my destination when my head began to swim. I stopped to wait for the dizziness to subside and prayed I would still be on my feet when it did, rather than lying on the ground.

"My lady, this is really too much for you," Ettu said as they caught up to me. "If you would tell us what is so urgent that you must go out tonight, perhaps we can help."

I didn't want to give them a reason to argue that finding the seer was not important enough to warrant continuing, but the ground swayed and tilted, and it seemed unlikely I could go much further. Perhaps I should turn back while I could still walk, rather than suffer the humiliation of my maids having to summon a guard to carry me. And of course, if they did, it would be Khaemmalu who came.

He was probably watching from the shadows even now. I had nothing to say to him, though, and even if he showed himself, I would simply hold my head high and walk away. Or I would if I was still capable of walking.

"I need your help," I admitted to Ettu and Merytre. "I must speak with the seer, but I find myself too weak."

"Perhaps I could take a message for you," Merytre suggested. "I could ask that she come to you."

"She won't," I said. "If I want to speak with her, I must find her."

"How do you know that?" Ettu asked. "I only recall you speaking with her once and she certainly didn't say any such thing then."

How did I know indeed? Khaemmalu had said it, but I couldn't tell them. More than that, though, it was a feeling I had. A certainty that one such as a seer would not make it easy to get information from her. But that's exactly what I intended to do tonight. I'd had enough of her clues and cryptic replies. It was time for real answers.

"If you would walk one on each side of me and let me hold your arms, I think I can manage," I said.

Ettu must have noticed I didn't answer her question, but she didn't ask again, only held out her arm for me. On my other side, Merytre did the same, and we set off again. At first, I tried to use their support as little as possible, but it wasn't long before I leaned heavily on them. To their credit, neither woman complained and they gave little sign of discomfort. Merytre carried her broken sandal but still wore its pair. She limped a little and likely regretted whatever incident had resulted in the damage to her shoe.

We were not far from where I had previously spoken with the seer when the bushes rustled. From the corner of my eye, I saw Ettu turn towards the direction of the noise. She shot me a look, which I pretended not to see. Merytre gave no sign she had noticed.

"Keep going," I said.

The bushes rustled again, but then we were past them. No doubt Khaemmalu crept through the shrubbery keeping pace with us. I longed to look for some sign of him, but didn't let myself turn my head. There were no further noises from the bushes, other than the startled squawk of a bird which sounded as if it had been abruptly woken from sleep.

As we drew near to the place where the seer was before, I was certain she would be waiting for me. She had said she knew I was looking for her, so of course she would be there again. But as we rounded the last bend in the path, she wasn't there. I stopped, drawing Ettu and Merytre to a halt since I still clutched their arms.

"Is this where you expected to meet her?" Ettu asked.

"She will be here." I strained to peer into the darkness. Surely she was nearby. She must know I searched for her. Was that patch of darkness beneath the tree over there merely another shadow or could it be her?

"There is nowhere for you to sit," Ettu said. "Unless you wish to sit on the grass."

I would have liked to say I could remain standing, but weariness washed over me and I stumbled. They grabbed me before I could fall.

"Sit down," Ettu said. "We will help you."

Between them they managed to lower me to the ground. Ettu fussed over my skirt, straightening it so it wouldn't wrinkle. There seemed little point in such a thing. After all, who would notice the creases in the dark?

"Shall I go fetch a blanket for you to sit on?" Merytre offered.

I waved away the suggestion. I was already on the grass, so it hardly mattered now. Ettu was muttering about cushions and something else I couldn't catch, when I became aware of someone nearby.

She wasn't quite in the shadows, but neither was she far enough out of them to see her clearly.

"Oh," Merytre said, apparently only just noticing the woman.

Ettu's mumbles died.

The four of us studied each other.

"I knew you would come," I said, and immediately felt like a fool.

She seemed to cock her head to the side, but said nothing.

"Do you intend to show yourself or will you stay in the shadows?" I asked, somewhat peevishly now. I had gone to much effort to get here, and the least she could do was come out to speak with me.

"Something which is hidden is not always what you think it is," the seer said.

She shifted slightly and a beam of moonlight fell on her face, making the scales glisten.

"What is that supposed to mean?" I asked. "Are you trying to say it is not really you hiding there?"

"You will make your own interpretation," she said. "One can deliver a message, but it is up to the receiver as to how they interpret it."

"Enough with this nonsense." I had no patience for her mysterious replies today. "I demand answers."

"I have told you that you already have the information you seek." She seemed unbothered by my irritation and continued to study me as calmly as always.

"Then help me understand it."

"What do you not understand?"

"My dreams."

I tried to pretend Ettu and Merytre weren't there. There was no way to avoid them hearing unless I sent them away, and that would only make it obvious I hid something from them. Ettu, at any rate, knew I had dreamed about the narcissus talking to me.

"Tell me your dreams," the seer said.

"I'm sure you already know."

I had dreamed of her, after all. She told me to leave while I still could. If she could send me a dream like that, she was undoubtedly responsible for the dreams about lions and narcissus as well. Someone was trying to send me a message and it seemed unrealistic to think I might be important enough to receive dream messages from two different people.

"What do you think the dreams tell you?" she asked.

Frustration welled within me. I wanted to lash out at her, to force her to tell me what I needed to know. Instead, I slapped my hand on the ground. It felt ineffective, and a little foolish, but I needed a physical way to convey my frustration. The seer's expression didn't change.

"I could have you arrested," I said. "Held until you give me answers."

"On what charge?" Her tone was as mild as ever. "Walking in the gardens of my home? A magistrate will see no crime in that."

She was right. Unless I fabricated a crime, the administrators wouldn't help me. I couldn't even threaten to use my position as Ornament to force her to talk since I didn't know whether I was still within Pharaoh's favour. Perhaps the birth of a girl child meant he would turn his attention elsewhere. Despite the relief of no longer having to feign politeness to a man I so despised, it would also mean I couldn't do what my father had sent me here for: to advocate for Babylon and to strengthen relations between our two countries. I shouldn't hope Pharaoh would no longer pay me attention.

"Please," I said. "I need to know who the lion is."

The image of Khaemmalu's inking was burned into my mind. I tried not to see it. If the seer could look inside my head and see my thoughts, I didn't want her to know why I was so desperate to understand.

"What do you think the lion represents?" she countered.

"Danger." I spoke without thought. Merytre made a small noise, a gasp maybe, but it was too late to take back the word. "A threat, both to me and my babe."

The seer made a small movement that might have been a

shrug, but could equally have been simply a straightening of her back.

"It seems to me you have the information you seek," she said.

"I need to know who the lion is," I said. "Which person."

"If you believe the lion represents a person, then it would seem you already know who that person is."

"Argh." I slapped the ground again, even though it made me feel like a child. "Why do you never give me a proper answer?"

"It is up to she who seeks answers to find them for herself," she said. "You surely do not expect to merely demand them and have the answers neatly presented to you?"

But yes, that was exactly what I expected. I *knew* she knew, but she clearly didn't intend to tell me. If she thought I had to find the answers for myself, perhaps I needed to show her I was trying.

"I saw something recently." Again, I wished Ettu and Merytre were not within hearing distance. "Something that might be what the dreams are trying to warn me of."

"Aah."

I waited, but she said nothing further.

"It was an inked marking on skin," I said. "Of a lion."

"And you believe the person who bears this marking is the lion from your dreams?" She gave me no hint as to whether I was right.

"He must be," I said. "I have been dreaming for months about the narcissus keeping me safe from lions, and then I encounter someone bearing the image of that very beast. Surely this is who the dreams meant for me to be wary of."

"And who or what does the narcissus represent?" she asked.

I had no answer for that. Who indeed could protect me from Khaemmalu? Not Pharaoh. He would sentence us both to death if he knew what we had done. The administrators might have such power, or Panouk anyway. Maybe he had the authority to fire Khaemmalu, or transfer him, at least. If Khaemmalu was no longer employed by the Palace of the Ornaments, he would lose his privileges to enter the grounds and I would be safe from him.

But my babe wouldn't be. Khaemmalu was in Pharaoh's employ, so he might merely be transferred to Pharaoh's palace. And there he would have easy access to Baby Ishtar.

The dreams weren't warning me to trust the administrators to keep both me and my babe safe from Khaemmalu. It was too obvious. The seer meant for me to figure out something else. The administrators weren't the narcissus.

"Beware your assumptions," the seer said, as if she could indeed read my thoughts. "Those we cling to the hardest are often false."

"If you won't speak plainly, I'm wasting my time," I said.

I thought that might encourage her to tell me something. Anything. I would take the smallest scrap of information she offered. But she seemed unbothered by my exasperation.

"That is as it is," she said. "I only urge you to set aside your assumptions and think for yourself."

CHAPTER 12

*E*ttu and Merytre helped me up from the grass and I discovered the brief rest had given the tremble in my legs time to stop. I was able to walk on my own, for now at least. I should have known the seer wouldn't tell me what I wanted. I had almost forgotten my companions until someone's sandal scraped on the path. Ettu cleared her throat.

"That was an interesting conversation," she ventured.

"Indeed." Perhaps if I made it clear I had no wish to discuss it, she would leave the matter alone.

Before she could reply, a bush rustled off to our left, and I restrained a sigh. Surely after I had ignored him earlier, Khaemmalu would know I had no desire to see him. But it wasn't true. Despite the narcissus's warning, I couldn't simply switch off my feelings.

"Lady Kassaya."

I was so immersed in my thoughts, I didn't even notice him waiting on the path ahead of me. As I met his eyes, the rest of the world fell away, and all I could think about was how it had been between us. He was gentle and thoughtful, and he made me feel alive. It was hard to believe it would be Khaemmalu who betrayed me, but the dreams had been quite clear.

I nodded an acknowledgement at him and went to walk past. His fingers grazed mine as I drew close.

"Kassaya." This time his voice was intended for my ears alone. "What is wrong?"

Mindful of Ettu and Merytre's presence, I glanced over my shoulder, only to find them huddled together some distance behind me with their backs to me.

"I'm tired, Khaemmalu," I said. "I must return to my chambers."

"I heard your babe has been taken to Pharaoh's palace." It wasn't a question. He already knew. Perhaps he thought that was why I was upset.

My throat choked at the reminder and I nodded, not trusting myself to speak.

"She will be well looked after." His voice was gentle. "You do not need to fear for her."

But I do, I wanted to say. And I'm afraid it might be you I should fear. But I said none of that, only nodded again.

"I must go," I muttered.

"Kassaya." His fingers grazed mine again. "Tell me, what happened between us? I don't understand."

My eyes filled with tears and I turned away so he wouldn't see them.

"Please?" he asked.

I hurried away. He didn't follow me, and I knew he wouldn't. It would draw too much attention from anyone who saw us. My heart hurt so much, I thought I might never feel anything other than pain again.

There had been too much pain in my life lately. My sister's

disappearance and the subsequent revelation of her fate. Ahmose's sudden death, unexpected to everyone except perhaps herself. My babe torn from my arms before I had time to nurse her, let alone memorise her every feature. And now the discovery that Khaemmalu wasn't who I thought he was. That he might be the very thing I should fear the most.

It was too much. How could any person be expected to bear so much pain?

Ettu and Merytre followed me in silence. As we reached the Palace entrance, Merytre cleared her throat.

"Do you need me to return to your chambers with you?" she asked.

Sutem must have finished work by now and would be waiting to walk her home.

"No," I said. "Go ahead. We will see you in the morning."

"Thank you, my lady." She bobbed me a quick bow, murmured something to Ettu, and hurried off.

Her step was jaunty now and that only made my heart ache even more. She was a young woman on her way to meet the man she loved, to go home with him, where they could have privacy and solitude and togetherness. All things I would never have.

Back in my chambers, Sehener gave us a cheery smile and seemed to fairly sparkle. Here was another woman who was able to be with the man she loved, even if it was only within the confines of my chambers.

"A messenger came for you, my lady," she said.

"It's rather late for messengers." Ettu paused by the table that held the remains of our dinner. She surveyed it as if trying to decide whether she was hungry.

"He brought word from Lady Henutmire." Sehener straightened her wig. If it had been crooked, I never noticed.

"Is something wrong?" I asked.

Perhaps she had received news of her brother. Pharaoh had kept him locked up for some weeks now, ever since their father sent him to Thebes to view Henutmire for himself and confirm she was indeed alive and well.

"She is holding a gathering tomorrow night," Sehener said. "The messenger implied it was quite a last minute decision and that was why he was sent so late with invitations."

"I assume you declined for me."

I dropped onto a couch. In my distress about Khaemmalu, I had almost forgotten my exhaustion, but now it rushed back over me, leaving me light headed and with trembling legs. I leaned back and closed my eyes, thankful for the sturdiness of the couch beneath me. My heart beat too fast and I breathed far harder than I should after walking at such a sedate pace.

"Actually, I said you would be pleased to attend," Sehener said.

I should probably open my eyes. Glare at her or something. But my eyelids seemed fixed shut and I didn't have the strength for such an effort as would take to open them.

"Am I not supposed to be resting and confined to my chambers?" A party was the last thing I felt like. The healer would surely not approve anyway.

Sehener stammered a reply, clearly not having expected me to object after how determined I had been to go out earlier. Ettu came to her rescue.

"Some socialisation will be good for you," she said. "And you like Lady Henutmire."

"I'm not sure I particularly like anyone right now," I muttered.

I could feel Ettu's glare.

"I should go let the men out," Sehener said.

The sound of her footsteps left the chamber. A nearby couch squeaked as Ettu lowered herself into it. Footsteps coming back preceded Sehener, Tall and Half, followed by the sounds of them settling themselves on various couches.

"Was your walk enjoyable, my lady?" Half asked.

"Not particularly."

The silence stretched for some time before he spoke again.

"I should like to be able to take a walk, even if it was only through the Palace grounds after dark. I find myself growing weary of our circumstances here. Not that I am complaining," he added hurriedly. "I am most grateful to have accommodation and food without having to perform for Pharaoh each night, and the company is quite enjoyable, too."

A pause in which I imagined him and Ettu looking fondly into each others eyes. They were probably holding hands. Tears welled again and I squeezed my eyes more tightly shut so they wouldn't spill over. Half might wish for freedom, but at least he and Ettu had each other. Tall and Sehener had each other, too. Merytre had Sutem. Who did I have? Nobody, and I never would.

Show Pharaoh what the women of Babylon are made of. My mother's voice rose unbidden in my mind. What would she think if she could see me now? Sulking on the couch, too angry with the world to even be civil to the folk who were probably my closest friends. No matter whether Pharaoh ever saw me like this, it was certainly not what my mother expected of me.

I sat up and took my time straightening my wig and smoothing my skirt so as to avoid looking at anyone. But when I finally looked up, they were all watching me.

"What?" I asked.

"I suppose we are waiting to see if you intend to explain," Ettu said.

I didn't know whether she meant for me to explain about Khaemmalu, or the seer, or my reluctance to attend Henutmire's gathering. Maybe she meant all of it, or none of it. I couldn't, though. It would sound mad if I told them I thought the seer was trying to communicate with me through my dreams.

And I didn't yet have the words to tell anyone what had been between me and Khaemmalu, or to admit I had made a terrible mistake. Even not wanting to socialise with the other Ornaments was too entangled with the other matters for anyone else to make sense of.

The only way they would understand was for me to tell them everything, and I couldn't do that. Better they knew as little as possible. If my affair with Khaemmalu was somehow revealed, I might yet protect my companions if they were ignorant of it. With that, I buried any thought of telling them and gave Ettu what I hoped was a blank look.

"I'm not sure I know what you mean," I said.

She didn't even pretend to hide her scoff.

"It's true I've been feeling morose since Baby Ishtar was born," I said. "I didn't expect her to be taken from me so soon." My voice broke and I paused to compose myself. "That hurt more than I anticipated."

"It's perfectly natural for a woman to feel sad after childbirth." Merytre's voice was breezy. "Gautseshen told me."

"You have been speaking with Gautseshen?" The revelation startled me, although I wasn't sure why.

Given Khaemmalu and Sutem were friendly with each other, it wasn't unreasonable to think they might spend time together outside of work, if they were ever off duty together.

And perhaps Khaemmalu's sister, Gautseshen, would join them as well.

I hadn't really pictured any of them away from work before. Not even Merytre, but of course she went home with Sutem every night. She had a whole other life I knew little about, and apparently that included Gautseshen.

"I saw her recently." Merytre's voice was hesitant, as if she wondered whether she revealed something she shouldn't.

"How lovely for you." It sounded daft and insincere, but I wanted her to know she didn't have to keep such a thing a secret.

"I quite liked her the one time I met her," Ettu said. "And not just because she stitched Half back together. I could see myself being friends with her if the situation was different."

If she didn't spend her days and nights attending to me and without any time for something as mundane as friendship with someone outside of my chambers.

"I am with child," Merytre blurted out.

Everyone turned to look at her. I was thankful their attention was on her, because hopefully it meant they all missed how I flinched.

"That is why I was speaking with Gautseshen," she added.

"That's wonderful." Sehener's voice was warm. She went to Merytre and leaned down to hug her. "I am so happy for you."

"As am I," Ettu said, although she didn't go to Merytre. It was only because I knew her as well as I did that I noticed the hesitation in her voice.

Merytre looked to me, and the way her chin wobbled told me she was anxious about my reaction.

"Congratulations." I did my best to make my tone as warm as Sehener's. I might not have quite managed it, but at least I didn't burst into tears as I thought I might.

"I know the timing is terrible," Merytre said.

I waved away the rest of whatever she was going to say.

"Nonsense," I said. "It's wonderful news and I am sure we will all be pleased to have such a distraction."

How would I bear it? It would be a constant reminder of my separation from my own babe. Watching Merytre's belly grow rounder, listening to her complain about the morning sickness and how her body ached and that her ankles had grown puffy. Listening to her screams and groans during the birth. Hearing the babe cry for the first time. Watching Merytre hold her babe, feed her babe. Do all the things I would never do.

Or at least, I assumed I would have to watch. I had paid little attention to the various small children around the Palace, other than to assume they were children of servants. After all, if they were conceived by Pharaoh, they would be taken from their mothers like Baby Ishtar was.

I left, trying not to look like I hurried out. The sitting chamber was silent as I went and it was only once I was in my bedchamber with the door closed that voices arose again. No doubt they discussed why I had left like that. But I had to. I didn't want to spoil Merytre's proud moment, but I couldn't sit there and listen to them speculate about whether the babe would be a girl or a boy. Not yet.

CHAPTER 13

*E*ttu, Merytre and Sehener spent what seemed to be an unnecessary amount of time preparing me for Henutmire's gathering. At least nobody suggested summoning the rest of my lady's maids, a thing for which I was both thankful and mystified. Since when had Ettu considered it appropriate for just the three of them to dress me for an event? I didn't question this unexpected good fortune, though, for fear she might change her mind if she thought about it. At least preparing me for the gathering distracted them from endless speculation about Merytre's announcement.

The matter of which gown I should wear became the subject of fierce debate amongst the three women. I didn't particularly care what I wore so long as I was suitably covered, a thing which was not necessarily guaranteed with Egyptian fashions. At length, they settled on a pale blue gown which flowed loosely over my body. My belly still protruded from the months spent carrying my babe and I was grateful the gown didn't put too much focus on it.

I didn't feel like my old self yet, and perhaps I never would.

It wasn't just that my body had yet to return to its earlier shape — my hips were more rounded and my breasts were larger, although they no longer ached with unneeded milk — but something within me was different. I wasn't the person I had been and I didn't know how to change that.

It was only as I left my chambers that evening that I realised this would be the first time I had interacted with other Ornaments since Baby Ishtar's birth. I prayed to Marduk they wouldn't ask too many questions. My emotions were still fragile, tears were constantly ready to spill over, and the wrong question was likely to set me off.

I had cried when Henutmire and Gilukhipa both sent me bouquets of flowers from the gardens the day after the birth. A messenger brought Neferu's congratulations, which also sent me into tears. Tiye was the only one I hadn't heard from, although that hardly surprised me. She was not the type to commend another woman on producing a child for Pharaoh.

Henutmire let me into her chambers with what looked like a genuine smile.

"Kassaya," she said warmly. "I wasn't sure you would come. Are you recovered?"

"More or less," I said. "Thank you for inviting me."

She gestured towards a table where Gilukhipa and Ineni were pouring mugs of wine.

"Get yourself a drink," she said. "We will eat soon. I hope you are hungry."

"Starving," I answered, although I wasn't really. My appetite had been poor since the birth, but I made myself eat so as to escape Ettu's attention.

Someone behind me caught Henutmire's notice, and I made my way over to Gilukhipa and Ineni.

"Oh, you came," Ineni said. "We thought you wouldn't."

"Henutmire said the same thing." I selected a bottle and studied the label. A red wine from Thebes. Expensive, no doubt. Henutmire wouldn't serve anything less. "Thank you for the flowers, by the way. I'm sorry I didn't think to send a message in reply."

"Oh, but you did." Ineni gave me a surprised look. "It was a lovely thank you. I was quite touched."

"How silly of me." I forced a chuckle, although it felt awkward. "I forgot."

One of my maids must have arranged it, probably Ettu. If she told me she was doing so, I had no recollection of the conversation. Henutmire sidled up beside me and poured herself some wine.

"We will eat as soon as Tiye arrives," she said. "Although the food will be quite cold if she doesn't hurry up."

The door opened just as she finished speaking and Tiye bestowed a smile on us. She was elegantly dressed as always — they all were — in a creamy-coloured gown which clung to her curves. It reminded me how big my belly still was and I held my mug low in front of it, hoping to hide it somewhat.

"Kassaya, I am surprised to see you." Tiye came straight to me and made a show of looking me up and down. "I hear your recovery has not been easy."

How had she heard such a thing? None of those who shared my chambers would spread such gossip, and I couldn't imagine the healer talking about one of her patients. A kitchen maid, perhaps. Someone who had glimpsed me but knew nothing of my condition.

"I am well enough." I aimed for a breezy tone and thought I pulled it off until I saw Henutmire's frown.

"You look positively awful," Tiye pronounced. "You should sit down. I fear you will fall over as soon as stand there."

"Do sit, Kassaya," Henutmire said. "You can tell me what you want and I will fill a plate for you."

Having other Ornaments wait on me made me uncomfortable, but Henutmire had sent away her maids as was usual for these gatherings, and the short walk to her chambers left my legs shaking. So I sat and Henutmire fussed around me, fetching food and topping up my wine even though I had drunk no more than a sip. Their light-hearted chatter turned serious as soon as everyone was seated.

"Have you had any word of your brother?" Ineni asked Henutmire around a mouthful.

Henutmire set down the hen leg she had been gnawing on and gave a heavy sigh.

"Nothing," she said. "And Pharaoh has not called for me since I begged for my brother's freedom. I fear I have angered him greatly. He might never summon me again."

Personally, I didn't see that as a bad thing, but I kept my thoughts to myself, aware I might now be perceived to have a level of security in my position that those who hadn't borne Pharaoh a child didn't have.

"I told you I will ask after your brother when I can," Tiye said. "But I must wait for the right moment. If Pharaoh is in the wrong mood, I will only risk alienating him and that will not help our cause."

I thought the cause she meant was getting Henutmire's brother released, but the decided nods from the other women made me suspect it was something more.

"Speaking of causes," Neferu said. "I received a message from my cousin last week. He says support for change is growing amongst the common folk."

"He didn't write that, did he?" Gilukhipa asked. "You know the scribe reads everything."

"Of course not." Neferu shot her a withering look. "He obscured his meaning, but I knew what he meant. He's working to ensure the people will support us when the time comes."

"As is my brother," Tiye added. "He is speaking with the military chiefs. They are not quite ready to commit, but he believes they will be soon. We must be ready to act as soon as we receive word from him."

"And we have support for your son?" Ineni asked. "It's not enough for folk to merely support a change of government. They must be willing to support Pentaweret taking the throne."

"His support grows every day." Tiye tossed her braids back and looked nothing but confident. "He's actively working in the community, letting them see how dedicated and skilled he is. I believe he will have the support he needs very soon."

Although they appeared to talk casually, I sensed there was more to the conversation than I understood. Tiye, Ineni, Gilukhipa and Neferu were too tightly wound, and the looks that passed between them seemed to say more than their words did. This was not merely about removing Pharaoh from the throne. There was something more at stake. Only Henutmire seemed unaffected, eating with gusto and jumping up from time to time to refill our mugs. Had I misunderstood their plan?

"What will happen to Pharaoh?" I feigned concentration on pulling apart a piece of bread, hoping it would make me look only half-interested in the answer and thus encourage them to talk more freely.

"He will be taken care of," Tiye said quickly. She sipped her wine as if to give herself a reason to say nothing further.

"How exactly?" Henutmire finally looked up from her plate. "I just realised we haven't discussed this."

"We will finalise that sort of detail later," Tiye answered. "It is not something you need concern yourself with at this point."

Her obvious avoidance of a proper answer confirmed my growing suspicion, which was only further reiterated by the look that passed between Gilukhipa and Neferu.

"I would like to know what the plan is, though," I pushed. "Will he be imprisoned? How do we ensure he doesn't take back the throne? No matter how much support there is to remove him, there must surely still be those who want him to remain in power."

"Like Hori," Henutmire said. At my blank look, she explained. "He is the governor of Thebes and son of the high priest of Ptah. Very influential. He's a great supporter of Pharaoh."

Tiye and Neferu exchanged glances. Neferu seemed to give a small shrug, perhaps indicating Tiye should tell us whatever was being held back. Tiye rejected it with the slightest shake of her head.

"Everything is in hand," she said. "We shall not discuss those details today."

From the look on Henutmire's face, I guessed she was more confused than suspicious. Tiye changed the topic to Palace gossip and Ineni, Gilukhipa and Neferu were only too pleased to contribute. The evening was late by the time the gathering ended, and although nothing else had been said about the plot to depose Pharaoh, I left convinced there was more to Tiye's plan than she was saying.

iye's obvious evasion was still on my mind when I woke the next morning. I had little time to ponder what was left unsaid, though, when Merytre arrived bearing a letter.

"From your father," she said as she handed me the scroll. "I ran into the runner just down the hallway and took it from him."

My father's seal was broken, a clear sign the scroll had been read. Pentau would have reviewed the letter whether the seal appeared to be broken or not. I didn't know whether to be pleased or offended he didn't even try to hide his spying. The others settled themselves on nearby couches and watched me expectantly. I started to unroll the scroll, but hesitated.

"Oh, you probably want some privacy," Ettu said, jumping up. "We should leave you alone to read it."

"No, no." I waved at her to sit back down, even though that was exactly what I wanted. But they would only expect to hear the details later. "You may as well stay."

I allowed myself a small smile when I realised Father's

message was once again written in Babylonian cuneiform. That would have frustrated Pentau, since he didn't, as far as I knew, read our language. So unless he had found someone who could read it for him, he didn't know what the letter said.

It was briefer than I hoped, barely half a dozen lines. I skimmed it, wanting to know what it said before I decided how much to share with the others. There might be something I wanted to keep to myself.

My dear daughter, it began. *I received your letter regarding your sister earlier today. Thank you for sending word of her. I look forward to confirmation of the safe arrival of your child.*

Of course, he wouldn't have yet received my most recent letter. This reply was for the two I sent some weeks ago, one official message sent through Pentau and a second which Merytre sent secretly for me.

I trust you are doing everything in your power to make the alliance between Babylon and Egypt worth what we have given for it, the letter continued.

Did he mean the ships of tribute, which Pharaoh probably never even inspected? Or was this an allusion to the two daughters Father had sacrificed to the treaty?

Your mother sends her best regards. The letter ended with Father's name and titles.

That was it. The entire contents of his reply to the news that my sister had disappeared and was believed to have been murdered. I set the scroll in my lap as I sorted through my thoughts. Father's tone was cool and he made no mention of being sorry to receive my message.

I was grateful he didn't mention my second letter, although I had no way of knowing whether he was being discreet, or if he never received it. He might know only as much as was included in the official message. It was my second, secret letter that told him of my sister's death.

His aloofness hurt, regardless of whether he knew she had been murdered, or only that she had disappeared. Where was any mention of regret for her disappearance? Where was the sadness at the fate of a daughter who was sent so far from home? Or the request for me to write again as soon as I had word of her?

He is a king, I reminded myself. This was his official response to correspondence from a daughter who was traded for an alliance. But still, I would have liked some sense of my father in the letter. The man, not the king.

"Well?" Ettu prompted. "What does it say?"

I paused to compose myself, then read it out to them, translating it into Egyptian as I did.

"Is that all?" she asked when I finished.

"It's a very short letter," I said.

"He sounds very…" Merytre's voice trailed away.

"Official," Ettu said quickly. "We must remember he is a very busy man. I suppose my lady is grateful he had time to send a reply. There must be Ornaments who never receive letters from their families."

Although Ettu's words were correct, they did nothing to soothe the sting of my father's coolness. Did he truly care so little for his daughters that this was all the reply he could be bothered to make?

"Besides," Ettu continued. "He wouldn't want to risk angering Pharaoh if the scribe reads it."

The others were swift to add their agreements that this must surely be the reason for such a cold reply. I nodded and pretended I accepted their pronouncements. There was no point provoking an argument by telling them they were wrong.

At least Father had replied, and he would surely write again when he received word of my babe. Pharaoh, on the other hand, had yet to acknowledge her. Was he angry she wasn't a boy? Did he not know? Did he have so many children already that the birth of yet another was too insignificant to acknowledge? I wished I knew.

"Send for a runner," I said over the top of their conversation. "I want him to deliver a message to Pharaoh."

"I will go." Merytre was already on her way to the door.

Ettu gave me a considering look.

"You think it a bad idea?" I asked.

"No," she said, although she didn't sound certain. "I just wondered what you intend to say."

"Maybe he doesn't know I have delivered my babe."

I couldn't say what I really feared: that I had angered him by giving him a daughter.

Ettu only shrugged. Half said something and she turned her attention to him. I was grateful for the distraction as it meant I could pass the time by planning my message.

At last, Merytre returned with a runner. With Tall and Half safely locked away, the boy came to stand in front of me. He was a little older than the runners typically were, maybe as much as twelve years old. He was just as skinny as always, though. I supposed his busy occupation left little opportunity for weight gain.

"You will deliver a message to Pharaoh for me." I spoke sternly, hoping to impress on the boy the seriousness of his errand.

He nodded solemnly and I regretted my sharpness. The runners were always diligent with their duties. I didn't need to tell him a message to Pharaoh was of the utmost importance.

"Tell him the Lady Kassaya, daughter of Marduk-apla-iddina of Babylon, has safely delivered a girl child. The babe's name is Ishtar. Lady Kassaya would be very grateful to receive news of her child. Now, repeat that back to me."

The boy dutifully recited my words, stumbling a little over my father's name. I made him repeat it until he could say it correctly.

"Return to me as soon as you have delivered the message," I said.

He gave me a little bow and hurried off. I tried to mask my impatience while I waited for his return. After all, he had to walk all the way to Pharaoh's palace, which was a journey of at least an hour, even with legs as young as his. Then he would have to wait until Pharaoh could see him, deliver his message, wait while Pharaoh composed his reply, and walk all the way back.

It would probably be at least three hours before I might expect Pharaoh's reply, but it could be much longer. If he was busy, he might not have time for the boy until tonight, or perhaps even tomorrow. I shut down that line of thought before I could dwell on whether Pharaoh might keep the boy waiting for several days.

To my surprise, he returned only a few hours later.

"Go on," I said. "What is the reply?"

"There is no reply, my lady," he said.

"Did you not deliver my message?"

"I did indeed, my lady. I went straight to Pharaoh's administrator and told it to him. He nodded and said I could leave."

"I told you to deliver it to Pharaoh." Frustration made my tone sharp. Had my instruction not been clear enough?

"But, my lady, messages are always given to the administrator." The boy shot a desperate look around the chamber, as if hoping someone would come to his rescue. "I have never delivered a message directly to Pharaoh."

"I believe the boy is correct, my lady," Merytre said. "It's quite common that messages for Pharaoh are delivered to his administrator. The man will then decide which are relayed to Pharaoh."

"But who tells Pharaoh the message?" I asked.

"The administrator, I presume," she said. "It would be highly irregular for a runner to present a message directly to Pharaoh himself."

My cheeks heated as I realised my foolishness in assuming Pharaoh would have time to receive every messenger who asked for him. Of course there would be a process where someone else took the messages and decided what was important enough to warrant Pharaoh's attention and what could be dealt with, or ignored, without disturbing him. It wasn't like I hadn't grown up in a palace. I knew how such a bureaucracy functioned.

Ettu must have noticed my dismay, because she dismissed the runner. He cast a worried glance at me as he headed to the door, as if wondering whether I intended to make a complaint about his failure to deliver the message to Pharaoh. Ettu followed him into the hallway, presumably to reassure him.

"Is there no way for me to contact Pharaoh directly?" I asked while she was gone.

"Could you request Panouk sends a message to Pharaoh's administrator?" Sehener suggested. "Perhaps that would ensure it would be passed on to him."

"But if the fellow has already decided such a message doesn't justify Pharaoh's attention, he's hardly likely to change his mind just because it comes via another administrator," Merytre pointed out. "Indeed, we don't even know he won't pass it on."

"We know someone who might have an idea of how to get to Pharaoh," Sehener said, nodding towards the hallway that led to the bedchambers.

Of course, she wouldn't risk saying anything more while the door was still open and the runner presumably within earshot. Once the runner was gone and the men returned to the sitting chamber, Sehener asked if they had any ideas. Half studied the wall as he pondered the problem, a thoughtful expression on his face. Tall only frowned.

"What is it?" Sehener asked, reaching for his hand.

Tall flinched a little as she touched him, although he didn't pull away. He never liked being touched when he wasn't the one to initiate the contact, but he tolerated it better from Sehener than anyone else.

"Worry!" he said. He flapped his other hand, the thing he always did when he was anxious.

"Of what, my love?" Sehener asked.

Tall frowned again and flapped harder. She waited patiently while he found a word.

"Bad!" he said at last.

"You think it is a bad idea?" she asked.

"Bad!"

"There is a person who is bad?"

He stopped flapping and stared intently at her.

"The administrator is bad?" she guessed.

Tall nodded and resumed his flapping.

"I think he's worried about my lady drawing attention to herself," Sehener said. "He doesn't trust Pharaoh's administrator. Is that right, love?"

Tall nodded again. His mouth worked as he searched for a word.

"Feel!" he said.

"I know," Sehener said. "It's just a feeling, but you have good instincts. If you think the administrator cannot be trusted, we should trust that."

Ettu cleared her throat and gave me a pointed look.

"Yes," I said quickly. "Thank you, Tall. Perhaps trying another message through the administrator is not a good idea."

"What exactly was your aim in sending a messenger to Pharaoh?" Half asked. "Are you seeking his acknowledgement of the birth or trying to obtain information about your babe's welfare?"

"The latter, of course," I said.

I cared little enough for Pharaoh or his opinions to concern myself with whether he acknowledged Baby Ishtar's birth, but I desperately wanted news of her. Just to hear she was well, that she was eating and sleeping as she should be, would ease my mind immensely. Of course, it wouldn't be enough. I would want more news of her, and more, but I would make it last me for now.

"If I may be so bold, then," Half said, "I would suggest your lady's maids may be able to obtain such information for you."

"Of course," Ettu said. "Merytre and Sehener have extensive networks amongst the maids, and there are many here who know folk working in Pharaoh's palace. My own network is considerably smaller, but I might also have some connections who could help. Why don't the three of us put out word to ask for news of your babe?"

"I can do that," Merytre said.

Sehener also gave an enthusiastic assurance of her eagerness to help.

"I would be most appreciative if you could get word of her

for me." I felt rather daft I hadn't thought of it myself. I hadn't yet encountered a maid who didn't like to gossip, and they were only too pleased to pass on any news.

Actually, there *was* one maid who didn't seem to care for gossip: Abar. I hadn't seen her since before Baby Ishtar's birth, as my maids had been told I didn't need their assistance while I recovered. I had interacted with Abar little since she accused me of having both her sister and mine killed, and said she would make me sorry if I had lied about what happened to Atahar.

I had my own network, too. I could put word out amongst the Ornaments. Many likely had access to information from Pharaoh's palace, not least of all Tiye.

But seeking information from Tiye wouldn't be free. She would expect something in return and I had little enough of my own to give. In exchange for word on Abar's sister, Tiye had taken my hairbrush with the handle carved from the tusk of a beast that was supposed to be the size of Babylon's Great Temple. And I had given Amanitore the promise of a favour of her choosing for her aid in speaking with my sister after her death, a deal I knew was not in my favour.

I had nothing else to trade but my jewels, and the other Ornaments had enough of those. It would be better to let my maids use their networks to get information for me.

CHAPTER 15

*O*nly half a day passed between Henutmire's gathering and the arrival of a runner boy bearing an invitation for a gathering that evening in Tiye's chambers. Ettu accepted on my behalf and sent the boy on his way.

"That's rather strange," she said as she returned to her spot beside Half on the couch. "It's so soon after the last party."

It must be about the plan to depose Pharaoh. I could think of no other reason why the runner would stress the urgency of the invitation, nor why Tiye was hosting us in her own chambers, an offer she had never made before, and which surprised me more than the timing.

A few short hours later, I was on my way to Tiye's chambers, which were not far from my own. As I turned down her hallway, Henutmire hurried up behind me. Her two maids dawdled some distance back, seemingly too busy with their conversation to pay attention to what their mistress did.

"Kassaya." Henutmire was slightly out of breath as she greeted me. "Hurry up," she called over her shoulder to her maids. "You will wait here for me."

So I wasn't the only one who expected tonight's gathering to be brief. I had already told Ettu and Sehener to wait rather than return in a few hours as they normally would. Surely little enough had changed since last night to warrant a lengthy conversation.

Our maids halted at the end of the hallway and made themselves comfortable for the wait. Tiye was very particular about who entered "her" hallway.

"This is unusual," Henutmire murmured to me, presumably trying to avoid either her maids or mine hearing. "Do you know anything?"

"Only as much as the runner said."

Tiye opened the door herself, something I had never before seen her do. But of course her maids were absent and there was nobody to do it other than herself. She greeted us graciously, thanked us for coming at such short notice, and invited us to pour ourselves some wine. She gave no reason for the urgency of the summons, but I supposed she wouldn't with the maids just a short distance down the hallway.

We were the first to arrive and I felt rather awkward as Henutmire and I waited together. I sipped my wine sparingly, wanting a clear head for the discussion. Tiye stood by the door, seemingly busy inspecting her fingernails. The others came one by one, first Ineni, then Neferu. Gilukhipa was the last to arrive.

"Quickly," Tiye said as soon as she had ushered Gilukhipa inside. "Get yourselves some food and sit down. We have much to discuss."

The food laid out for us was as elaborate as ever, with a selection of baked fish and hen, roasted root vegetables, and a salad of lettuce, cucumber and little onions, along with several types of bread and cheese. The chamber was silent as we served ourselves other than the sounds of spoons against platters and an occasional "excuse me" or "no, you go first" as two women reached for the same thing.

We settled ourselves on the cushions. My stomach growled and I had a hen's leg halfway to my mouth before I noticed nobody else was eating. Reluctantly, I set it back down again. I hoped we wouldn't have to wait to eat until after the discussion. But Tiye didn't hesitate. As soon as everyone was seated, she cleared her throat.

"I received a message from my brother this morning," she said, giving us a look that seemed loaded with significance.

"The one liaising with the military chiefs?" Ineni asked.

"The same," Tiye said. "He's also helping garner support amongst the residents of Thebes. He says details about Hydna's unfortunate fate have reached the common folk and animosity towards Pharaoh is higher than he has ever seen."

"But—" I started, then realised perhaps I shouldn't share my suspicion that Panouk had failed to carry out Hydna and Weren's death sentence.

Besides, surely I wasn't the only one who suspected their fates weren't what we had been told. If the others thought it a good idea to use the information that was publicly available, maybe I should keep what I knew to myself. Or, rather, what I thought I knew. Panouk had hinted they weren't executed, but I didn't actually know anything, and perhaps I had been eager to misinterpret what might have merely been his hesitance to discuss a deeply unpleasant matter.

"But?" Tiye's voice was cool and she raised her eyebrow at me, a clear challenge in both face and voice. She never liked being questioned.

"Nothing," I muttered.

"My brother feels it is time to act." Tiye deliberately met

the eyes of each of us. "So now is the time for you to decide whether you are in or out. If you are involved with our plan past this, you will be involved until the end."

"I'm in," Neferu said, without hesitation.

"Me too," Ineni said.

Tiye's gaze landed on Gilukhipa who was visibly paler than before.

"Well?" Tiye asked her.

"You know my reservation," Gilukhipa said. "And I have not changed my mind on that."

"Nevertheless, you understand why it must be this way," Tiye said. "So make your choice."

After another moment's hesitation, Gilukhipa sighed.

"I'm in," she said.

Tiye looked to Henutmire next, who quickly nodded.

"Say it," Tiye said. "I want to hear everyone make the same commitment in front of all of us. There will be no confusion later about who committed and who didn't."

"I'm in," Henutmire said, almost fiercely. "And when the throne is taken from him, I will expect my brother to be immediately released."

"That has already been agreed," Tiye said, then turned to me.

"What exactly is our aim?" I asked.

She cocked her head to the side and studied me.

"I'm sure you already know," she said.

"I want to hear you say it." I tried to match her forcefulness. "I doubt you want anyone committing without fully understanding the aim."

"We will send the hawk to the West," she said.

Although I hadn't heard the phrase before, I was familiar enough with the way the Egyptians danced around the topic of death. For folk who seemed so fixated on it, they did everything they could to avoid actually talking about it.

"You intend to kill him," I said.

Henutmire gave a little gasp, followed by a laugh.

"Oh, no, Kassaya," she said. "You misunderstand."

But when nobody else laughed, she looked around at the other women.

"She misunderstands, doesn't she?" she asked. "That is not the plan."

Gilukhipa, Ineni and Neferu all looked to Tiye. It had never been more clear to me that she was the one making the decisions. The other women might have their own reasons for getting involved, but this plan was Tiye's. How she must loathe Pharaoh to do such a thing. She acted the adoring Ornament so perfectly, never giving even so much as a hint of her hatred. I wondered if he would ever know that hers was the mind who orchestrated his downfall.

Tiye looked evenly at Henutmire, seemingly unperturbed.

"What did you think we were going to do?" she asked. "Taking the throne from him is one thing, but how would we ever stop him from simply taking it back? He still has support amongst the military, as we discussed last time. There are still those who will do as he says, however hideous and immoral, merely because he is Pharaoh and a living god."

"But to kill him?" Henutmire's voice was faint. "That is so... final."

But it wasn't about revenge. It was about protection, and not only for those women who suffered his cruelty. Tiye had privately confessed to me that she knew of only two women who had ever retired from the Palace. What happened to the thousands of others who had lived in this place? Perhaps they were sent home, or somewhere else. Maybe Pharaoh didn't want to be reminded of a woman he no longer had interest in. But perhaps something more sinister occurred to them.

Every Ornament here was in jeopardy, if not from Pharaoh himself, then from whoever removed those women once they were past their childbearing age. So was every woman who would come after us. He had to be stopped in order to protect ourselves and all those who would follow.

"I'm in," I said.

Henutmire gave me an aghast look.

"No," she said. "I expected it of the others, but you, Kassaya?"

My thoughts were too complicated to share, and I didn't know if the others knew Pharaoh liked to abuse the women he was intimate with, or how few Ornaments ever retired. I was reluctant to share what Tiye had told me in front of her. If she hadn't told them, she had her reasons for it, and I didn't want to be seen to cross her.

"Think of your brother, Henutmire," Ineni urged. "Once Pharaoh is gone, he will be freed."

"And Pentaweret is a good man," Neferu added. "Think of what he will do for the economy, for the lives of the common folk. We live in luxury and it shields us from reality, but the commoners make do with very little. Their existence is far harsher than ours. If Pentaweret will work to improve their lives, then he has my support."

"He will also advocate for better relations with our allies," Gilukhipa said. "I myself am eager to see a less hostile relationship with Mitanni. I was sent here to strengthen our alliance, but it is difficult when Pharaoh is only willing to act in Egypt's favour."

Henutmire bit her lip as she looked around the circle of women.

"I don't know," she said.

"Make your decision," Tiye said. "If you do not intend to help, we cannot discuss anything more in front of you."

Henutmire's mouth wobbled a little. I could imagine what she was thinking: that if she didn't join us, she would forever be on the outside of this little group of friends. She would never again be a confidante of any of us. This thing we were about to do — the death of a living god — was too big and it would always lie between us.

"Can I think about it?" she asked.

Tiye shook her head and it seemed to me there was sadness in the action.

"You must decide," she said. "Are you in or out?"

Still Henutmire hesitated.

"My brother," she said. "Will you promise me on your own life that if we succeed, you will ensure he is released unharmed and allowed to return home?"

"I promise you on the life of my son, Pentaweret," Tiye said. "For his life is more dear to me than my own. All our futures depend on him."

Henutmire let out a shaky breath.

"I'm in," she said at last.

CHAPTER 16

*N*ow we had all given the commitment Tiye demanded, the conversation turned to specifics of the plan, and I was dismayed to discover that despite the talk about shoring up support amongst both commoners and the military, a key part of the plan was yet undecided: the matter of how, exactly, Pharaoh would die.

"I was thinking poison," Neferu said. "Something odourless and tasteless. We could slip it into his wine and he would never know until it was too late."

Just like the potion I dropped into his goblet before he bedded me. It had been Ahmose's idea, a concoction that would supposedly enhance his ability to get me with child. Baby Ishtar was evidence of its success. Thinking about Ahmose made me miss her all over again with a sharpness that brought tears to my eyes. I quickly blinked them away. I didn't want anyone thinking I cried over Pharaoh's impending demise.

"Someone would need to smuggle it in," Tiye pointed out. "And there is the possibility of discovery in the moment of putting it in his wine. It would be a death sentence for the woman who is caught."

"Do we not all already face death if our plan is exposed?" Gilukhipa asked.

The chamber fell silent. For me, the realisation was like a slap in the face. I had known, of course, that such a crime was punishable by death, but I had avoided thinking about it. Much the same as how I had refused to consider my possible fate, or Khaemmalu's, if our affair was uncovered. By the time I did, I was already too in love with him to let it stop me. Not that it mattered anymore. The threat of execution mightn't keep me away from Khaemmalu, but the knowledge he was a danger to my daughter certainly would. There could never be anything between us again.

For the first time, I also comprehended the very deep trust I had put in these women. My life was literally in their hands. If any one of them were to betray us, we would all be executed.

"That is true," Tiye said. "I am merely pointing out that if a woman was discovered slipping poison into Pharaoh's goblet, she and she alone would pay the price."

"Assuming she kept her mouth shut and didn't incriminate the rest of us," Neferu said.

Tiye gave her an odd nod that seemed to mean neither yes nor no, but both at once. Perhaps she didn't believe any of us would hold our tongues if we were caught.

"Going back to Neferu's suggestion," Ineni said. "Poison can be unpredictable. The dose might be wrong or it might not affect him in the expected way. A blade would be more reliable."

"None of us would ever get close enough with a blade,"

Tiye said. "His guards still search my body every time, even after all these years."

"There might be a way to arrange for the guard who checks her to be one who is loyal to us, rather than Pharaoh," Ineni said.

"Possible, but if it went wrong, she would have no defence." Tiye dismissed the idea with a wave of her hand. "There is no other plausible reason for a woman to be carrying a blade when she meets Pharaoh."

"He is a rather large man," Henutmire said. She sounded uncertain, as if she wasn't sure she had anything to contribute, but wanted to show she tried. "And certainly much bigger than any of us. Would we have the strength to overpower him if he realised what was happening?"

"We have a man in his personal squad, don't we?" Ineni asked. "He would be well placed to get close to Pharaoh. Perhaps he could sneak up on him when he is sleeping."

"Or eating," Gilukhipa added.

But Tiye shook her head and it was clear the decision had been made. Pharaoh's demise would not be by blade.

"Who is our man within Pharaoh's squad?" I asked.

"His name is Bebi," Tiye said, somewhat absently. "I doubt you would know him."

But I did. Bebi was Khaemmalu's childhood friend, the man he considered his brother. If Bebi was involved with the plot, did that mean Khaemmalu was too? If they were as close as he claimed, surely there would be no secret so big as this between them.

But if Khaemmalu was involved, did that suggest my dreams were wrong? Why would he take my babe if he was fighting to bring Pharaoh down? I could make no sense of it and I didn't have the luxury of pondering it right now. I couldn't afford to miss a crucial detail in the conversation.

"Given we have one of his bodyguards, what about suffocation?" Ineni asked. Clearly, she favoured a fast and violent approach. "Even with a single guard, if one or more of us were there to help, surely we could manage it between us?"

"But what is to stop the other guards from coming to his aid?" Tiye pointed out. "Suffocation is not a swift means and Pharaoh will hardly sit still. He will fight and call out and someone will hear."

"And if they do," Gilukhipa added, "they will certainly come. They would be accused of complaisance otherwise."

They fell silent for a while. I wracked my brain to come up with a suggestion, but I had never before considered the possibility of killing a man and had no idea how to go about such a thing. Khaemmalu would know. If things were different, I could ask him. Ahmose, too, would have known. She killed the man she was given to. When I first learned of that, I wondered what would make a woman so desperate to escape that she would kill.

"Kassaya, do you have any ideas?" Tiye's gaze held a challenge and I remembered something she said to me not long after I arrived at the Palace. *Surely every group of women has their secrets,* she said. *An outsider would need to prove herself before such things are revealed.* I had asked how I could do that. *You will know when the time comes,* she said, and it seemed the time had indeed come.

"Snake bite?" I suggested. The idea seemed daft at first, but as my thoughts came together, it didn't feel quite so absurd anymore. "I saw a snake charmer not long ago. Tiye, you probably saw him too. It was at the festival for Min."

Tiye gave a slight nod.

"At the end of his performance, the snake went up his sleeve," I continued. "I don't know how such a thing is possible, but if a snake can be transported like that, could one be smuggled in and somehow made to bite Pharaoh?"

"They press on the snake's neck," Ineni said. "It makes the snake go rigid and that's how the fellow can carry it up his sleeve."

There was silence after Ineni's comment. I was a little surprised nobody rushed to say my idea was foolish, but the look on Tiye's face told me she actually considered it.

"It's not a terrible idea," she conceded. "Let's keep thinking, but if we can't come up something better quickly, we might go with that. Pharaoh needs little encouragement to hold a banquet and he might be persuaded to request a snake charmer. It would be unfortunate if one of the fellow's snakes got away from him, and even more unfortunate if Pharaoh was bitten."

"The snake charmer would have to disappear," Henutmire said. "And quickly. Once Pharaoh is bitten, the charmer's life is forfeit, for negligence if nothing else."

"We could arrange for him to flee the country," Ineni said. "Amun knows we all have jewels and whatnot of enough value to fund a new life for him elsewhere."

"Another idea if there were to be a banquet," Tiye said, "is an overdose of poppy."

"I have heard Pharaoh is quite partial to it," Gilukhipa said.

"I have seen him partake many times," Tiye said with a nod. "He will only take it if prepared by one of his personal guards or by me. I have mixed it for him on many occasions."

"He trusts you," Neferu said.

"He does indeed," Tiye said. "And that might well be his downfall."

Her mouth turned up in a grim approximation of a smile. We all fell silent. Were the others, like me, pondering the gravity of our discussion? This was treason we planned. Would we even receive a trial if we were uncovered? Or would Pharaoh himself determine our fate?

Regardless, there seemed no other option. Nobody else would do this. If we didn't act, Pharaoh would continue his reign of horror unchecked. I didn't know what kind of person that would make me if I allowed such a thing to continue.

CHAPTER 17

*B*efore anyone could offer other ideas for Pharaoh's demise, Neferu cleared her throat.

"There is something we haven't yet discussed and I think it timely we talk about it tonight." She seemed to look to Tiye for permission to continue and received a nod in reply. "Although I am fully in agreement we must act, something that has been bothering me is the potential impact of his death."

It seemed to me only good things could come from it, other than the possibility of our capture and execution.

"The sun," Neferu continued. "And the annual floods."

They all nodded and it seemed I was the only one who didn't understand.

"What do you mean?" I was reluctant to ask, since it showed my ignorance, but with the magnitude of what we planned, I had to understand every last detail.

"Without Pharaoh on the throne," Neferu explained, "the sun won't rise. The floods won't come when we need them. It's due to Pharaoh, and the rituals he conducts every day, that the world continues as it does. The sun rises because he bids it to. The floods come when we need them, and to the right height, neither too much nor too little, because of him. Without Pharaoh, chaos will overtake the world and it will be all our fault."

"Well, not really our fault," Ineni said. "It's Pharaoh's fault. We are merely remediating his wrongdoings."

I restrained my scoff since they all looked so serious. Surely, they didn't actually believe Pharaoh had the power to make the sun rise and the floods come? But then, I had been told over and over that Pharaoh was a living god. I still didn't understand how a man could be born of a mortal woman and yet also somehow be a god, but the Egyptians treated this as a fact. Something that needed no discussion or explanation. It simply was.

"Regardless," Neferu said. "We should discuss how to avoid these things coming to pass."

Tiye's face implied she disagreed, but she said nothing.

"Every Pharaoh dies eventually," Ineni said. "There must be measures in place to hold chaos at bay until the heir is coronated."

"Magical measures," Neferu said with a nod. "But how would we access magic strong enough for such a thing?"

"Pharaoh has two magicians." Tiye's prior disagreement seemed to have faded and now she merely looked thoughtful. "Iyroy and Prekamenef."

"Iyroy," I repeated. "I thought he was the royal physician?"

"He looks after Pharaoh's bodily health," she said, "using both magic and science."

I didn't realise Iyroy was a magician when he came to examine me during my pregnancy. Had he used magic on me? Did he use spells to look inside me and see how the babe was growing? Could he have told me even then I would have a daughter and not the son I expected? I wished I had known such a thing might have been possible. This didn't seem like the time to ask such questions, though.

"What kind of magic?" I asked instead.

"Pharaoh needs to withstand everything the forces of chaos throw at him on a daily basis," Tiye said. "The magicians perform rituals every day for his protection, and they aren't the only ones who do so. There's a whole network of priests spread across the country who share this duty."

"So there are many magicians?" I asked.

"Most of them are merely priests," Tiye said. "Iyroy and Prekamenef are the only ones I know for certain to be magicians."

We knew a woman magician, too, although nobody mentioned her. Amanitore.

"What do we know about their alliances?" Ineni asked. "Would they be open to an approach by us?"

Tiye shook her head. "I don't know enough about either to be certain. Both give the appearance of being loyal to Pharaoh."

"We all know appearance is not necessarily truth." Neferu gave Tiye a pointed look, which Tiye accepted with a slight incline of her head.

"I only mean I have never heard any suggestion they aren't loyal," Tiye clarified. "We can't risk it unless we are certain."

"What about the books of magic?" I didn't realise I had said it aloud until they all looked at me.

"What books?" Henutmire asked.

I had assumed the spell books were common knowledge, but perhaps not. Hopefully nobody would ask how I knew about them.

"Pharaoh has books containing spells," I said. "Supposedly every known spell is stored in his library, and there are only two librarians who have access to them."

"Messui and Shotmaadje," Tiye said. She gave me an odd look, her eyebrow raised just slightly, as if to suggest she knew their names would be familiar to me.

I shrugged and tried to pretend the names were of little consequence. If Tiye knew I knew who they were, did she also know they had been smuggling scrolls out of Pharaoh's library and passing them to Henuttawy, who in turn gave them to Ahmose? I had to assume Tiye knew everything Ahmose had.

I had thought to hold Pharaoh accountable for his crimes without involving myself in Tiye's plan, not that I knew any details of it at that point. My plan to make myself powerful enough to force Pharaoh to confess shattered when Henuttawy absconded with Ishtar's gem, which was meant to pay for the scrolls. I never even knew Ahmose had given it to her. Henuttawy was also my only means of contacting the librarians. Ahmose died shortly afterwards, her heart likely broken by her daughter's betrayal.

"My son knows them," Tiye said. "Although perhaps not well. He could make a subtle overture to find out whether they would be receptive to helping us. If there are spells for Pharaoh's personal protection, there must also be spells to ameliorate it."

"What can be given can also be taken away," Neferu said.

"Exactly," Tiye agreed. "I will get a message to Pentaweret."

"But we still have the problem of Pharaoh's death unleashing chaos," Gilukhipa said. "And that worries me. Obviously, this is something of a mystery to me, and probably

Kassaya too, but if it is a likelihood, as you say, we need a plan to manage it."

She acknowledged me with a nod. Of course, we were the only two in the chamber who weren't born Egyptian. She, like me, probably didn't understand how Pharaoh's death could possibly unleash chaos on the whole world.

"Pentaweret will see if the librarians can help with spells for that, too." Tiye waved away her concern.

Gilukhipa didn't look reassured, but she made no further comment.

"What else do we need to discuss?" Ineni asked.

"I think that will do for now," Tiye said. "We should continue to think on these issues, though. We need to be ready to act very soon and we must have resolved all possible complications before then."

The other women started to get to their feet.

"How soon?" I asked.

They all paused to hear Tiye's reply.

"Soon," she said.

"But what does that mean?" I pushed. "Weeks? A couple of months?"

She gave me an amused look.

"A week," she said. "Or two, at most."

Then she was ushering us out the door and there was no further opportunity for questions. Our lady's maids sat at the end of the hallway looking rather merry, far more than was warranted for merely waiting for their mistresses. Perhaps they had shared a few bottles of wine while they waited. Not that I minded if they had. It must be boring to sit and wait for hours.

Ineni made a sharp comment to her maids, so it seemed I wasn't the only one who wondered if they had been imbibing.

Sehener gave me a cheerful smile and even Ettu seemed less uptight than usual as we headed back to my chambers. It wasn't until we were inside with the door safely barred that Ettu asked about the reason for such an urgent gathering.

"I think Tiye just wanted the company," I said with a shrug, feigning nonchalance.

"Indeed." Ettu gave me a look that said she didn't believe me.

Merytre had stayed late with the men and left to meet Sutem as soon as we got back. I asked Tall and Half how they passed the evening, hoping it might distract Ettu.

"He had a nap," Half said, with a nod towards Tall.

Tall beamed and made a show of yawning.

"I tried to nap, but he was snoring too loudly," Half added.

Sehener giggled.

"He does snore rather loudly," she said. "I hear him from my bedchamber almost every night."

I had never noticed, but perhaps my bedchamber was far enough away from the men's that the sound didn't travel that far.

"Half can hardly claim to be as innocent as he pretends," Ettu said, poking the little man with her elbow. "He snores equally as loud as Tall. I wonder sometimes that either of them get any sleep at all, with them both competing to be the one who snores the loudest."

"You couldn't possibly hear us," Half said. "Not over the sound of your own snoring. It's as loud as an elephant."

They all laughed merrily and I pretended to join them, although the conversation left me feeling hollow. I didn't know whether Khaemmalu snored, having never had the opportunity to spend enough time with him for us to fall asleep. I never would either. I couldn't imagine what such intimacy would be like.

I would never spend the night with a man, not unless Pharaoh required me to stay with him, and I would rather not have the experience at all if that was the only way it could happen. But if our plan succeeded, and Pharaoh truly had only a week or two left to live, perhaps my situation afterwards would be different. I didn't dare let myself think about that.

As I lay in my bed that night, my mind whirled with thoughts of our plan. I wanted to prove myself useful, but how? If I could come up with some crucial part of the plan, perhaps solve one of the problems we had identified, that would demonstrate my usefulness and also my loyalty. I must never forget Tiye had told me I would have to prove myself before they trusted me. I wasn't yet sure I had done that.

Just before I fell asleep, I realised something. Tiye didn't know I knew Bebi. Apart from the fact it meant she probably knew nothing of my affair with Khaemmalu, I had a connection she knew nothing about. I knew our man in Pharaoh's personal squad and I could get a message to him if I needed to. That might be useful at some point in our plan. Perhaps it might even be how I proved myself.

CHAPTER 18

*J*hadn't yet risen when Merytre arrived the next morning. Usually she would sit and chat with whoever was already up, but today she came straight to my bedchamber.

"My lady," she whispered, cracking open the door. "Are you awake?"

"Sort of." It seemed like too much trouble to even open my eyes.

"I must speak with you."

I finally opened one eye and the somber expression on her face made me sit up too quickly. My head spun and I clutched the bed while I waited for it to subside.

"What is it?" I asked once I was sure I wouldn't fall off the bed. "Has something happened to Sutem?"

Or their babe. That should have been my first thought. Apart from Merytre's initial announcement, they had been discreet with their chatter, perhaps not wanting to upset me. Merytre looked well, though. Too well to have suffered the loss of a babe.

"It's not Sutem," she said. "I have a message for you. From Khaemmalu."

Now I understood why she came to speak with me privately. Sutem likely knew — or had guessed — something of our affair, and he surely would have shared it with his wife.

"Go on." I tried to make my voice disinterested, but I knew I failed.

"He says he must speak with you urgently."

To beg me to take him back, probably. To pretend he didn't know why I had pulled away. To pretend he was no threat to either me or my babe.

"You may consider your message delivered." I lay back down and closed my eyes. She would leave if she thought I had fallen asleep. But she didn't.

"My lady," she whispered. "He asked for me to seek confirmation you would go to him tonight."

Once I would have been thrilled by such a message from Khaemmalu. I would have spent the day studying the sun's painfully slow movement through the sky and wishing it was dark already so I could go to him.

"My lady?"

"No," I said. "You may tell him I will not go to him."

A moment of silence that stretched so long, I wanted to open my eyes to see what she was doing.

"May I tell him why?" she asked at last.

"He knows why," I said. "He just doesn't think I know."

"I confess I am confused. Sutem told me you are as in love with Khaemmalu as he is with you."

My thoughts were tangled and it took me too long to find a reply. Merytre must have assumed I didn't intend to answer.

"I'm sorry to have disturbed you," she said.

Her footsteps left my chamber and the door closed.

I wanted to call her back and tell her that of course I would go to Khaemmalu, but I was also proud of myself for refusing. If I had only my own safety to consider, I would probably take the risk, but I had to think of Baby Ishtar now. For her sake, I could resist Khaemmalu.

I lay in bed for so long that Ettu came asking if I was unwell and didn't look convinced when I told her I wasn't. The way she lingered in the doorway told me the conversation wasn't over.

"I have been thinking perhaps it's time for the rest of your lady's maids to resume their duties," she said.

I groaned. The noise escaped my mouth before I thought better of it and Ettu frowned at me.

"They are employed to attend to you," she pointed out. "If you have no further need for them, the Palace might not keep them in service."

"Surely there is no shortage of Ornaments wanting more maids," I said. "And new Ornaments arrive from time to time. They, too, will need maids. I doubt they will lose their positions."

Ettu shrugged.

"You don't know that," she said. "If you are willing to take the risk, I can tell Panouk you no longer require their services, but I thought keeping them employed would be important to you."

She was right. I had no wish to be the cause of a woman losing her position through no fault of her own.

"Very well," I conceded. "Tell them I will require them. Not tomorrow, though. The next day, perhaps?"

Ettu made a small sound, but she didn't argue any further, so I assumed she was satisfied enough. She didn't leave, though, but went to my dresser and rearranged the cosmetics.

So there was something else she wanted to say. I waited while she adjusted the placement of the jars.

"I want to ask you something," she said at last.

"Go ahead."

"Have you..." She lapsed into silence.

I waited. She would say whatever it was without me pushing. Maybe she intended to ask whether I would release her even though my babe was a girl. On our journey from Babylon, I promised to release her with funds for a new life once I bore Pharaoh a son.

"Have you considered leaving?" she asked.

I blinked in surprise. She couldn't know Khaemmalu had urged me to do that very thing.

"This place." Now she had started, the words rushed out of her. "It's not what I expected. There are rumours..."

Her voice trailed away again. I resisted the urge to tell her to hurry up. To demand she tell me the rumours. Were they about me and Khaemmalu? Or about Tiye's plan? Both would mean my death.

"Something is going to happen," she said. "Something bad, and I think you should leave before it does."

"What will happen?" I asked. "Tell me what you have heard."

Ettu shrugged and turned to face me. Her brows were furrowed and her eyes unhappy.

"I don't know." She sounded frustrated now. "I hear things here and there, but only snippets. Nobody seems to know the whole story, or if they do, they are not telling."

"Give me an example."

"The residents of Thebes are unhappy. Very unhappy."

"The common folk are always unhappy," I said. "They don't live like we do, knowing our accommodation is secure and that our meals will arrive on schedule. They have much more uncertainty. They have jobs and…"

My voice faded as I realised I didn't really know anything about how the commoners lived, only that they didn't have palaces and expensive gowns and lavish meals twice a day.

"The workers keep striking," Ettu said. "Supply lines are disrupted. Folk are unhappy that Pharaoh keeps building temples instead of seeing to the security of the borders. Grain is ever more expensive, and people are struggling to feed their families."

"None of that is anything to do with us," I said. "Nor do we have any control over it."

"There is more," Ettu said. "Something to do with the military. I cannot quite figure it out. An uprising of some sort. Perhaps they intend to oust one of their captains."

"That also doesn't impact on us."

My voice sounded a little breathless. The success of a plan as large as Tiye's relied on garnering much support. She surely expected there would be whispers. That didn't mean anyone outside of our plan actually knew the details.

"There is a rumour about Pharaoh's magicians," Ettu said. "But nobody seems to know quite what it is, or maybe they just aren't willing to share it."

"There are always rumours about folk like that. I'm sure you told me there were rumours about Amanitore, too."

Amanitore, the Kushite woman who folk called a magician, had allowed me to talk to my sister. Only briefly, but it was enough for me to tell Ishtar I loved her and for her to express her wish that someone would stop Pharaoh. It was what finally persuaded me to get involved with Tiye's plan. That and the failure of my own plan which died with Ahmose.

"Something is going to happen," Ettu said. "And I fear it will be bad. I think you should leave before it does."

"I cannot leave," I said. "Ever."

"What if…" She hesitated and seemed to swallow hard. "What if we could get Baby Ishtar? Would you leave with her?"

"That is not possible, so there is no point discussing such a thing."

I hoped the firmness of my tone would stop her from speculating further. Nobody could get to my babe. As the child of Pharaoh, she would be guarded day and night. Not even Bebi would get near her unless he was assigned to personally guard her, and removing her from Pharaoh's palace would be another thing altogether.

If our plan failed, there was no hope for either me or Baby Ishtar. She would grow up knowing she was the daughter of a cruel and stupid man, and I would spend the rest of my life — which might be short indeed if we failed — watching her suffer for it.

CHAPTER 19

*T*hat night, I dreamed again of the narcissus and the lion. I stood in the middle of a bed of narcissus. Nearby, more of the flowers sheltered my babe, now a young girl. I greedily drank in the sight of her. Her dark eyes. Her shaved head where only a sidelock — the traditional hairstyle of young children here — was allowed to grow. Her awkwardly long limbs, much like my own were at her age.

A lion prowled between the two beds, seemingly undecided as to whether to focus his attention on me or my babe. I wasn't bothered by his presence. The narcissus had shown over and over they would protect both her and me. The lion couldn't get to either of us.

He poked at a flower with his paw, and drew back hissing as if stung. Then he turned his large head to look me right in the eyes.

As my gaze locked with the lion's, the rest of the world fell away and I forgot this was my enemy who would take my babe. I sensed he tried to communicate with me. Like the narcissus, he too had a message for me, but his was no clearer than that of the flowers.

"What is it?" I asked him, frustration growing within me. "Why do you want my babe?"

He growled, a grumble which had sounded terrifying before, but now seemed almost comforting. It was still fierce, but his ferocity wasn't directed at me. Then he turned back to my babe and the connection between us was severed. He was once again merely the beast tying to get to my child.

He reached out to swat a narcissus and I felt his irritation when the contact hurt him. Then he crouched down, gathered himself up, and jumped right into the middle of the flowers.

He let out a yowl as they stung him or burned or bit or whatever it was they did. Despite his pain, he didn't flee. Instead, he stoically made his way through them to stand beside my babe. She barely reached his shoulder as he rested his enormous head against hers.

My child stood calmly beside the lion and showed no fear at his presence. In fact, she reached up to wind her fingers through his mane. Together, they studied me. Her gaze calm and unafraid, while his showed the pain he felt at his contact with the narcissus, but also his determination to remain at my child's side.

I woke bewildered, barely knowing where I was. The bird outside my window sang its pre-dawn song and it took a few moments to realise I lay safe in my bed. The lion had never tried to communicate with me before. It was like he told me not to be afraid. That he intended no harm to either me or my babe.

Was I wrong about the message in the dreams? I thought the narcissus protected me from the lion, but maybe it was the other way around. Maybe the lion protected me from the narcissus. If Khaemmalu was the lion, as his inking signalled, was I wrong about him? Or, rather, had I been right to trust him before I let the dreams sway my mind? I was so confused.

A rap at the door interrupted my thoughts.

"My lady, are you out of bed?" Ettu called.

"Almost."

"Your lady's maids will be here shortly. I didn't think you would want them to find you still abed."

Ettu knew I didn't care about such things, even if she did.

"I am getting up right now," I said.

"Do you need any help?"

"Perhaps you could pour me some melon juice? My throat is dry."

And once my maids arrived, there would be no opportunity to either eat or drink until such time as they were satisfied with my appearance.

"Very well." Ettu's footsteps retreated down the hallway.

My maids arrived mere moments later, their voices a veritable cacophony as they greeted Ettu, Merytre and Sehener, who some had not seen for weeks. I quickly got out of bed, set a wig on my head, and headed for the sitting chamber before Ettu came to find out what was taking me so long.

"Oh, there you are," she said as I encountered her in the hallway. "Your lady's maids have arrived."

"Thank you," I said, raising my voice to be heard above the giggles and squeals from the sitting chamber. "I wouldn't have realised if you hadn't come to tell me."

Ettu narrowed her eyes, but made no further comment. I followed her into the sitting chamber and my maids gathered around me. I had forgotten quite how loud they were with their constant chatter and laughter, their many congratulations on the birth of my babe, and their enquiries after my health since then. They swept me off to the bathing chamber, stripped me naked, and sat me on the stool where they were swift to pour warm water over me.

"I have heard she is the most beautiful baby," Tuya cooed, scooping a handful of natron salt from the tub they kept in the corner of the bathing stall.

"I heard she has the most darling personality already," Nebetah said. She took some natron, too, and she and Tuya began rubbing it over my skin, starting with my shoulders and working down my arms.

Meanwhile, Ipu scrubbed the calluses from my feet while Hemetre cleaned my face. Khensa and Mutnofret waited behind them, razors in hand. They would be responsible for ensuring not a stubble of hair remained on my body, even in the most intimate parts. Ettu watched them carefully, scrutinising the women's work to ensure it was to the standard she required as their supervisor.

Not all my maids could cram into the bathing chamber. Neither Merytre nor Sehener were here. Presumably they were busy making decisions about my appearance, from which gown I would wear today, to which wig would pair best with it, and which cosmetics, perfume and sandals would perfect the look. And, of course, Abar, was nowhere to be seen.

"I have a friend who is a wet nurse in the royal nursery," Khensa said. "Not for your babe, my lady, but she has nursed several others. She said yours is one of the sweetest she has ever met. She plays with her when she can."

Tears welled at the unexpected news that one of the nurses cared enough to play with my babe.

"Please thank her for me," I managed to say. "I am very appreciative of any attention she is able to give my daughter.

In fact, Ettu, would you fetch a jewel or two for Khensa to give her friend?"

"Of course, my lady." Ettu hurried out, although not without giving me a look I couldn't decipher.

Perhaps she disapproved. That didn't matter. Once word got out that I would reward anyone who paid special notice to my babe, she would be inundated with attention. I might have an influence on her life after all.

"Oh, my lady." Khensa wiped her eyes, seemingly overcome with my offer. "My friend would not expect such a thing. She is merely doing her job."

"I want to give her something," I said. "I trust you will ensure she receives it?"

"Of course," she said. "I would be most honoured. My friend will know I work for the most generous of all the Ornaments."

Fortunately Ettu returned just then, saving me from having to figure out a reply. She showed me a pair of earrings set with small green gems. Emeralds, I thought.

"Are these satisfactory?" she asked.

"Whatever you think," I said.

Ettu passed them to Khensa who stared, mouth agape, at the jewels in her hand.

"Oh," she said. "My lady, I cannot even imagine what it would be like to receive such a gift. I will be so proud to give her this."

I only nodded, hoping she would take it as a signal the conversation was finished. The hands on me disappeared as the women gathered around Khensa to ooh and aah over the earrings. As I watched, I finally noticed Abar was missing. She rarely assisted the women with their duties, but she usually at least waited in the doorway.

"Ettu." I spoke quietly, not wanting to attract any attention but her's. "Where is Abar?"

"In the sitting chamber." Ettu cleared her throat, her displeasure apparent. "She refused to come in."

"I suppose it doesn't matter," I said. "It's not like she helps anyway."

"That isn't the point," she said, rather directly. "She is supposed to attend to you, but she refuses. I have said before I think you should dismiss her and I haven't changed my opinion."

I wouldn't, though, and she surely knew it, even if she didn't understand why. I saw too much similarity between Abar's situation and mine. Neither of us was here by choice. We had both endured the death of a beloved sister in this place. And neither of us was allowed to leave.

By the time my maids filed out, offering me their good wishes as they departed, I was quite exhausted. I never even saw Abar. Presumably she slipped away as soon as it became apparent their duties were complete.

"You do look lovely, my lady," Sehener said. She gave me a broad smile, seemingly invigorated by the morning's work, and went to unlock the door to the men's bedchamber.

The kitchen maids had brought our morning meal some time ago and my stomach grumbled at the aroma of fresh bread. The gruel would be cold and probably inedible by now, but there was still bread, cheese and an assortment of fruits. I filled a plate and went to sit down.

"I have a surprise for you." Merytre looked almost shy as she picked up a folded piece of linen which hung over the back of a chair. "I finished the wallhanging for your bedchamber."

She unfolded the linen and I found myself face-to-face

with a yellow narcissus. Its petals were open like a mouth and I wondered what the flower would say if it could speak. An elaborate border resembled the edging of a garden bed, and a cord stitched to the top would allow the design to be hung.

"It's magnificent," Sehener said. She leaned in for a better look. "Your stitching is truly exquisite."

"Do you like it?" Merytre asked me.

I had tried not to look at the narcissus while Merytre worked on the piece. It reminded me too vividly of my dreams and seemed like yet another reminder the flowers had a message for me.

"It's very finely done," I said.

Merytre beamed.

"I will hang it in your bedchamber," she said. "If you wish."

"Of course," I managed. "Put it wherever you want."

"Tall, come and help me," Merytre called over her shoulder, already on her way to my bedchamber. "Sutem gave me a hammer and a nail, and you can hang it for me."

"I'm sure you can hang it perfectly well yourself," Ettu said. "It merely requires driving the nail into the wall and looping the thread over it."

Tall followed Merytre out and Ettu trailed behind them.

"Oh, I couldn't do it myself," Merytre replied. "I would be sure to hit my thumb with the hammer or break the nail. Better that Tall does it for me."

The three of them disappeared down the hallway and Ettu's reply was no more than a muffled murmur. I doubted she found Merytre's response satisfactory. Ever since she started wearing men's attire, Ettu had become quite strident about what women should do for themselves. I was torn between admiration for her bravery and the knowledge I would never have the courage to voice such opinions myself.

The brief sound of hammering reached the sitting chamber and they returned in short order.

"It looks very good in there," Merytre said. "We hung it in that dim corner furtherest from the window. It brightens the spot nicely."

Of course that would be the place she chose. It was right where I would see it from my bed. I briefly toyed with asking her to move it, but I had said she could put it wherever she wanted, and she would be disappointed if she thought I didn't like it. She had spent a very long time stitching it for me.

"Since you are dressed, perhaps you would care for a walk?" Ettu's tone was the pointed one she used when she offered something she considered more than a mere suggestion.

I didn't want to go out, but at least if we were walking, my maids would likely talk amongst themselves, leaving me free to ponder last night's dream.

"Very well," I said. "Who would like to accompany me?"

After a brief discussion, it was decided Merytre and Sehener would come. Ettu didn't argue very hard about it and I didn't miss the look that passed between her and Half. No doubt they would be pleased for some time alone.

CHAPTER 20

*O*utside, the air was fresh with just a hint of coolness. The season had certainly turned, with the days now a more temperate heat and the nights cool enough to welcome a woollen blanket over me. Sehener and Merytre quickly fell behind, too immersed in their conversation to pay much attention to me, for which I was thankful since it left me free to ponder the lions that had surrounded me ever since my arrival in Egypt.

The beast at the ceremony for Isis and Nepthys. Ineni's offering for Nebtu. Merytre's wallhanging of Sekhmet, which still hung in her old bedchamber. The tiny wooden carving of Bastet Half made for Ettu. She was a cat, not a lion, but yet another feline couldn't be a coincidence. And, of course, there were the dreams.

Before I had time to think about who the narcissus represented if the lion was Khaemmalu, movement ahead of us caught my attention. The edge of a gown as its owner disappeared around a bend in the path. A glimpse of dark hair between the branches. A hand, the skin so white as to be almost translucent, reaching up to caress a leaf. She must have heard me behind her, for she turned and gave me a chilly look.

"Hilde." I made my voice as warm as I could. "I haven't seen you in such a long time."

"I heard you were delivered of your babe," she said stiffly. "I congratulate you. Your father must be very pleased."

"He would have been more pleased were she a boy." The words slipped out of my mouth before I could think better of them.

Hilde gave me a slightly friendlier look.

"I am sorry if that is the case." She resumed walking and didn't object when I fell in beside her.

If her maid was nearby, she was nowhere to be seen. From somewhere behind us came Sehener's merry laugh.

"Would your father not want you to produce a boy?" I asked.

Hilde shrugged a little. "I am not sure he cares whether I bear a child or not, let alone whether it be a boy or a girl. He sent me here to prove his loyalty to Pharaoh and he has done that. It matters little, though, since I don't expect to be here much longer."

"You don't?" I tried to conceal my surprise, but her side-ways glance showed I did a poor job of it.

She had said she intended to ask her father to call her home. He wouldn't, though, of course. No man would risk angering Pharaoh by demanding the return of one of his Ornaments.

"I wrote and told him what I understand of recent events here," she said. "I asked that he send for me and he surely will as soon as he receives my letter."

I hesitated, wondering how to tell her that Pentau, the Palace scribe, would never send such a message.

"I am not so daft as that." Her tone was scornful as she guessed my thought. "I didn't send it through the scribe."

"Of course not."

She must have other maids, not just her cousin, and they would be able to leave the Palace grounds. They could carry a letter out for her, just as Merytre did for me. If only I had realised it was that easy sooner.

"I expect to hear from him any day now," she said.

Despite her apparent confidence, I sensed her uncertainty. She wasn't as sure of her father as she pretended.

"I do hope you say goodbye before you leave," I said.

"We are not friends, Kassaya. We might have been, had you made different choices, but it is too late to change that."

Too late for me to warn her that Pharaoh liked to hurt a woman before it happened to her.

"I'm sorry I didn't tell you," I said.

I would regret not doing so for the rest of my life. I should have warned my sister, too. But I would atone for my mistakes. I would ensure Pharaoh never hurt another woman again.

"I believe you," she said, to my surprise. "But what are you going to do about it?"

"Do?"

Why did she assume I would do anything? Ettu had done the same thing when we learned the body of an unknown woman had been taken to the House of Life. *I suppose you intend to try to see the body,* she said to me. It was the first time in my life that someone thought I would do something important, and here was Hilde thinking the same thing.

"Of course you intend to do something," she said. "Your

face gives away your guilt, and you would have answered much sooner if you weren't busy trying to find a reply that didn't reveal your secret."

"Nonsense." Fortunately, right at that moment, my foot landed partly on the path and partly on the grass. My ankle turned and I went toppling sideways.

"Oh, my lady," Merytre called as she and Sehener rushed to help me up. "Are you hurt?"

I let them haul me to my feet before I tested my ankle. It was painful, but I could put weight on it.

"Not badly," I said. "I will be able to make it back to my chambers."

"You cannot possibly walk like that." Sehener crouched in front of me to examine my ankle, her fingers cool against my skin. "It's already swelling."

"I will fetch a guard," Merytre said. "We can have someone carry you back."

At least it wouldn't be Khaemmalu. He didn't come on duty until sunset.

"Please don't," I said. "I don't want to be a bother and it would be embarrassing to be carried through the grounds."

"It wouldn't be the first time," Merytre said.

"Exactly." I shot her a look. "I will walk on my own feet. If my ankle pains me, I will lean on you and Sehener."

The two women exchanged glances and Sehener shrugged. At least they were both tractable enough to do as I said. If Ettu were here, she would likely have already marched off to find a guard to carry me. I had almost forgotten Hilde.

"If we do not encounter each other again, I wish you well." She sounded almost sincere.

I wanted to prove to her that I really did try to make up for my mistakes. But it wasn't my decision to bring anyone else in on the plan, so I only smiled and returned her well wishes.

"Lady Hilde is so lovely," Sehener said as we started our slow, limping way back to my chambers.

My ankle hurt much more than I anticipated and I clenched my jaw to avoid crying out. When someone nearby cleared their throat, my heart leaped, and for a moment I thought it was Khaemmalu, until I remembered it was too early. Instead, it was Sutem.

"My lady, are you injured?" he asked.

He and Merytre exchanged fond looks and she blew him a kiss. Sutem reddened and straightened his back as if making a show of looking professional.

"Just turned my ankle," I said.

"I can assist if you need it," he offered.

I waved him away and set off again.

"No, no, I am well enough," I said.

Sutem exchanged another look with Merytre, and I tensed. I got the feeling he prepared himself to say something.

"My lady," he said.

I knew what was coming.

"Khaemmalu asked me to give you a message if I saw you."

I hobbled another few steps, hoping he would leave if I didn't answer. But Sutem merely waited. He would tell Khaemmalu I had hurt myself. Good. Let him know I was hurt and he wasn't here to help. I immediately felt ashamed of myself for thinking such a thing.

"May I give you his message?" Sutem asked when I still didn't reply.

"Very well."

"He said to tell you the lion will protect the one he loves."

Surprised, I let out a gasp. Sutem's face showed no hint of

duplicity. If he knew the message might hold a sinister meaning, he gave no sign of it. With a bow, and a smile for Merytre, who blew him another kiss, he headed off down the path.

I barely noticed his departure, too busy puzzling over his words. Something about them bothered me, but I couldn't quite figure out why. The lion will protect the one he loves. Where had I heard those words before?

Lost in thought, I forgot my sprained ankle until I stepped too hard on it. The pain that shot up my calf almost sent me toppling to the ground again. Sehener and Merytre rushed to my side and I clutched their arms as we resumed our ponderous journey back to the Palace.

A particular bed of narcissus caught my attention. Its position beside a dom palm gave the flowers a somewhat sheltered location, although they obviously received enough sunlight to thrive. Between them, something in the dirt caught a ray of sun and sparkled. Without thinking, I let go of Sehener and Merytre, and left the path.

"My lady?" Merytre asked as they kept pace with me. "Do you not think it would be safer to stay on the path? The ground is somewhat uneven here and you might turn your ankle again."

"I want a closer look at those flowers," I said.

"Your favourite," Sehener murmured.

No, narcissus had never been a flower I particularly liked. But I kept dreaming about them. Narcissus and lions.

The flower bed was freshly weeded. I couldn't see what it was in the dirt that caught the sunlight. Perhaps it was no more than a sliver of rock. Something about the dirt's disturbance brought a forgotten memory to my mind. The narcissus, the freshly disturbed dirt. The lion will protect the one he loves.

"That was what she said to them." I said it out loud without realising.

"Who, my lady?" Sehener asked.

I had dreamed about the seer stopping at this very flower bed. She spoke to the narcissus, but by the time I woke, the memory of what she said was gone, leaving me with only the knowledge that it had been important. *The lion will protect the one he loves.* That was what she said to them. How was it possible for Khaemmalu's message today to contain exactly the same words I had dreamed all those months ago?

I had it all wrong. The narcissus were never protecting me. It was the lion who did. The lion who tried to save me from the narcissus. If Khaemmalu was the lion, and it seemed obvious he must be, then who was the narcissus? Pharaoh? The Palace? Someone or something I didn't yet realise was a threat to me?

The lion will protect the one he loves. In my dream, the lion had jumped into the middle of the narcissus, despite the pain they caused him, to grab my babe. It wasn't just me he would protect, but also Baby Ishtar. He was never stealing her away from me. He was saving her from the narcissus.

CHAPTER 21

With Sehener and Merytre's help, I made it back to my chambers and spent the day enduring the repeated application of wet cloths to my ankle. It had swollen, although not to an alarming extent, and I resisted their suggestions to summon a healer. I had well and truly had enough of being examined by both healer and physician.

If Khaemmalu was the lion — and I was certain he must be — then I was wrong about the lion's intentions towards me. Before I knew about the beast inked on his chest, I wouldn't have questioned whether I could trust Khaemmalu. There was never a single moment in which I felt like he was dishonest with me, or that I was unsafe with him.

But I had misinterpreted the dreams. The lion would protect me from the narcissus — whoever or whatever that was — not the other way around. *Something which is hidden is not always what you think it is,* the seer had said. She all but told me I was wrong about what the dreams meant.

Despite my desire to unravel exactly what the lion was supposed to protect me and Baby Ishtar from, I paid closer than usual attention to the chatter between Ettu, Merytre and Sehener, which left me little time to ponder the problem. After Ettu's vague warning about some kind of plot, I didn't want to miss any suggestion of rumours that might actually hold some truth. Not that I knew what I would do if I heard something. Tell Tiye, probably. She was the architect of the plan, after all, and she was the sort of woman to prepare for every outcome.

In the moments when the conversation lapsed between the women, Hilde was on my mind. I wanted to show her I did intend to act, and she seemed trustworthy; the kind of woman we might bring into our plan. She certainly had reason to want to see Pharaoh relieved of his position, but would it be fair to involve her in a plot to commit both treason and heresy? Given the ramifications if we were uncovered, perhaps it would be kinder to leave her out of it. If I owed her for not warning her before Pharaoh abused her, maybe it was by not involving her in our plan that I could make it up to her.

If only she knew she didn't have to wait for her father to summon her home. When Pentaweret allowed the Ornaments to leave if they wished, as Tiye said he would, I hoped Hilde would somehow know I had been involved in the plan that set her free. That I had done something after all, as she had thought I would.

As the sitting chamber finally grew darker, Sehener set about lighting lamps while Ettu closed the shutters. I got up to test my ankle. The pain wasn't as bad as it had been and I thought it might hold up long enough to find Khaemmalu. After all, I wouldn't decipher the puzzle of the lion and the narcissus by sitting around in my chambers. As I took a few steps, Ettu cleared her throat.

"I hope you are not thinking about going somewhere," she said. "Your ankle is still very swollen."

"It hardly hurts at all anymore." I avoided her eyes and hoped she wouldn't hear the lie in my words.

Ettu made a sound that said quite clearly she didn't believe me.

"I am going home shortly," Merytre said, "if my lady permits. I can pass on a message for you."

My cheeks heated at how easily they read me. There was no privacy when one lived in such close quarters. Not that I had been raised with any expectation of such a thing, but sometimes it would be welcome.

"I thought some fresh air might make me feel better," I said.

"It's a little stuffy in here." Sehener's gaze went to the windows. "Perhaps we could open one shutter a tiny bit? It might be enough to let in some fresh air without too many bugs."

I waved away her suggestion. The last thing I felt like was spending the night huddled under a blanket to escape the biting insects that descended with dusk. I wouldn't be the only one who suffered, and all because I chose to pretend my only reason for wanting to go out was fresh air.

By the following evening, the swelling was gone and the pain had greatly lessened. I had taken several walks around the sitting chamber throughout the day in an attempt to prove my ankle was better. If they believed me to be recovered, they wouldn't argue when I wanted to go out tonight. I couldn't wait any longer to speak with Khaemmalu. I had to determine the truth of the lion's intentions.

"You're still limping," Ettu observed, watching me take yet another turn around the chamber.

"It doesn't hurt any more, though," I said.

"You wouldn't limp if it didn't hurt," she retorted.

I restrained my sigh and returned to the couch. Clearly, I wouldn't be going anywhere tonight.

When my maids arrived the following morning, they were full of chatter about a parade that had been held at Pharaoh's palace.

"I heard he assembled the entire palace staff," Hemetre said as she and Tuya scrubbed my skin with natron salt.

"They were all invited to a banquet, too." Nebetah's voice was envious. "I heard the food was very fine. It's the first time I have ever wished I worked in Pharaoh's palace."

She and Khensa sighed at the same time. They went on in a similar way for so long that I closed my eyes and tried not to listen while I pretended I wasn't sitting naked in front of so many women. It was Mutnofret's comment which caught my attention.

"I heard the babes were brought out," she said.

My eyes sprang open. "Which babes?"

"Well, all of them," she said.

"All the babes delivered within the last year," Tuya clarified.

"Ishtar, too?" I asked.

"Of course," Khensa said. "My friend who is a wet nurse said she looked very beautiful. She wore a creamy coloured gown which was made specially for the parade."

"Do you know anything else about her?" I asked Khensa.

"She is well and happy," she assured me. "I gave my friend the earrings and told her she must send me a message immediately if your babe is ever unwell. I will know if she has even the slightest sniffle, and I will come to tell you straight away."

"Thank you," I said. "It gives me much peace to know she has a friend nearby."

Khensa beamed.

"My friend was very pleased to receive the earrings," she added. "At first, she told me she couldn't possibly accept such a gift, but I said my mistress had insisted she have them. She said for me to give you her most sincere thanks."

I acknowledged her words with a nod, too busy puzzling over why Pharaoh hadn't summoned me for such an event to pay much attention to the conversation. Surely the occasion of a babe being presented warranted her mother's presence? But perhaps he considered me irrelevant. Maybe he saw no need for a mother in a child's life.

I knew Tiye didn't see her son often, but I had assumed it was because he was old enough to be busy with studies and military training and whatever else occupied a son of Pharaoh all day. I hadn't let myself consider it might never have been any different when he was younger and less busy. At some point, she must have gotten to know him enough to trust involving him in her plan. It gave me hope that one day I, too, might have the opportunity to know my daughter.

When dusk fell that evening and I got to my feet, Ettu made no comment. I took that to mean she was in agreement my ankle had healed enough for a walk.

"Who will accompany me?" I asked.

Ettu and Sehener looked at each other.

"I went last time," Sehener said. "I can stay."

By now, it seemed they assumed Merytre would always come with me in the evening, so she could go home with Sutem afterwards.

I walked slowly as we made our way through the Palace, careful not to make any sudden movements.

"Are you in pain?" Ettu asked. "You are walking rather oddly."

"Just trying to be cautious," I said.

"If it hurts, we should go back. It will heal faster if you rest."

"It doesn't hurt." Irritation flared within me, but I was being unfair. I had given her little reason to believe when I said I wasn't in pain. "Thank you for your concern, though."

She didn't reply and we walked in silence after that. As we emerged outside, I took a deep breath of the night air. What a welcome relief after being confined to my chambers again.

"Ouch," Merytre said as she slapped her neck. "Something has bitten me already."

"They are swarming around me too." Ettu waved her hand in front of her face to shoo away the insects.

"They are no worse than usual." I slapped away a bug that landed on my arm. I wouldn't let a few bites disrupt my chance to speak with Khaemmalu and discover his real intentions.

We headed along the torch-lit path until we reached the place where a branching path disappeared into the darkness. Neither woman commented as I led them away from the torches. We were barely out of sight of the main path before the bushes rustled.

"Wait here," I said, and made my way into the shrubbery.

As the darkness enveloped me, I could feel Khaemmalu's presence, although he didn't reveal himself.

"Khaemmalu?" I whispered. "I know you are here," I added crossly when he didn't reply.

I heard his sigh and turned in the direction it came from. I could still see nothing of him.

"Come out," I said. "You're scaring me by hiding like that."

"I'm sorry." He emerged from his hiding place, but was no more than a shadow. "I didn't mean to scare you."

We were both silent after that. I assumed he, like me, waited for some explanation.

"Why are you angry with me?" he asked at last. "I don't understand."

I knew he would ask, but hadn't yet figured out how to tell him without revealing I had trusted my dreams more than I trusted him.

"Whatever it is, Kassaya, you can tell me."

The tenderness in his tone convinced me. I should never have doubted him. Of all the folk in this place, Khaemmalu was no threat to either me or my babe.

"I've been dreaming about lions." Once I decided to tell him, the words came out in a rush. "For months now. And narcissus."

"Lions and narcissus?" He sounded bewildered and I could hardly blame him. "I don't understand."

"Ever since I arrived here, I've been surrounded by lions."

"So when you saw the lion on my chest, it scared you?" He spoke slowly, obviously still piecing the parts together.

"I thought the dreams warned the lion was a threat to me."

"You thought I was a threat?" He sounded offended now. "To you? Kassaya, surely you know I would never hurt you."

"I know, truly I do. The dreams kept showing me what I thought was the narcissus protecting me from the lion, but it was the other way around. The lion protected me from the narcissus."

"This isn't making any sense," he said.

"I dreamed my babe was in the middle of a bed of narcissus. The lion jumped in even though the narcissus hurt him. He snatched her up and ran away with her. I thought they warned he would take my babe, but then I realised the lion was you."

"So you thought I intended to take your babe from you."

His voice was flat now. I had hurt him. I rushed on, desperate to convince him before the damage was irreparable.

"After I figured out the lion was you, I realised he was trying to protect both me and my babe, not take her away," I said.

"Where are these dreams coming from? Who is sending them?"

"The seer." My voice was confident. It was the one thing I was certain of. "I dreamed of her, too. She told me I should leave while I could."

"I have also told you to leave," he said.

"But I cannot. I wish everyone would stop saying such a thing."

"Did she also warn you when you spoke to her in person or does she communicate with you only through dreams?"

"She won't give me a straight answer. I was looking for her when I came out the other night, before I sprained my ankle."

"Are you recovered now?" he asked. "You're still limping."

"It only hurts a little." I longed to reach for him. Surely his concern meant he didn't hate me. He might yet forgive me.

"Regardless, why is the seer warning you? Why does she use dreams to do it, rather than merely tell you? And why you? Of all the women here, why is it you she is warning to leave?"

"Maybe it isn't just me. Others might be having similar dreams but not talking about them."

"I doubt other women are dreaming of lions if the lion is me," he said. "There is no point to it if they are, since there is not another woman here I would risk my life to save."

My heart pounded as my hand reached for his. I had hurt him and he might push me away. But he allowed his fingers to twine through mine.

"I cannot believe you thought I was a threat to you," he said. "Even if you thought the lion was, I would have thought you'd know you had it wrong once you realised it was me."

"I should have. I'm sorry." His hand was warm, and his grip firm but gentle. There was a point where I thought I'd never touch him again.

"Are you keeping any other secrets from me?" he asked.

I hesitated. There was, indeed, one very large secret, but I suspected he already knew something about Tiye's plan. Perhaps he didn't know I had joined them, though. I couldn't imagine Khaemmalu saying nothing if he knew.

"Kassaya?" His voice was sterner now. "What else are you hiding?"

When I still didn't answer, he squeezed my hand. "You can trust me. Please, be honest with me. That's all I ask. I cannot protect you if I don't know what you're getting yourself involved with."

"What makes you think I need to be protected?" I countered.

He hesitated. So, he did know something.

"What are you keeping from me?" I asked, hoping to push my advantage.

If he was distracted at my realisation that he, too, kept a secret, he might forget about mine, for a while at least. Long enough for me to figure out how much he knew and how much I should tell him. I didn't want to put him in danger, and even knowing about our plan was perilous.

"Kassaya," he started, then stopped.

"What is it?" I asked. "Tell me, Khaemmalu. Whatever it is."

He sighed. His secret obviously lay heavily with him. I could feel his reluctance to tell me.

"There are things you don't know about this place," he said.

"I probably know more than you think."

I could feel the way his gaze searched my face, although I could still see little more of him than a shadow in the dark.

"That may be," he said, "but even so, I don't want to involve you in some of the things I know. Believe me, Kassaya. If I have not told you everything, it's for your own safety."

"Do I have no right to know what affects my safety? Why do you assume I am safer if I know nothing?"

He sighed again and rubbed his eyes with his spare hand. He had come to a decision. I waited, hardly daring to breathe for fear any distraction would give him reason to change his mind.

"There are plans being made," he said. "Plots being laid. You might know some of it, but you don't know it all."

"You mean Tiye's plan."

"Hush," he said quickly. "Lower your voice."

I could feel his surprise that I said it so baldly, but there was no point dancing around the subject. If we were to establish what we both knew, we had to speak plainly.

"You wouldn't have said so much if you believed anyone to be nearby," I pointed out.

"Still," he said. "It pays to be cautious. Yes, I mean that plan. Tell me what you know."

"You tell me first."

"No, Kassaya. I don't want you involved. It's a dangerous plot she makes and I am not happy if she has drawn you into it."

"She hardly drew me in," I said. "I agreed to join her. He must be held accountable."

There was no need to name the person I spoke of. We both knew who I meant.

"Kassaya, trust me on this," he said. "Whatever you have agreed to, it is not too late to walk away. We can go together, all three of us. I will find a way to get to your babe and we can flee."

"My sister wanted someone to stop him. I have to do this. For her."

"It's too late for your sister. She won't know you risked your life for this."

"She doesn't have to. I know. That is enough."

"It doesn't have to be you. There are enough of us working to put an end to it. You don't need to be involved."

"But I do." I squeezed his hand, hoping touch would help him understand what my words didn't. "I failed to protect her from him, but I can still protect the women who will come after her."

He sighed again.

"Kassaya, you put yourself in more danger than you know. Think of your babe if you won't think of yourself."

"I understand the risk," I said. "I know it's both treason and heresy, and I know the punishments for both."

That made him pause. I had surprised him.

"Tell me what you understand the plan to be then," he said. "Prove to me you truly comprehend what you're getting involved with."

"I cannot say it," I said. "It's too dangerous."

"So you do know. Anything else, you would say, but this, this is the one thing we cannot say."

"Why didn't you tell me?" I asked. "You kept this from me as much as I kept it from you."

"I already told you. I wanted to protect you. Save you from the knowledge of what was being planned. Protect you from the consequences if it goes wrong."

"And if those consequences come for you?" If he was executed, I meant. "Did you consider what would become of me then?"

"I hoped you would be safe." His voice was achingly tender now. "I hoped that if you knew nothing, your life here would continue as it has."

"How would I survive without you?" I asked. "Tell me that, Khaemmalu."

"You would go on," he said. "In time, you would forget me. Forget what we had. It's only been a few months, after all. Hardly a significant portion of your life. You would hurt at first, but with time, you would move on. Maybe you would find someone else in this place. I hoped you would. But if not, your life would continue, and it would be better than it was, because of what our plan achieved."

A glimmer of moonlight showed me the tears on his cheeks. How hard it must have been for him, to be involved in such a momentous thing, knowing it might mean his own death, and that he would leave me alone. But then, it was no more than I myself had done when I agreed to become involved.

I, too, knew the consequences and I had chosen to get involved anyway. Because the cause was too great to ignore. Because however severe the punishment might be for an individual, it would leave the world a better place for all the women who came after us.

CHAPTER 22

left Khaemmalu reluctantly. He kissed me sweetly, but his hands didn't wander as they usually would, and I was grateful for his restraint. My body wasn't yet ready for intimacy, and discussing Tiye's plan felt like a big enough risk for one night.

The following morning, I paid Tiye a visit in her chambers. I hadn't spoken to her privately since the day I told her I would join her plan. Funny how both Khaemmalu and I thought of it as Tiye's plan, I mused as I traversed the short distance to her chambers. Would it ever become our plan or would we always think of it as hers?

Ettu walked in silence for a change, then propped herself against a wall at the end of Tiye's hallway. When I first learned Tiye allowed nobody but her visitors and her own maids down her hallway, I had thought it a pretension. Now I knew the kind of plans being made within her chambers, I realised it was probably a security against the wrong ears hearing anything.

It was Nammu who opened the door for me. I had almost

forgotten she still served Tiye. She sneered when she saw me and I half expected her to slam the door in my face. She, like I, was no doubt remembering the last time we spoke when she accused me of being pleased about Ishtar's death. I had hoped today's visit would prompt Tiye to reveal more details of her plan to me, but not with Nammu there.

Tiye, as usual, was adorned as exquisitely as if she expected Pharaoh himself to visit. The thought amused me. As if Pharaoh would deign to visit a woman's chambers. When he wanted to see one of us, he sent a messenger with a summons.

Nammu didn't wait to close the door behind me, but went immediately to a chair by the window. She folded her hands in her lap and fixed her gaze outside, although I had no doubt she would be listening for any opportunity to cause trouble for me. I closed the door myself and went to sit with Tiye. As our eyes met, I flicked my gaze towards Nammu, hoping she would understand I wanted her to send the woman away, but Tiye only watched me settle myself on the couch.

"Are you well, Kassaya?" she asked after I had finish smoothing out my skirt. "I heard you sprained your ankle."

How she managed to know such insignificant details always puzzled me. There were, it seemed, many within the Palace who reported even the smallest event to her. I supposed when one laid plans of the magnitude she did, such a network was necessary. If she knew about my ankle, did she also know why I was out in the garden that evening?

"It has healed well," I said. "I'm afraid I injured it being my usual inelegant self."

I laughed, expecting her to laugh with me, but Tiye only regarded me with an expression that seemed part amusement, part puzzlement. She, of course, would never be so inelegant as to sprain her ankle while merely walking.

"Nammu." Tiye's voice was sharp and she never even looked in the woman's direction. "You are dismissed for the rest of the morning. Return to me when the sun reaches its peak."

Nammu didn't bother to reply, only got to her feet, strode across the chamber, and left with a slam of the door.

"We had something of a disagreement earlier," Tiye said, obviously noting my surprise. "That woman does not know when to keep her mouth shut."

"What was it about?" I asked.

Tiye's combative relationship with her lady's maids intrigued me. I would have expected her to be the kind of mistress a maid wouldn't dare talk back to. She dismissed my question with a wave of her hand.

"Nothing of significance," she said.

She studied me, clearly waiting for me to make the next move. I didn't want to seem too eager. If I asked about her plan, she probably wouldn't tell me.

"Have you heard from Henuttawy?" I asked instead.

"Not a word," Tiye said. "Nor do I expect to. She knows I won't accept her back into my service after the way she left."

"I would be interested to know if you do hear from her."

I doubted there was a possibility of retrieving Ishtar's gem from her, but I didn't want to miss any opportunity to try. Henuttawy had probably already traded it for what she needed to start her new life. Transport, perhaps. Somewhere a long way from Egypt.

Belatedly, I noticed Tiye's bemused expression.

"What is it?" I asked.

She gave an elegant shrug. "I am merely surprised."

"At what?" I hid my irritation at the way she made me draw it out of her. It would only encourage her.

"That you would want to know about her. Especially after what she did."

"What is that?"

So, Tiye knew about the gem. It shouldn't surprise me, really. Henuttawy probably reported everything to her. If she knew Henuttawy had Ishtar's gem, she probably also knew we were procuring magic spells from Pharaoh's library.

"Pretending to be your servant's daughter, of course," Tiye said.

I gaped, too stunned to hide my ignorance.

"Oh, you didn't know?" she asked.

I closed my eyes for a moment, searching for calm. Tiye would never apologise. There was no point saying she should have told me.

"How long have you known?" I asked instead.

"From the beginning," she said. "I never knew her mother, but one of my previous lady's maids did. Henuttawy's mother was a childhood friend of hers. I took Henuttawy on at her recommendation."

"But Henuttawy must have known you knew," I said.

Tiye shrugged. "I never told her my maid had recommended her, and she and I never spoke of her mother."

"So how do you know it wasn't Ahmose?"

After all, any childhood friendship of Ahmose's must have been a very long time ago. The old woman was fifty at least when I first met her, and she had been in Babylon for more than thirty years. That was a long time in which childhood friends could lose touch.

"Because her mother was about to go to the West at the time I hired Henuttawy," Tiye said. "My maid hoped to ensure a good position for Henuttawy so her mother would go to her rest knowing she had secure employment."

"So Ahmose was definitely not Henuttawy's mother." My voice was flat.

"I'm afraid not." She watched me carefully, no doubt analysing my reaction.

How had Ahmose been so taken in? She was certain she had found her daughter and she trusted Henuttawy with far more information than she should have. Not only did Henuttawy lie to an old woman who desperately wanted to find her daughter, but she absconded with a jewel worth more than she would ever earn. A jewel she wouldn't have been entrusted with if Ahmose hadn't believed Henuttawy to be who she said she was.

Was Ahmose's death from the shock of Henuttawy's unexpected departure, or the realisation that she couldn't really be her daughter? After all, surely no daughter would leave without farewelling the mother she had been separated from for so long.

"You could have told me." I didn't even know why I bothered. Tiye wouldn't care, and nor would she ever change her ways.

She raised one eyebrow at me.

"Had you asked, I would have," she said.

A friend would have offered the information, but I left the thought unsaid. As Tiye had previously pointed out, we weren't friends. I didn't want her to have to remind me again.

"What other information are you waiting for me to ask about?" She wouldn't miss the bitterness in my voice, but I didn't care. I was tired of her games. Every time I thought I had reconciled myself to how she was, she did something like this.

"I am afraid you would have to be more specific," she said. "You can hardly expect me to recite everything I know."

I restrained the sigh that wanted to come out of me. Showing my annoyance would get me nowhere with Tiye. If I wanted information, I needed to be strategic.

"Do you know Hilde?" I asked. Not that I intended to suggest we bring her into the plan. I just wanted to see what Tiye would do if she thought I might tell someone. I wasn't yet sure I had earned her trust. "She is from Britain, rather newly arrived."

Compared to me, at any rate, although even I was probably newly arrived from Tiye's perspective.

"I do."

Her smug expression left me momentarily confused, until I remembered how Tiye made every new Ornament clean her bathing chamber each morning after someone, presumably not Tiye herself, had spilled a full chamber pot over the floor. I was the only one to have escaped such a duty after I climbed out her window.

"Of course you know her," I said.

"I assume there was a reason for your question."

"I merely wondered whether you had met her. And whether you had any intention of bringing anyone else into the plan."

"We have enough people involved." If she was at all concerned I might have told Hilde something, she gave no sign of it. "The more folk who know, the greater the risk someone will talk."

"You think there isn't already talk? You have folk out there recruiting the commoners. Persuading the military. You have no idea how many people know."

"That's all happening at a distance. You think I haven't

taken precautions to ensure folk don't know any true details? You think those who are out there soliciting support for my son are using my name? No, everything that is occurring can be explained as others trying to initiate change themselves."

"So you get them involved in your deadly plan and then abandon them if word gets out?"

How quickly would she abandon each of us if she thought it necessary? Would she turn on us to save herself?

"Everyone involved knows the risk." She eyed me flatly. "Including you."

"Everyone is expendable, aren't they?" I asked. "You use them as you want and you distance yourself when you are finished with them."

She narrowed her eyes at me. "You have been here long enough to know how this place works, Kassaya. You get nothing for nothing. Every accomplishment takes the right alliances, the correct preparation."

"And killing Pharaoh will be just another of your achievements."

She didn't respond, only continued to study me, and I could feel the chill emanating off her.

"Is this the first time you have tried to kill him?" I asked.

She waited a long moment before she replied.

"I'm sure you are aware it is not," she said. "I'm only surprised it has taken you this long to mention it."

It wasn't what I expected her to say. That it was not her first attempt, perhaps, but not that I already knew. Then I realised.

"The day we went sailing and the boat overturned." Both my sister and I would have drowned if we hadn't learned to swim as children.

"We barely knew you at the time," she said.

It was the closest thing to an apology I would hear from her.

"You knew Kia," I said.

"We did, although not well. Her death was unfortunate, but if we had succeeded, it would have been worth it."

"Not to her, maybe. Did she know what you planned? Did she agree to get on the boat that day knowing you intended to tip it?"

"Of course not," Tiye said. "But regardless, the life of one woman would have been worth it to remove Pharaoh. If we had succeeded that day, your sister would still be alive."

"How did you do it? Was it a spell?"

She dipped her head, a brief acknowledgement.

"What kind of spell? How did you know it? Who else was involved?" The questions tripped off my tongue. Although Ahmose had thought the wind that hit the boat on precisely the right angle to overturn it was probably the result of a spell, I had never been certain. It could as easily have been a stray gust, or the will of the gods.

"Henuttawy acquired the spell," Tiye said. I hadn't thought she would give me any detail. "She obtained it from Pharaoh's library with the help of one of the librarians."

A spell procured in exactly the same way as Ahmose and I had intended for my plan to make myself powerful enough for Pharaoh to fear me. Whose idea was that to start with? Perhaps Henuttawy had planted the idea in Ahmose's mind. She might have played a far longer game than any of us realised.

"Kia wasn't the only woman to lose her life that day," I said. "A maid servant died as well."

"Unfortunate."

Tiye would shed no tears over the death of a servant. I

143

didn't even know why I pointed it out, except someone had to acknowledge that two women were sacrificed to Tiye's plan that day.

Neither Tiye nor I mentioned how I helped save Pharaoh from drowning. Surely she knew, yet she never accused me of interfering. She wasn't the kind of woman to forget such a thing, though, and I couldn't help wonder whether she still harboured resentment over my contribution to the failure of her plan.

CHAPTER 23

*L*earning Tiye would have considered the deaths of both my sister and me a justifiable loss shocked me. As much as I agreed Pharaoh needed to be removed from the throne, I didn't accept that the deaths of others who had done no wrong should be tolerated.

"Is that the only time you tried to kill me?" The words were out of my mouth before I thought better of it.

Tiye cocked her head to the side as she studied me.

"You know the importance of what we do," she said.

"Answer me," I demanded. "How many times have you tried to kill me?"

"None." She looked me right in the eyes as she spoke. "It was always Pharaoh we targeted. But you got in the way once or twice."

"The time my sister and I were ill after dining with Pharaoh. Did you try to kill him then too?"

She inclined her head ever so slightly.

"Did you poison our food that night?" I asked.

"The details are unimportant," she said. "What matters is that we failed. This time, we must succeed."

There was no point pushing her for details. If she had decided she wouldn't tell me how she made us ill, I wouldn't get it out of her.

"Was Pharaoh ill that night as well?" I asked instead.

She sighed. "No, unfortunately. You and your sister must have gotten some of the dose, but not enough to be lethal, and it seems he was not affected."

So she did poison our food.

"Or he is immune to it," I said.

She gave me a sharp look, but didn't respond.

"What?" I asked. "What does that look mean?"

"He is not immune," she said. "But he is protected. By magic. He is, as one might expect, cognisant of the possibility of assassination, and he is by nature extremely superstitious. He takes every possible precaution for his own safety."

We had talked about Pharaoh's magical protections the night she summoned us all to her chambers, but the discussion didn't reveal much more than that he had both magicians and priests ensuring his safety. I hadn't quite understood the impact of his defences. If Pharaoh was so well protected, failure was possible, perhaps even probable. He wouldn't be an easy man to kill.

I left soon after. There were too many new thoughts in my head for me to focus on a conversation, especially with Tiye.

Ettu must have known from my face I had much to think about because she took one look at me and suggested a walk outside. As we made our way through the Palace, I received a number of congratulations on the birth of my babe. I recognised the faces of most of the women who spoke to me, although I didn't always know their names. Gossip travelled fast in a place like this and the birth of a child of Pharaoh would be big news.

I was thankful nobody stopped to talk, but merely offered their well wishes as they passed. I'd probably burst into tears if someone asked whether I had seen my babe, but they surely all knew any child would be swiftly whisked away, leaving the mother with both empty arms and an empty heart.

It was a relief to be outside and away from anyone who might comment on my babe's arrival. Ettu trailed behind me, seemingly lost in her own thoughts. With nothing to distract me from my conversation with Tiye, I mused on whether the other Ornaments involved knew about the previous attempts on Pharaoh's life. Ineni, Gilukhipa, and Neferu probably did. Not Henutmire, though. She hadn't known the plan to remove Pharaoh from the throne also included his death until our gathering in Tiye's chambers. I couldn't imagine she had known they tried to kill me and didn't tell me.

"My lady." The exasperation in Ettu's voice suggested she had tried more than once to get my attention. "Lady Henutmire is some distance behind us. She called out to you."

"Thank you," I said. "I didn't hear her."

"Hmm," Ettu said, no doubt wondering what I had been thinking so hard about.

"Kassaya." Henutmire was a little out of breath as she caught up to us. "I thought you mustn't have heard me."

"I didn't," I said. "But Ettu did."

Henutmire gave Ettu a small nod of thanks, then came to walk beside me. She linked her arm through mine, giving the appearance we were out for a companionable stroll together. Ettu dropped back to walk with Henutmire's maid.

"Why don't you two find a shady spot to sit and wait for us?" Henutmire suggested over her shoulder to the two maids. "Kassaya and I will take a short walk and then return to you. There is no need for you to tire your legs following after us."

Her maid readily set off for a tree. Ettu hesitated, her gaze flicking between me and the maid.

"Go on, then," I said. "It would be unfair of me to require you to walk with us when Henutmire's maid is permitted to rest."

Ettu hurried after the maid and Henutmire and I strolled away. She set a leisurely pace, which I was forced to match since she still had her arm linked through mine.

"I must speak with you in private," she whispered as we walked.

"So I gathered."

She hesitated, taking a deep breath as if steeling herself for whatever she wanted to say.

"I didn't fully understand," she said at last. "I feel rather foolish now, of course, but I didn't know they meant to…" She paused and gave me a look filled with significance. "You know."

She didn't know they meant to kill him. That much had been clear from her reaction in Tiye's chambers. Henutmire gave a troubled sigh.

"I know I committed, but I'm reconsidering," she admitted. "If we were to be uncovered…"

"It would mean death for all of us," I said.

"Suicide, most likely."

"Really?" Her revelation took me aback. Given what I knew of the penalties for an affair, I had expected the method of execution to be more savage.

"It's the most common death sentence for those of noble birth," she said.

"How would…" My voice trailed away. I couldn't say it, but she knew what I meant.

"For a man, it would most likely be a blade," she said. "For a woman, poison, perhaps. I cannot imagine they would expect us to have the strength to stab ourselves through the heart."

I tried to picture it. Locked alone in a chamber. A knife on the table. It would be sharp, perhaps not overly large, but small enough for a woman to wield. I would take it up, wrapping my fingers around the handle. Turn it so the tip pointed towards my heart. Rest it against my skin. Feel it pierce me, perhaps a small trickle of blood, as I steadied myself. Then a thrust, pushing it deep into my chest.

Would it sink in easily? Would I have to force it? Would it catch on bone? Could I even do such a thing? It would require great physical strength to push the knife into one's own chest — the angle would be awkward, after all — but I couldn't comprehend the mental strength it would require. To keep forcing the blade into my body, despite the pain, despite the blood, despite the knowledge it would kill me. I didn't think I could.

"Kassaya?" Henutmire's voice drew me from my gruesome thoughts. "Are you well? Did I shock you?"

"Somewhat," I admitted. "I was trying to decide whether I would be able to stab myself in the heart."

"I have thought about it, too," she said, "and concluded I couldn't. It wouldn't matter how long they gave me. If my method of death was to be by blade, someone would have to do it for me."

We walked in silence for a while and I assumed she, like me, still contemplated the difficulty of stabbing oneself through the heart.

"Did you know?" she asked at last.

"That the plan was to kill him? I suspected."

She exhaled sharply. "Why did you agree then? The others, I can understand. They are more ruthless. But you. I cannot figure out why you would knowingly agree to such a thing."

I glanced at her, trying to glean clues from her face or her body. Surely she understood. She knew what he did.

"Tell me why you agreed first," I said. "Then I will give you my reason."

"For my brother," she said promptly. "I wouldn't have gotten involved for anything less. I begged Pharaoh to release him, but he only laughed at me and told me he doesn't care to. So I will support whoever wants the throne as long as he will send my brother home."

She looked at me, gauging my response.

"Now you," she said.

"For my sister. For Nebtu. For Hilde. For every other woman he will hurt if he is allowed to do what he does."

"Nebtu? What does Nebtu have to do with this? Or Hilde? Or your sister, for that matter."

"You know what I'm talking about," I said. "The way you reacted when I asked if Pharaoh had ever hurt you tells me you do."

I had told her before the last time she went to Pharaoh. That if he put his hands to her throat, she mustn't fight him. Surely she had figured out what that meant for Nebtu.

"I know he sometimes hurts the women he is intimate with," she said. "It's not something anyone talks about, other than in whispers. But he never did it to me, nor to Nebtu as far as I know. She would have told me."

Her face gave no suggestion of duplicity. How could she not know?

"He killed my sister." I watched her carefully. This was shocking news and I didn't know how she would react.

"He…" Henutmire's voice trailed away and she stopped walking, drawing me to an abrupt halt. She swallowed hard. "Are you certain?"

"I am."

"But…" She took a moment, seemingly gathering her thoughts. "How do you know? Do you have any proof?"

"A witness who saw her go to Pharaoh that night. Not a single person who can testify she left alive. I know which guards disposed of her body and where she was interred. This is what he does."

"What he does." Her voice was flat as she repeated my words.

"Yes."

She covered her mouth with one hand, her eyes shining with tears.

"No," she said. "Kassaya, I am so sorry for your loss, but I cannot believe it. He is cruel, and I believed you when you said he likes to hurt a woman, but he would never kill one of us. We are his wives. We belong to him. Everything you see around us is for our pleasure. He wants us to be happy."

"He wants us to be confined," I said. Was she really that naive? "However beautiful this place is, it's still a prison."

"We have everything we need. If there is something we desire, we only have to ask the administrators and they will arrange it. New gowns, jewels, wigs, a particular wine or food. Nothing is too much trouble for Pharaoh's Ornaments."

That was exactly what the administrators told me when I arrived. My chambers could be re-painted, the floor tiles replaced, new chests for my clothing. Anything I wanted, they said. When I demanded bigger chambers, they moved me.

When I requested more beds so my female companions could sleep in my chambers instead of the maids' dormitories, they brought them.

"We are permitted no contact with anyone outside the Palace unless it is sent through the scribe," I said. "I cannot even write to my own father."

"It is for our safety."

"How is preventing me from communicating with my father for my safety?" I asked. "That is ludicrous."

"Well, not your father specifically," she said. "But other folk."

"Who? Who could I possibly write to that would jeopardise my safety in a place like this?"

Henutmire shrugged. "I don't know. I have never really thought about it. It's merely one of the rules."

"But that's my point," I said. "There are all these rules we must follow and no good reason for them."

"There are reasons. They mightn't be clear to us, but if you asked the administrators, they would explain it for you."

"What about the rule that unmodified men are not permitted within the Palace?" I asked. "And that no man may touch an Ornament."

"To keep us safe," she said. "We never need fear being attacked within our own home because the men who attend us don't have that kind of urge. And if they do, they know it will result in their execution, so they don't even try."

"What if you wanted to touch one of them?"

"Me?" The look she gave me was aghast. "I would never."

"You might want to. One day, you might encounter a man and fall in love with him. What then? Would you be happy to live the rest of your life knowing you can never be with him?"

"I belong to Pharaoh." She sounded less certain now,

though. "Even if there was a man I desired, I would never act on it. I know you wouldn't either."

When I didn't respond, she glanced over at me.

"Kassaya? You wouldn't, would you?"

I spent too long trying to find a reply. She gave a little gasp.

"Tell me you haven't. Oh, Amun. Kassaya, you know the rules."

It was too late to deny it. She wouldn't believe me now.

"The rules are unfair," I said. "And they are not for our benefit. They are solely designed to control us. So Pharaoh has the pleasure of knowing no other man has touched a woman he has claimed."

"I cannot believe you would do such a thing." She lowered her voice. "Who was it?"

I shook my head. "I cannot tell you."

"Amun," she said. "Tell me you haven't..."

I waited. I knew what she wanted to know, but she would have to say it.

"You haven't been intimate with him, have you?" she whispered.

My cheeks heated and she gasped.

"Oh, Kassaya."

I shrugged, already regretting that she knew.

"Is it one of the modified men?" she whispered. "I have heard things about them. That they know how to pleasure a woman."

Now it was Henutmire's cheeks which heated. I kept my mouth firmly closed. If she knew he was unmodified, that certainly narrowed down the possibilities, and she would only have more questions. I couldn't possibly tell her about the things Khaemmalu had done to me.

"Regardless." Henutmire cleared her throat. "Back to what we were discussing. You said you had proof Pharaoh killed your sister."

I only nodded, hoping she would put the pieces together for herself. That I wouldn't have to be the one to tell her he had also killed Nebtu.

"But why?" she asked. "Why would he do such a thing? He adores his Ornaments."

"Because he gets pleasure from seeing a woman think she might not survive." My tone was flat. No matter how many times I said this, it never got easier. "And if she fights him, he has to make sure she knows he is more powerful, and sometimes he goes too far."

Henutmire flinched.

"Poor Ishtar," she said. "I didn't know her well, but no woman deserves such a fate."

"No, no woman does."

Still I waited. Surely she had figured out what this must mean for Nebtu? But if Henutmire had, she didn't say it. So eventually I did. I had to be sure she understood. If she was to be involved in the plan to kill Pharaoh, she deserved to comprehend exactly why we did it.

"He killed Nebtu, too," I said.

"No." Her denial was swift. "The administrators said she returned to her father."

"I know you don't believe that. You never did."

"They wouldn't lie to us."

Maybe it was too much for her to take in at one time. Perhaps I shouldn't have told her, or at least, not today. Henutmire had been certain the administrators were lying after Nebtu disappeared. There was no reason for her to deny it now, especially to me.

"You sent a secret message to Nebtu's father," I reminded her. "You wouldn't have done such a thing if you believed the administrators."

"I was merely surprised she left without telling me. I thought we were friends."

"You were, Henutmire." I squeezed her arm. "And she would have told you if she was leaving. She didn't tell you because she never expected she wouldn't return. She went to Pharaoh that evening and she died."

"There must have been an accident. Perhaps she had too much wine and she fell over and hit her head. Or she got bitten by a snake. Or..."

"Henutmire, you know that isn't true. You never for a moment believed what the administrators said. You always knew something had happened to her."

"But not..."

"I tried to get evidence of her death for you."

She gave me a sharp look. I had surprised her.

"How?" she asked.

"I snuck out to the House of Life one night. I hoped to see her body being prepared."

"No," she whispered. "You didn't. You wouldn't be that foolish."

"It wasn't long after she disappeared. I heard the body of an unknown woman was taken to the House of Life and I wanted to see if she was Nebtu. I would have told you if it was. I wanted to give you that certainty."

"But it wasn't her, I assume," she said.

"No, it was Atahar."

She shot me a questioning look. "Who?"

"My maid's sister. She was sent to work in Pharaoh's palace and she must have caught his eye."

"So you believe he killed her, too? Along with Nebtu and Ishtar? Kassaya, surely you understand how ludicrous this sounds. That Pharaoh could be responsible for three murders? I'm very sorry for your sister, and also your maid, but it's simply not possible."

"Not just three."

She shook her head, obviously still refusing to let herself believe.

"There have been many women," I said. "My maid, Mery-tre, knows of at least fifteen who have gone missing in the time she has worked here."

"Women run away all the time." She sounded less confident now.

"No, they don't. How do you think an Ornament would get out of the gates without permission? Pharaoh summons them and they are never seen again. It has happened over and over, Henutmire. Why don't you believe me? Do you think I would lie to you?"

"Of course not," she said quickly. "I merely think you are mistaken. That you want so badly to have certainty of your sister, you have put together pieces that don't actually fit and created a story that never happened."

"You were the only one who didn't believe Nebtu had gone back to her father," I said. "I don't understand why you're so unwilling to believe me now. I've been looking into this for months. There is so much evidence, it can't be ignored. There is no other possible answer that makes sense of everything."

"I cannot believe you," she said. "I will not. Kassaya, if what you say is true, that means we are all at risk. Every single one of us. I cannot believe such a thing."

"All of us," I said. "And every woman who will come after us. Are you really able to stand by now you know the truth? I cannot. I will not let a single other woman die at his hands if I can do something about it."

"I'm sorry," she said, unlinking her arm from mine. "I truly am. But I cannot be involved with such craziness."

"Ask Tiye, then. If she is honest, she will tell you exactly the same as I have. They all know, Henutmire. That's why they made this plan."

"No, there are other reasons," she said. "The economy, for one. It's a disaster, with all the workers' strikes and supply issues. There are many reasons we need a change of government. I'm not convinced we must go to the extreme they're planning, but I suppose they want to be certain he won't merely take the throne back after everything is done."

With that, she turned and strode back to where our maids waited, walking fast enough to make it clear she had no further wish to converse with me.

CHAPTER 24

"You and Lady Henutmire appeared very deep in conversation," Ettu said as we headed back to the Palace.

"Hmm," I answered, hoping she would let the matter drop if I appeared uninterested. Of course, she didn't.

"There is much colluding happening at present," she said.

"Colluding?" I studied her profile, wondering just how much she had guessed.

"Plans being laid. Plots being made."

"And colluding."

"Yes," she said. "There is definitely colluding going on."

"And what are all these plans and plots and colluding about?" I asked.

"That is what I don't know." She shot me a sideways look. "I don't suppose you know anything about them?"

"Me? I hardly know anything." My cheeks heated, giving immediate evidence of my lie.

"My lady." Ettu hesitated, as if choosing her words carefully.

My heart pounded a little faster. When she did this, it was always because she had something serious to say.

"I told you the other day I thought something was about to happen," she said.

"You did. Have you heard anything more?" I tried to keep my tone easy. She might have put some of it together, but she surely didn't know of my involvement or she wouldn't be telling me.

"If I am right, it's bigger than big," she said. "I can hardly fathom it."

"Tell me."

She shook her head. "It's too dangerous. It's better you know nothing, and I am only guessing anyway. I know nothing for certain."

"How is it any less dangerous for you to know?"

Ettu shrugged. "I am merely a maid. You, however, are an Ornament. Nobody pays attention to what a maid might know. An Ornament, on the other hand. Folk listen when an Ornament speaks."

"Whatever it is, you can tell me. I won't tell anyone."

She shook her head.

"I will say nothing of it, only to repeat what I said earlier. You should leave. We will find a way to get your babe. Half and I will come with you, for now at least."

"For now?"

"I haven't yet decided whether I wish to attach myself to a man. I have said before I want to be free to make my own decisions and that hasn't changed."

"I thought there was something between you and him."

"There is, but however different he may be, he is still a man. And I am not so sure I want one of them."

"Does he know you feel that way?"

"Of course." She gave me a disparaging look, as if she was offended at my suggestion she might have kept such a thing from him.

"And it doesn't bother him?"

"Of course it does. He is a man, after all. But he listens when I tell him what I think and he tries to understand."

Ever since we smuggled Tall and Half into my chambers, Ettu had worn a *shendyt* and shirt like a man. She said it was so when we sent the men's clothing off to be washed, folk would think it was hers. I wondered that nobody questioned the varying sizes of the men's items, but I supposed since there seemed a logical explanation of why men's clothing was included in the laundry from my chambers, nobody thought too hard about it. Maybe they even thought others of my maids wore such garments in private.

After all, it must be incomprehensible to think I might have men living here. With the number of folk who were in and out of my chambers every day — my lady's maids, the kitchen staff, the servants who came to clean — it must seem impossible that anyone could be there without folk knowing.

"He's a good man," I said, finally realising she probably still waited for my response.

"He is, and if I wanted to align myself with one, I would choose him in a heartbeat. I'm just not sure it's the kind of life I want for myself."

"I promised to release you once I bore Pharaoh a son," I said.

"You did."

I hesitated before I said anything more. I didn't want Ettu to leave, but it would be better if those I cared about were as far away as possible before Tiye's plan was enacted. I didn't want any of my companions involved, even inadvertently, and

I certainly didn't want them sharing the blame if we were uncovered. It was reasonable to think that if my role in the plan was revealed, folk would assume my maids had known as well.

"You may go," I said. "There is no need to wait any longer. You may take Half with you, or not, as you and he both choose."

"My lady?" She gave me a confused look. "Have I displeased you?"

"Of course not."

"Then why do you want me to leave?"

I could hardly tell her the truth.

"I suspect I may never bear a son," I said. "Some women only have daughters, no matter how many times they try."

"Your mother bore five sons and only two daughters," she pointed out. "I think there is a very good chance you will bear a son. You have only one child and you are young yet. There is plenty of time for sons."

"I don't intend to produce another child for that man." The words surprised me, but they were out of my mouth before I could think better of them.

"Hush," she said quickly. "You mustn't let anyone hear you say such a thing."

"You should go. Don't wait to see if I manage to bear a son. Just go and make the life you want."

Her words about wanting to be free to make her own decisions resonated with me. They lit a flame inside me, but I tamped it out. That sort of life would never be for me and there was no point longing for it. I didn't even let myself think about what my life might look like if it was within my control. Such thoughts could only ever lead to unhappiness.

CHAPTER 25

y maids were still fussing over my appearance the following morning when a knock came. Ettu slipped away to see who it was. I heard a brief conversation, but couldn't make out the caller's voice or anything that was said.

"It's Lady Henutmire," Ettu said when she returned to my bedchamber. "She's in the sitting chamber. I told her you might be some time yet, but she insisted on waiting."

"Did she say why she's here?" I asked.

"Only that she needed to speak with you and it was most urgent."

Something to do with yesterday's conversation, no doubt. I couldn't think what else might have prompted her to pay me a call. I tried not to show my frustration as my maids changed my wig twice and my sandals three times, even though surely nobody would even notice my shoes. As I had no plans to go out today, it all seemed pointless, but I knew better than to complain. Ettu would only remind me it kept my maids employed.

When they were finally satisfied with my appearance, Abar was first out the door as usual. In the sitting chamber, Henutmire stood by the window, as if she was looking out, but I sensed she saw nothing of the meticulously maintained gardens.

"Henutmire, this is a surprise," I said as I joined her at the window.

"I hope I'm not intruding." It was only when she turned to face me that I saw the dark circles under her eyes.

"Are you unwell?" I asked.

"Oh, no." She raised one hand to her eyes, as if wanting to rub them, but stopped. She probably didn't want to risk her maid's wrath if she ruined her kohl. "Just tired. I hardly slept last night."

No doubt because she spent the night thinking about our conversation. I knew I was right when she spoke next.

"Would you send your maids away?" she asked in a low voice. "I have something to say which would best be said in private."

"Of course." I turned back to Ettu, Merytre and Sehener who had already made themselves comfortable on the couches. "You do not need to stay," I said to them. "Henutmire and I will be quite fine to look after ourselves for a while."

"It's no trouble," Sehener assured me. "I'm perfectly happy to do some needlework, and should you happen to need anything, we will be right here."

I looked to Ettu and she, at least, seemed to understand.

"Come," she said to the others. "Let's leave my lady and her friend to talk without us listening in the background."

She ushered them out of the chamber. Merytre seemed unbothered, but Sehener gave me a hurt look as she left. Perhaps she thought I didn't trust them. I wished I could explain I only tried to protect them. The door to one of the bedchambers closed and I turned back to Henutmire.

The dark circles weren't the only evidence of her worry. Her face was pale, and she scratched at a red welt on her wrist.

"Why didn't anyone tell me?" she blurted out. "There were others, earlier. I never knew any of them personally, so I understand if nobody thought to tell me, but everyone knew I was close to Nebtu. Why didn't they tell me what happened to her?"

"I suppose they wanted to protect you," I said. "You were so upset when she disappeared, but it would have been even worse if they told you what they knew."

"But then I wouldn't have wondered," she said. "I could have made my peace with knowing she would never come back. That I would never receive a message explaining why she left so suddenly and without any farewells."

"Did you really expect that? You always thought something had happened to her. I'm sure there are others who don't believe the administrators when they claim a woman decided to leave, but you were the only one willing to say it."

Henutmire sighed and turned her gaze to the gardens. We watched a guard make his way around the perimeter. Gardeners trimmed shrubs and one weeded a flower bed on his hands and knees. It was such a normal scene. Domestic. Tranquil even. To see it, no one would guess at the horrors this place held.

"I never believed them," she admitted at last. "Despite what I said to you yesterday, I think, deep down, I knew she had gone to the West, but I didn't know how, or why. Knowing... knowing makes it harder."

Her voice trembled and she seemed about to burst into

tears. I put my hand over hers on the window sill, hoping to comfort her.

"This is supposed to be a safe place," she burst out. "We are supposed to be safe here. *He* is supposed to protect us. What do I do now I know he is the person we are most at risk from?"

"You help us," I said. "You know the plan. We are going to make it right. To make this a safe place for all the women who come after us."

"I want to burn this gods-damned place to the ground," she said. "And never let another woman enter through its doors."

"Maybe we can do that, too. Once we have achieved our aim."

Once we have killed him. There was no need to say the words. We both knew what I meant.

"When I first understood what they intended, I thought they didn't mean it," she said. "That it was a game. A fantasy about taking control of their lives."

"It's not," I said.

"I know. I understand that now."

"So, are you in?"

She wouldn't miss the significance in my use of Tiye's words from the other night. Henutmire nodded and her previous reluctance was gone.

"I am," she said.

CHAPTER 26

*I*neni was the next to send a runner with a message of a gathering in her chambers.

"There have been an awful lot of gatherings lately," Ettu observed after the runner left.

She eyed me carefully, watching my reaction. I shrugged and tried to look nonchalant.

"I suppose everyone's a bit bored," I said. "It's a pleasant diversion for a few hours."

"Hmm." The look she gave me said she knew there was more to it than that, but she was wise enough to not say anything else in front of the others.

As she and Sehener walked me to Ineni's chambers the following evening, I could feel Ettu restraining herself. We turned down the final hallway and she could keep her thoughts to herself no longer.

"Are you sure you want to attend tonight?" she asked. "You look very tired. Perhaps an early night would be better for you."

"Oh, you shouldn't feel obliged to go if you are too tired,"

Sehener said quickly.

The innocence in her voice told me she didn't suspect Ettu had any reason other than my apparent fatigue for suggesting I skip the gathering.

"It's only a couple of hours," I said. "I can sleep all day tomorrow if I feel like it."

It wasn't like I had anything else to do, other than endure my maids' attentions, sit in my chambers, and maybe take a walk. Perhaps I should take up needlework after all. At least it would give me something to pass the hours with.

"You are still recovering from childbirth," Ettu pointed out. "Nobody would be offended if you were too tired."

"But I'm not," I said.

"I don't think you should go," she burst out.

Sehener was so surprised, she stopped walking and had to hurry after us.

"Why?" I asked.

"Why ever would you say such a thing, Ettu?" Sehener asked. "If my lady wishes to go, that is her prerogative. It's not up to the likes of us to tell her what to do."

"Sehener, hold your tongue." Ettu's voice was curt now.

We stopped to face each other in the hallway and she looked me right in the eyes.

"I don't know what is going on," she said, "but I fear you are caught up in it. No good can come of whatever those women are planning."

Her direct accusation caught me off guard.

"Ettu—" I started, but she cut me off.

"My lady, please. Think of your babe if you will not consider your own safety. What retribution might fall on her for your involvement?"

"They wouldn't."

My babe was a child of Pharaoh. She was safe. Impervious. If we were caught, they wouldn't harm her. Would they?

Ettu held my gaze and shrugged.

"As you say," she said.

"What have you heard?" I asked, my voice low. "Tell me."

"No more than I have said previously. But I have a bad feeling about it."

So she knew nothing. That should have reassured me, but it didn't. There was too much chatter. We were going to come undone.

"Wait for me," I said. "I don't expect to be long."

That was probably what this latest gathering was about. To discuss the rumours, maybe cancel our plans since folk were talking about it. If that was the case, I would make a new plan. *One day, someone will stop him,* my sister had said to me. *One day, someone will be brave enough.*

Nothing would prevent me from doing that for her. No matter how many times the plan fell apart, I would try again.

One day, I would be the one who stopped him.

CHAPTER 27

*W*hen Ineni answered my knock, I discovered I was the first to arrive.

"Kassaya, how lovely to see you," she said, gesturing for me to enter. "The others should be here soon."

Despite Ineni acting like this was just another casual gathering, I sensed an undercurrent of tension in her. While we waited, she flitted around, seemingly unable to stand still. I poured myself some wine and pretended to sip at it. I had no desire for it, though, and suspected I would need a clear head for the discussion to come.

Henutmire arrived next. Her face was pale and her eyes red, but she gave me a determined look, poured some wine, and gulped it down, before refilling her mug. So, she was still adjusting to what she knew. I wondered whether she would ask them why they never told her what happened to Nebtu.

Neferu and Gilukhipa arrived together, and Tiye was not far behind them. We chatted as we served ourselves dinner and made ourselves comfortable on the cushions. The food looked as superb as ever, and I knew it would be delicious, but the mere smell of it made me nauseous. Ineni was already spooning baked fish into her mouth, eating with relish as if it was her first meal today. How could she be hungry when we discussed such a perilous plan?

My fingers went to my wrist, seeking the comfort of knowing the Eye of Horus pendant was there. It had protected me before and I must have faith in its continued protection. But the skin where the pendant should have been was bare. The cord must have broken at some point. I couldn't remember when I'd last had it. Hopefully it was somewhere in my chambers. Thoughts of the missing pendant fled my mind when Tiye spoke.

"My son has spoken to the royal librarians," she said abruptly.

I set down the piece of bread I had been pretending to nibble. Henutmire froze, but Ineni kept eating. She had finished her fish and moved onto some salad. The crunch of her onion seemed almost obscenely loud.

"They have access to spells which will reverse the ones protecting Pharaoh," Tiye continued.

"And they have agreed to help?" Neferu asked.

"They have." Tiye looked around at each of us. "That is one of the most significant items we had yet to resolve and now we have the solution."

"What have they requested in return?" I asked.

"Only that they be permitted to continue in their positions once the transition has occurred," she said.

The transition. Such a tidy name for what we were about to do. Much better than murder or sedition or insurrection. More palatable than heresy or treason.

"You expected something else?" Tiye's voice gave no hint of her thoughts.

Did she know I had offered Ishtar's gem in return for access to spells? Did the librarians even know such a reward was available, or had Henuttawy always meant to keep it for herself? I never realised folk might want to see Pharaoh ousted badly enough to help without payment.

"What about the chaos that will ensue when Pharaoh dies?" Gilukhipa asked. "Do they have spells for that?"

"Yes," Tiye said. "They will assist with that as well. I think we can be secure the magical aspects will be covered."

"Where are we at with military support?" Ineni asked as she arranged a slice of cheese on some bread.

"Negotiations are still in progress," Tiye said. "It's going well. Pentaweret is confident we will have a full commitment from Bonemwese and Pasai within the day."

"Who?" I hadn't heard either name before. This, it seemed, was a part of the plan I didn't know about.

"Bonemwese is in charge of the archery division," Tiye said. "And Pasai is a general. As soon as Pharaoh has been dealt with, we will send messengers to them. Their men will be ready and waiting."

"You intend an armed revolt." I hadn't expected violence, other than in the manner of Pharaoh's death.

"But of course." Tiye's face said she thought it was inevitable. "We need to ensure any disunity is promptly put down."

"People could get hurt," I said. "Or killed."

Henutmire frowned, but the others looked unconcerned. This was detail they already knew and had agreed to.

"You intend to kill anyone who opposes you," I said.

"Bonemwese and Pasai's men will deal with anyone who tries to stand in their way," Tiye clarified. "We cannot afford anything but full support for the transition."

"But killing people?" I asked. "That could include folk we know."

Like Khaemmalu's friend, Bebi, who was our man in Pharaoh's personal squad. I hoped he wouldn't have to stand against an armed force invading the palace. As long as he didn't resist, he should be safe. Khaemmalu was involved somehow, too, and surely he would warn Bebi if he thought there was any danger to him. At least I didn't need to fear for Khaemmalu. The violence would be at Pharaoh's palace, not here.

"It is necessary." Tiye waved away my objection. "Pharaoh has his own plans for what will occur on his departure to the West. He has an heir, and there are men whose job it is to ensure Ramses takes the throne with as little disruption as possible. We need to ensure that doesn't happen. Pentaweret must claim the throne first."

I had forgotten Pharaoh already had an heir. But of course he did, and of course Ramses would expect to succeed his father. I had never met Ramses, but I heard him speak at the festival for Min. His speech was long and ponderous, just like those of Pharaoh himself.

"He won't be hurt, will he?" Henutmire asked. "The boy, Ramses."

"He's hardly a boy," Tiye said with a scoff. "He's a man in his twenties."

"He's not responsible for his father, though," Henutmire said. "He has done nothing wrong."

I was surprised, and rather impressed, she pushed back.

"He won't merely stand aside," Tiye said. "He leads one of the army divisions and has men who will fight for him. We need him out of the way as swiftly as possible."

"Can we not lock him up?" I asked. "Does he have to be…"

My voice trailed away. I couldn't make myself say it.

"Killed?" Ineni asked baldly.

"Any potential source of opposition must be dealt with," Tiye said. "Our plan needs to be comprehensive for us to succeed."

The look on Henutmire's face said she was reconsidering her agreement. I, too, wavered, until Gilukhipa spoke. It was the first thing she had said since we sat down.

"We must remember why we do this," she said. "This is about stopping Pharaoh. There is no other way. He will not merely desist because we ask him to. How many more will suffer at his hands if we don't act? Yes, there might be casualties, but that is as it is. We fight for the future of every Ornament in the Palace."

"And what happens to us once the plan is enacted?" I asked. "Once Pharaoh is dead, and his heir, and Pentaweret takes the throne, what happens to the Ornaments?"

"The Palace will continue as it is," Tiye said, "except that he will compel no one to stay. Any Ornament who wishes to return to her father's home will be permitted to do so. The rest will remain in service to Pentaweret."

"As his Ornaments?" I asked.

"But of course." She frowned at me, clearly not understanding my confusion. "Every Pharaoh has Ornaments. Pentaweret will be no different. He will choose new Ornaments of his own, but he won't turn out anyone who doesn't want to leave or who has nowhere to go."

"So the Palace of the Ornaments will go on," I said.

Women would still be confined here, subject to Pharaoh's whims, forced to bear children for him, and to amuse him when he called for them. It might be a different man, but how different would the Ornaments' lives be? Tiye cocked her head as she studied me.

"Did you expect something else?" she asked.

I shook my head, unwilling to tell her. My thoughts had been focussed on protecting the women who would come after us, so I supposed I always expected the Palace to continue, even if I hadn't consciously thought about it. If I was given the option to leave, would I take it? And where would I go? Would my father allow me to return home if the new pharaoh willingly let me leave?

"Pentaweret will still send my brother home?" Henutmire asked.

"That has already been agreed," Tiye said.

"I want to go with him," Henutmire added.

Tiye nodded. "Of course. That will be your choice."

"And what of you?" I asked Tiye. "Will you stay?"

She gave me a bemused look. "As Ornament to my own son? Of course not. I intend to retire."

"He will give you a villa in Thebes?" I asked.

"I will move to Pharaoh's palace," she said. "Pentaweret will have a wing prepared for me. He needs someone to perform the role of queen, of course, until such time as he chooses a bride. I will do that for as long as he needs me and then I will retire."

So, Tiye had angled herself into position as queen after all. How long would she cling to that role before she allowed her son to take a wife? And she would help choose the woman who eventually replaced her. Tiye would wield a tremendous amount of power over both the new pharaoh and his queen.

How much of her plan was about ensuring power and an extravagant retirement for herself? I pushed away the thought. No, Tiye was doing exactly what Tiye always did:

taking the opportunity to grasp any benefit for herself. That didn't mean she acted for the wrong reasons. This was about the women Pharaoh had killed and all those he would harm in the future. If we could prevent that, it would all be worth it. Even if Tiye managed to get herself into position as queen, it wouldn't take away from what we had achieved.

CHAPTER 28

"We have yet to finalise the means of death," Tiye said. "We need to be ready to act very soon and we have not made a decision on this."

"After we last spoke about it, I was thinking about mandrake poison," Neferu offered. "I know the fruit is safe to eat, but consuming the plant itself causes death within minutes."

"Isn't it also a cure for insomnia?" Gilukhipa asked.

"It is," Tiye said. "And Pharaoh has used it previously. I myself have prepared the wine for him, as he trusts very few people to do such a thing. You can't even taste the mandrake powder once it is mixed in."

"Has he mentioned having trouble sleeping lately?" Ineni asked. "If not, I cannot see you would have a reason to offer it to him."

"Not to me, he hasn't," Tiye said. "And we cannot afford to wait. If our plans weren't time critical, mandrake poisoning might be a good option, but let's forget about it for now."

Neferu shrugged and didn't seem disappointed it wouldn't be her idea that was used.

"I still think an overdose of poppy would be a good choice," Gilukhipa said. "It takes a couple of hours to be fatal, but it is practically guaranteed to work if you use enough."

Tiye nodded. "He will gladly take wine dosed with poppy from me, and it would not be hard to convince him he wants it, but we need a plan that doesn't rely on him calling for me."

"Well, that makes it more difficult," Neferu said. "I've thought of other options, but they all rely on you being able to put it in his food or wine. Castor-oil plant, for one. It would only take a few seeds to kill him. Nightshade berries. I doubt he would recognise them. He would probably willingly eat them if they were included in a bowl of berries."

"All good ideas," Tiye said. "And we could readily source any of those if he called for me. However, for an option that doesn't rely on my presence, snake bite, as Kassaya suggested, has to be one of the top ideas."

She acknowledged me with a queenly nod. Perhaps she was already practicing for when her son became Pharaoh.

"It wouldn't be all that difficult to get a snake into his chambers," she added. "The tricky part would be ensuring it bites him."

"Death won't be fast, though," Ineni said, her tone thoughtful. "I believe a carpet viper bite can take a week or more to cause death, and a saw-scaled viper even longer. Two weeks, perhaps."

"But he would be incapacitated in the meantime," Neferu pointed out. "Internal bleeding, haemorrhages, eventual unconsciousness. Does it matter if it takes some time? Death is all but certain."

So many folk probably viewed the Ornaments as purely

decorative. Pretty women, elegantly dressed, without a thought in their heads other than getting close enough to Pharaoh to bear him a son. I'd certainly heard such comments, but these were strikingly clever women with the ability to be both practical and tactical. They were almost terrifying with the meticulous way they planned Pharaoh's downfall.

"If he has enough time, who knows what might go wrong?" Ineni was already shaking her head. "If his magicians know the right spells and potions, they might reverse the effects, and what happens then? They go searching for an explanation of how the snake got into his chambers."

"That in itself is easily explainable," Tiye said. "Snakes sneak in all the time. They find somewhere to hide and might not reappear until days later. Nobody would spend much time wondering how a snake got inside."

"You know how suspicious he is, though," Ineni said. "If he is bitten, he will immediately assume an assassination attempt. Whether his magicians can save him or not, he will have time to put such thoughts in their heads. They might well open an investigation after his death."

"And what would they find?" Tiye asked. "They would need a witness willing to testify it was he who deliberately released the snake into Pharaoh's presence to bite him."

"Torture a man and he will say anything you want him to," Gilukhipa said.

"But our man will already be well away from here," Tiye said. "We will have him release the snake, then flee immediately."

"You have someone in mind?" I asked. Perhaps she intended to recruit the snake charmer from the festival for Min.

"There is a butler in Pharaoh's palace," Tiye said. "He has

some skill as a snake charmer, although I think hardly anyone knows."

"He is receptive?" Ineni asked.

Tiye shrugged. "I have never had much to do with him, but if we approach him at the moment we are ready to act, we could get the job done swiftly, pay him, and send him away. He will be gone before he has time to confess."

"Assuming he is willing," I said.

"Everyone can be bought," Tiye said. "I have individual jewels worth many times more than a man will earn in his entire lifetime. Half a dozen of those, and who would refuse? We don't need to fear an investigation anyway. Pentaweret would never allow it."

"I suppose there is another option," Neferu said thoughtfully. "He has men who are responsible for preparing his food, yes? He won't be suspicious of anything that comes from them. Perhaps we don't need Tiye to be there to administer a poison in his food or wine."

Tiye frowned. "I'm not sure enough of either of them," she said. "Paibakamana *might* be amenable — I have seen the look on his face when Pharaoh is being cruel to me — but I wouldn't be willing to take a chance with Mastesuria. He always looks the other way. If I had to guess, I would say he is still loyal to Pharaoh."

"Could we have Bebi approach Paibakamana?" Ineni suggested. "Try to ascertain whether he might be willing to work with us."

"And if he is not, that could go wrong very quickly," Gilukhipa pointed out. "I doubt Bebi would expose us if he is uncovered, but if we lose our man in Pharaoh's personal squad, it makes things that much more difficult."

Not to mention that Bebi might lose his life if Paibakamana reported him. But nobody seemed concerned with that. I supposed they would consider him just another casualty. Another sacrifice for the sake of the plan.

"I agree with Gilukhipa," I said quickly, before anyone could argue with her. "We should reserve Bebi as a last resort. Who knows when it might be useful to have a man so close to Pharaoh?"

Regardless of Bebi's kindness to me the first night I went to Pharaoh's palace, this was the man Khaemmalu considered his brother. If I could save Bebi, I would.

"A fair point," Tiye said. "We should not deploy him unless we have exhausted all other options. If things go wrong and I am there with Pharaoh at the time, Bebi is the one man who might get me out safely."

Just as he had done for me after my *senet* game with Pharaoh. I was hardly surprised Tiye wanted to reserve him in case she needed him, rather than for his own sake.

"What about a curse?" Neferu asked.

The look on Tiye's face said she hadn't considered this possibility before.

"Who would you suggest for such a task?" she asked.

Neferu shrugged. "I haven't thought it through. The idea only just came to me. One of his magicians, maybe. Or a priest."

"Amanitore," I said.

Tiye's assessing gaze came to me. "I heard she conducted a ceremony for you. Facilitated you speaking with your sister, didn't she?"

"She did," I said. "And I was most grateful for the opportunity."

"Could you be sure it was really your sister, though?"

Henutmire asked. "It could have been a demon, or Amanitore might have tricked you."

"It was definitely my sister," I said. "It was her voice and I could feel her presence. There were things she said that someone impersonating her wouldn't have known."

"So Amanitore has some ability," Tiye said. "Does anyone know her allegiance, though?"

They all looked to me, but I had no further information about Amanitore. In truth, I barely knew her, having had little else to do with her.

"I ate breakfast with her once," Neferu said. "She hadn't yet been summoned by Pharaoh at that point, if I remember correctly. She said little about him, only that she expected him to call for her imminently."

"I believe I've heard she has only been with him twice," Ineni said. "So she mightn't have a reason to act against him. We should proceed cautiously. She is a woman who would turn on us in an instant if she had reason to."

"We have to make a decision," Tiye said. She smoothed her skirt over her legs, perhaps to give herself time to think. "And preferably agree on a second option as well. It wouldn't do to still be finalising our plan when the moment comes."

"I vote snake bite," Neferu said promptly. "It might not be the fastest option, but I think it is the safest."

"For us, at any rate," Ineni added, her tone grim. "Not for him."

"No, not for him," Neferu agreed.

"I think it should be poison," Ineni said. "The risk of discovery is higher, but the end will be faster."

"And what would be your poison of choice?" Tiye asked.

I wondered whether her adept change of topic suggested

Amanitore was already involved. Was this another of Tiye's games? Did she even now withhold parts of the plan from us?

"Poppy, I think," Ineni said. "But we need to make sure he calls for you when we need him to."

"I could perhaps have Pentaweret tell Pharaoh he wishes to see me," Tiye said. "He might suggest inviting me for dinner and asking if Pharaoh would join us."

"The man won't turn down a banquet," Neferu said.

"Nor will he reject an evening with me." Tiye's voice was smug, considering earlier she hadn't been sure of Pharaoh calling for her.

Although I would never betray them, I did wish Pharaoh might somehow learn about how a whole chamber of very clever women conspired to murder him. He who thought he was so smart and the cause of every good thing would be brought down by mere women.

"What about his queen?" I asked. "Could she cause trouble if she knows Pharaoh intends to spend the evening with you?"

"She cares nothing for him," Tiye said. "I made an overture to her some time ago. She made it clear she will have no part of our plan, but nor will she stand in our way."

"Does she know what you intend for her son?" I asked.

Tiye gave me a scornful look. "Do you think she would stand aside if she did? No, she knows only as much as she needs to, and nothing more. She believes Pharaoh's removal will give her son access to the throne sooner than expected."

"And what will happen to her afterwards?" I asked. "If you intend to take her place, where does she go?"

"Wherever she wants," Tiye said with a shrug. "Pentaweret has said she may take whatever she wants from the royal treasury. Enough that she can live the most extravagant lifestyle for the rest of her life, as befits a former queen, as long as she absents herself from both the palace and the public view. He doesn't want the common folk seeing a reminder of the previous government in the continuing presence of the former queen."

So even Pharaoh's own queen didn't care enough to stand up for him. Perhaps she welcomed the day she could retire from public life and do whatever she wanted. Would she leave Thebes? She had borne Pharaoh many children — four boys and presumably girls as well. Surely she would want to be near them.

But then, I had only met her two or three times. We had probably spoken less than a dozen words. Perhaps she wasn't the kind of woman who wanted to be involved in her children's lives. Perhaps bearing them was enough. She had fulfilled her duty of producing children, and the rest of her life was hers to do with as she wished once she was no longer queen.

It was a strange idea, but who was I to judge another woman? I couldn't imagine feeling that way myself, but if she intended to remove herself without resistance, she was unlikely to become a target. That made her one less person who might get hurt when the uprising happened.

I couldn't help but wonder, though, what the queen might do when she finally learned Tiye hadn't told her the whole plan.

CHAPTER 29

As we left Ineni's chambers some time later, I spotted Nammu standing with the maids who waited for us. She watched as I approached and gave me a snide look before pointedly turning away. Beside me, Tiye made a soft sound of amusement.

"I don't know why you keep her," I muttered.

"She might yet be useful," Tiye replied softly.

I couldn't see what possible use a servant like Nammu might have. She was treacherous and disloyal, quick to gossip and slow to learn her lesson. But she was in Tiye's service and no longer my concern. Still, I would dearly like her to get her recompense for the time she stole Tiye's jewel and planted it in my clothing chest.

Ettu and Sehener leaned against a wall as they waited for me. Both women were sleepy-eyed, and Sehener restrained a yawn as I joined them.

"I'm sorry I was so long," I said, feeling bad for keeping them from their beds. "It went much later than I expected."

"Did you have an enjoyable time?" Sehener asked.

"I did," I said.

Ettu gave me an odd look as if she knew my response was inappropriate, but said nothing, and we walked to my chambers in silence. Merytre let us in and slipped away to meet Sutem. He would have been waiting for her ever since he finished work at sunset. Guilt twinged in me for keeping a pregnant woman up so late.

We needed a better way of managing such gatherings. Perhaps just one maid could wait for me, given she would be with others and not on her own. That would mean Merytre could go home at a more reasonable hour, and the remaining woman could stay in my chambers with Tall and Half. Not that it would be an issue for much longer. Once our plan was enacted, the late night gatherings would end. So, too, would my time in the Palace presumably.

If Pentaweret was being truthful when he told Tiye he would let any Ornament who wanted to leave do so, I intended to go, but only if I could take my babe with me. I couldn't imagine he would have any use for Pharaoh's children. They would mean nothing to him. Surely he would be pleased to let the children return to their mothers. After all, he knew only too well what it was like to grow up without his mother in Pharaoh's palace.

I passed a restless night thinking about various details of our plan. It didn't sit right with me, this plot to murder a man, however despicable he might be, and I particularly disliked that his heir would suffer the same fate. If I could have come up with another idea that appeared likely to succeed, I would have suggested it to Tiye. But nothing else seemed to have the same potential. If death was what it took to stop him, then that was as it must be, and I had to reconcile myself to it.

As my maids attended to me the following morning, I

yawned repeatedly, barely able to keep my eyes open. Too many sleepless nights had caught up to me and at one point, I almost dozed off sitting on the stool while Merytre did my makeup. When the women finally filed out, with chirpy well wishes for my day, I could hardly hide my relief. In the sitting chamber, I flopped down on my usual couch.

"Shall I fix you some breakfast?" Sehener asked. Despite our late night, she looked as fresh and cheerful as ever.

I started to reply when a spasm of pain gripped my belly. I doubled over, clutching it as I cried out. They crowded around me in an instant. There were questions and comments, but I could focus on nothing but the pain.

"Send for the healer." It was Ettu's voice which rose above the others, calm as ever. "Tell her to hurry. It might be some after effect of childbirth."

Merytre went off to find a runner while Sehener locked Tall and Half in their bedchamber. Tall grabbed a loaf of bread and a bottle of wine on his way out. The pain subsided and I leaned back against the couch, my body limp.

"No need for the healer," I said between gasps. "It's gone now."

Ettu gave me a disapproving look. "It came on too suddenly. You were feeling quite well earlier, weren't you? You never said you were unwell when you got up this morning."

"I'm just tired," I said. "I didn't sleep well."

"That would not cause such severe pain," she said.

There was little time to argue with her as Merytre returned with the healer. It was the same woman who had attended to me during childbirth. She made me lie down while she poked and prodded at me for what seemed like an age. At last, she allowed me to sit up again.

"There doesn't appear to be anything wrong with you," she said. "I can find no tenderness or swelling in your belly. There is no sign of fever or clamminess of the skin. Just how severe was this pain?"

"It was the worst pain I have ever felt," I said. "Even worse than when I gave birth."

She gave me a doubtful look, as if wondering whether I exaggerated.

"I can send a tonic for you," she said. "If you are sickening, it should help. Send for me if the pain comes again."

She was halfway out the door when another spasm gripped my belly. I cried out and she came running back. Her hands prodded the area I indicated, but she only shook her head.

"There is nothing," she said. "I don't disbelieve your pain, but there is no swelling or pulsing or heat, or anything else that suggests a problem."

"It hurts," I managed between groans. "Make it stop."

"I encountered your lady in the hallway so I have no herbs with me. I can go to my chambers and fetch some things."

She went to move, but stopped when I grabbed her hand.

"Am I dying?" I asked.

She shook her head.

"I highly doubt it," she said. "This doesn't..."

Her voice trailed away and she tapped her chin as she gave me a considering look.

"Search the chamber," she said to Ettu, Merytre and Sehener who watched us, their faces worried. "Look for anything that is not usually here. Whatever this is, it doesn't appear to have a physical cause."

"She has been spelled?" Sehener asked with a gasp.

The healer gave a brief nod.

"Possibly," she said.

The women immediately set to work, checking every shelf, behind curtains, under the cushions and rugs. Meanwhile, the healer inspected me. She pawed through my wig, inspecting each braid individually, and even examined the spaces between my fingers and toes.

Another spasm grasped me, this one even worse than the ones before, and I was insensible as I rocked and clutched my belly. When it passed, my face was wet with tears and my jaw ached from being clenched.

"Stand up," the healer urged, her hands already on my arms, pulling me to my feet. "We need to check the couch beneath you."

My legs trembled as she hauled me up. She wrapped an arm around my waist to steady me as Ettu pulled the cushions off the couch.

"Nothing," Ettu said and went to put the cushions back. "Wait."

She reached down and seemed to poke at the corner of the couch. She held up a tiny figure, no taller than the height of my littlest finger to the first knuckle. My eyes were blurry from the pain and the tears, and I couldn't make it out.

"Is this what we're looking for?" Ettu asked.

The healer took it from her, turning it around to study it from all angles.

"Yes," she said. "This is it."

"That's causing her pain?" Ettu's voice was doubtful.

An even stronger spasm gripped my belly and I screamed as I doubled over. When it was finally over, leaving me panting and gasping, the healer held the little object up to show me.

"See this?" she said. "It's crude but clearly effective."

"What..." I didn't have the breath to say any more than that.

"A woman," she said. "Made by somebody who is not a skilled artist, but certainly a skilled magician."

"Is that meant to be my lady?" Merytre asked.

The three women crowded around the healer to see the object. She set it on the palm of her hand and held it out to them.

"It doesn't have to look like the subject," the healer said. "It's merely a representation. The power comes from the spells said over it."

"What kind of spells?" Sehener reached out as if wanting to touch the little figure, but quickly withdrew.

"Spells to cause pain." The healer's voice was grim. "Pain which will continue as long as the object is in close proximity to the subject."

"So if we hadn't found it, my lady would..." Ettu didn't seem to know how to finish her question, but the healer obviously didn't need her to.

"The pain would continue," she said, matter of factly. "Eventually, my lady would will herself to death in order to escape it."

"Who would do such a thing?" Merytre asked.

"And to my lady?" Sehener added, shaking her head. "Everyone adores her."

Not everyone. Not Abar who blamed me for the death of her sister.

"This is not cottage magic," the healer said. "It takes much strength to infuse an object with such power. It cannot be done by someone who merely dabbles in healing magic or some such thing. This is priest-level magic. Maybe even magician magic."

And there was only one woman in the Palace with a reputation that suggested she might be that powerful.

"We know someone who is considered to be a magician," Merytre said.

"Amanitore," the healer said. "Yes, there may well be others here with such ability, but she is the only one I have heard of."

"You said this could be priestly magic," Ettu said. "There are both priests and magicians in Pharaoh's palace. Could one of them have done it?"

"Does your lady know any of them personally?" the healer asked.

"No," Ettu said. "Not as far as I know."

They all looked at me and I shook my head. I still didn't have enough breath to speak.

"Then it is unlikely," the healer said. "Such magic requires the maker to be familiar with the intended victim. To infuse the object with what she knows of the subject, and the final spells would usually be said within close proximity."

"I woke up thirsty last night," Sehener offered. "I came out to get a drink and thought I heard footsteps in the hallway which seemed to stop right outside." She gestured towards the door as if we might not know where she meant. "I put my ear to the door and heard someone breathing, so I asked who it was. I thought it might have been a runner come with an urgent message for my lady, but hesitant to wake everyone. There was no answer, but the footsteps went back down the hallway."

"Did you go out there?" Merytre asked, her eyes wide.

"Of course not," Sehener said. "Without knowing who it was, or what purpose they might have in loitering in the hallway so late, I wasn't going to open the door. I had quite forgotten about it until just now."

"That was likely the maker of the object," the healer said. "And then somebody planted it in these chambers this morning. If the pain only just started, it couldn't have been placed here any earlier."

"The kitchen servants come every morning," Merytre said. "At least half a dozen of them."

"And the cleaners," Sehener added. "Another half dozen."

"And the rest of my lady's maids," Ettu said. "Seven more women."

Something about her voice told me she had already decided who was responsible.

"You don't think…" I said.

"Can you think of anyone more likely?" she retorted.

I doubled over as another spasm gripped my belly. I understood how such pain might make a woman will herself to death. Already I didn't know how much longer I could tolerate it.

"I think we should send for Panouk," Ettu said. "If Abar is responsible, he needs to interrogate her."

"Get rid of it first," I managed between gasps. "I cannot take any more."

The healer hesitated, staring down at the object in her hand.

"Once I remove the figure, the pain will lessen," she said. "But this is your evidence. Will Panouk not want to see its effect on you?"

"Then tell him to hurry." The pain eased and I collapsed back onto the couch. I rested my head in my hands and realised my face was wet with tears.

"I will go myself," Ettu said.

"Perhaps I should wait in the hallway in the meantime," the healer suggested. "I can at least remove the figure from the chamber until the administrator arrives. The effect is likely to be slight, but it may give you some small amount of relief."

I only nodded, too exhausted to reply. She was correct that the improvement was only slight once she was out of the chamber. The spasms still came just as frequently and were almost as painful. The figure's removal from my proximity seemed to do no more than dull the pain a little, but I was grateful for even that much.

It took some time for Panouk to arrive, but at last, he bustled into the chamber, his face creased with concern. Ettu and the healer followed him.

"Lady Kassaya," he said. "Your maid says you are the victim of some terrible magic."

"Somebody has cast a spell on me," I said before the next spasm overtook me.

As I wailed and groaned, the healer's voice became part of the background. She must be telling Panouk about how her examination had found no obvious cause.

When the pain finally eased again, I found myself lying on the couch with my legs curled up to my chest and Panouk frowning down at me.

"Well, then," he said. "It seems quite clear there is indeed magic at work here. Do you know who might have reason to do such a thing?"

"Abar," I said. Ettu would tell him if I didn't. "My maid."

"The one from Nubia?" he asked. "A prisoner of war, if I recall correctly."

Ettu darted in to help me as I gingerly sat up. Merytre brought a soft cloth for me to wipe my face with.

"That is the one," I said. "You might remember her sister—"

It was all I had time for before the pain came again.

Ettu's voice took up the story, presumably reminding Panouk about how Atahar, had been assigned to work in Pharaoh's palace and had gone missing, presumed dead. She wouldn't tell him, of course, how we had seen her body when we snuck out to the House of Life.

"I'm not sure I understand why she blames Lady Kassaya for her sister's misfortune," Panouk said. "Surely she knows Lady Kassaya had no part in bringing either her or her sister here from Nubia, or in their respective work assignments."

The pain eased and I was able to speak again.

"She blames me for not finding her sister soon enough," I said. "I had told her I would try to find word of her, and by the time I did, Atahar had disappeared."

"But that is not your fault." The look Panouk gave me showed he was still mystified.

I shrugged. "She thinks it is, and I suppose that's all that matters. She swore revenge on me."

"Surely she doesn't have the skill for such magic herself," Panouk said. "Do you know who she recruited to cast the spell for her?"

"I suspect I do," I said. "But I would rather not name her without proof."

After all, Amanitore had given me the chance to speak with Ishtar, and I had promised her a favour.

Panouk gave me a nod.

"Very well," he said. "I will find Abar and bring her here to account for herself."

The pain came again and my only reply was a loud groan. If Abar was sensible, she would have fled immediately after planting her little spell figure in my chambers. No, I realised. She wouldn't have left. She would want to see her spell at work. She would anticipate returning tomorrow to find me insensible with pain. She was not the sort of woman who would flee without viewing her handiwork.

It seemed like a very long time before Panouk returned, a sullen Abar following. She directed a glower in my direction. She had, it seemed, already guessed why she had been summoned.

"There is a very serious accusation levelled against you," Panouk told her. "Somebody has cast a spell on Lady Kassaya and she has reason to believe you might be responsible. What do you have to say for yourself?"

Abar only gave him a shrug.

"I do not understand," she said stiffly.

Panouk took the little figure from the healer and showed it to Abar.

"Have you ever seen this before?" he asked her.

"I do not know what you ask," she said.

"Abar, you must be honest with us." Panouk's voice was stern. "What have you done?"

No matter how he asked, "I do not understand," was her only reply. Every time the pain came, her eyes lit up, and she watched me groan and writhe in agony with an eagerness that belied her pretended ignorance.

At length, Panouk dismissed her. She fled, slamming the door behind her.

"We will get nothing out of her," he said. "Not as long as she continues to pretend she doesn't understand anything I say."

He had to wait until the next wave of pain passed before I could focus on him again.

"What do you wish for me to do?" he asked. "I think it's clear from her response that she is indeed responsible.

However, her circumstances mean she is not entitled to a trial."

Her position as a prisoner of war, he meant. If Abar had no rights, then a sentence would be imposed and carried out without the need for a trial.

"I'm satisfied this could be classed as attempted murder," he continued. "Given your status, the harshest of penalties would be appropriate."

I understood quite clearly what he meant: if I wanted Abar executed, he would make arrangements. And I suddenly knew exactly what penalty I wanted for her.

"No," I said. "Send her home."

Panouk was so surprised, his eyebrows rose up until they were sitting at the top of his forehead, almost on his bald scalp. If I hadn't been in so much pain, the sight would have made me giggle.

"I'm not sure I understand," he said.

"She is not fit to be a servant here," I said. "The penalty I want is for her to lose her position and be sent home."

"Being sent home in disgrace would not normally be considered a severe enough penalty for such as she has done," he said.

"But there are times when the weight of a penalty far exceeds the crime."

We looked at each other. Was he, like me, thinking of Hydna and Weren? Panouk cleared his throat and studied the floor for a moment.

"Given she would be returning to a backwards nation with a standard of living far beneath ours," he said, returning his gaze to me, "I do think it might be appropriate in this case."

He seemed to consider it for another few moments, then gave me a decided nod.

"It will be as you say, Lady Kassaya," he said. "Abar will be sent home. It will be made clear to her that she is not permitted to ever return to Egypt."

Despite the agony she had subjected me to, I felt the satisfaction of that. I had managed to give Abar the one thing she wanted: to go home.

"I trust you can dispose of this… thing?" Panouk gave a disgusted look at the little figure in his hand, then handed it back to the healer.

She took it from him with a nod.

"I will see to it immediately." She was already on her way to the door. "You will feel its effects lessen as it gets further from you, my lady. It may take me a few hours to properly deal with it, but it will be gone by nightfall."

"What…" I started, but the pain gripped my belly again and I couldn't speak any further.

"What my lady means to say," Ettu interjected, "is what will you do with it?"

"I will remove it from her vicinity, to start with," the healer said, her fingers already on the door handle. "Then I need a magician to remove the spells on it. Finally, the object must be entirely destroyed. It will be burned until it is no more than ashes, then the ashes must be prayed over by a priest before they are deposited in the Great River, where they will be scattered to all ends of the earth."

I wanted to know how she knew what to do, but the latest wave of pain was stronger than the others, and I had no words available to me. I gestured for her to go, and she slipped out the door. Panouk followed her, after assuring me Abar's sentence would be carried out with all haste.

Then, finally, it was just the three maids and I left in the chamber.

"I will let the men out," Sehener said, already on her way to them. "They have been locked away for a very long time."

I lay limply on the couch, too wrung out to even attempt a reply. Already, I could feel a slight lessening in the spell's hold over me. The healer must be running through the hallways.

"That was well done," Ettu said. "I'm not sure I could find it within myself to be so charitable to her."

I acknowledged her words with a nod. There was no need for anything more and they would never understand why I had done it anyway. But however much she hated me, Abar and I were not so different. We had both been brought here against our will. We had both suffered the loss of a sister to this place. And we both wanted nothing more than to leave. She would never thank me for it, but I had given her something nobody else could.

CHAPTER 30

*T*he waves of pain continued through the rest of the afternoon, although each was slightly less sharp than the last. The healer must still be moving further away.

We were all gathered in the sitting chamber, with Ettu and Half on their usual couch, and Sehener and Tall in their accustomed spot. Merytre stood at the window and I guessed she watched for any glimpse of Sutem. Ahmose's chair was empty as usual. Nobody had sat there since her death.

"I wonder where she will find a magician?" Sehener asked at one point.

"Pharaoh's palace most likely," Merytre said. "There are probably other magicians in Thebes, but no doubt she knows where to find them there."

The woman could hardly go to Amanitore since she was the one most likely to have aided Abar.

"That would make sense," Sehener said. "And there are priests there too, if she needs one of those."

She lay on the couch with her head on Tall's lap. His hand idly stroked her shoulder, and I pushed down the jealousy that rose within me at seeing them so comfortable together. They would never know how badly I wanted what they had.

I had thought them an odd pair at first, but the more I saw them together, the more I understood. Sehener was an anxious sort, tightly wound and very concerned with knowing exactly what was expected of her. She always seemed to think before she spoke, as if checking her words wouldn't upset anyone. But she didn't hesitate in the same way with Tall.

She seemed to feel freer with him, perhaps because his difficulty in speaking meant she didn't feel judged. Unlike Ettu, who still had reservations about whether she wanted a man in her life, Sehener seemed devoted to Tall. I hoped that when our plan was carried out, they too could leave this place and go somewhere they could be together without having to hide.

The sun had long set before the pain finally stopped. I lay on the couch, too exhausted to move. My body was drenched with sweat and my bones felt like they had turned into honey.

"Your colour is a little better," Ettu observed.

"Is it over?" Sehener asked. "Do you think the healer found a magician?"

"I hope so." I didn't have the strength to even so much as raise my head.

"You should eat," Ettu said. "Sit up and I will fetch you some food."

The kitchen maids had brought our meal hours ago and the others had already eaten their fill.

"I'm not hungry," I said.

Ettu paid me no notice, already busy selecting from the vast array of food still remaining.

"Should I send for hot water?" Merytre offered. "A bath might make you feel better."

I waved away her offer. A bath sounded like far too much trouble. If I had to choose between the two, I could at least pretend to pick at some food. I managed to sit up, although my head spun and my whole body ached. It seemed I would be sleeping on the couch as I didn't have the strength to walk to my bedchamber.

"You should go home," Ettu said to Merytre as she brought me a plate of food. "Sehener and I can look after things from here."

"Are you sure?" Merytre eyed me doubtfully. "What if it starts again? I think I should stay tonight."

"No, go," I said. "I'm fine."

She left, although not without several glances back at me as if waiting for me to change my mind. Sehener brought me some wine and I nibbled at a piece of bread since Ettu was watching to make sure I ate.

Ettu was adamant I couldn't sleep on the couch, but when I tried to get up, my legs collapsed under me. In the end, Tall carried me to my bedchamber and lay me down with a gentleness that belied his physical awkwardness. I waved away Ettu's suggestion of changing into a sleeping gown and she must have decided getting me into bed was enough of a victory, because she left with far less argument than I might have expected.

I must have fallen asleep almost immediately, stirring only when the bird at my window jarred me into wakefulness with his pre-dawn song. I lay in bed a while longer, enjoying the absence of pain, until Ettu came knocking.

"Your lady's maids will be here shortly," she said, flinging open the window shutters.

The brightness made my eyes water, but I breathed deeply, enjoying the freshness that burst into the stale chamber. The sun's rays landed on Merytre's wallhanging, making the yellow narcissus gleam even brighter. I closed my eyes, hoping Ettu would think it was merely the sunlight I avoided, and not the wallhanging.

"Are you getting up?" She noisily rearranged the cosmetics jars on my dresser.

"I thought you might have told them they weren't required today," I said, somewhat peevishly.

"I assumed you would want a walk," she said. "You must be properly attired if you intend to go out."

That got me to sit up. A walk did sound like a good idea, provided my limbs would cooperate. When I gingerly slid off the edge of the bed, my legs held my weight, even if they felt weak.

"Are you well?" Ettu asked and I finally realised she must be waiting to ensure I could stand unaided.

"Well enough," I said.

"Good," she replied. "Oh, I think that's them arriving now."

It was indeed my maids, but only six of them. Abar, of course, didn't come. The others were subdued, barely speaking as they stripped me and sat me on the bathing stool. The silence between them seemed to grow thicker as they rubbed me with natron salt and rinsed it off with warm water.

"My lady." Khensa, it seemed, had been designated as speaker, for all hands on me stilled as soon as she began. "I hope we have not displeased you?"

She didn't look at me, and as I studied the women around me, I discovered the only ones who would actually meet my eyes were Ettu, Sehener and Merytre.

"Of course not," I said. "Whatever gave you that idea?"

"We heard Abar has been dismissed," Khensa said. "Sent back to her home country in disgrace. I suppose we are wondering if we, too, are to be sent away."

"Nobody else is being sent away," I said. "Not unless you wish to leave. I will gladly release anyone who wants it."

After all, I didn't expect to be here much longer myself. I hadn't yet dared to think about where I would go — it seemed premature to assume the success of our plan — but I had to trust Tiye was truthful when she said her son would release any Ornament who wanted to leave. The women seemed to perk up at my reply.

"Oh, my lady," Tuya said. "I was so unhappy thinking we had all displeased you and didn't even realise."

"I thought we were all to be dismissed," Hemetre said with a relieved laugh.

"I was just miserable at the thought," Mutnofret added.

"This is the best position I've ever had," Ipu said.

"No other Ornament has ever provided a picnic for her maids," Nebetah said. "I wouldn't want to serve anyone else."

What would become of them when I left? Should I make some kind of arrangements for them? I didn't know how to go about such a thing, other than to offer them some jewels and tell them to leave if they wished. I would have to do something before we enacted our plan.

When the women departed, they were full of their usual chatter and laughter.

"Why did they think I would dismiss them all?" I asked after the door closed behind them.

"Most folk know Abar has been sent away," Merytre said. "It was already being talked about when I arrived this morning. But I don't think anyone knows why."

"So they thought it was because I was unhappy with her service?" I asked.

Merytre shrugged. "There are all sorts of rumours, as always. I haven't heard anything that was even close to the truth, though. Folk are guessing, so I suppose your lady's maids did the same."

I sighed and sank down onto the couch. My legs already trembled with the effort of standing for only a few moments. Despite the absence of pain, it seemed there was some recovery ahead of me yet. Sehener brought me a mug of melon juice and as I sipped the sweet liquid, my stomach growled. At least one part of my body seemed to have recovered.

Before I had a chance to eat, Panouk arrived. Tall and Half had only just been released from their bedchamber after the departure of my maids, and they went tiptoeing back in before Merytre opened the door for Panouk.

"Lady Kassaya, I trust you are much recovered?" he asked smoothly, folding his hands in front of his belly.

"I am," I said. "I heard Abar has left."

"She departed at dawn," he confirmed. "She asked to see you before she went. I didn't think you would want to speak with her, given the circumstances, so I refused her request. I did, however, agree to pass on a message for her."

"What did she say?" It seemed unlikely she would have wanted to apologise. Perhaps she meant to thank me for sending her home? She surely knew she departed at my request.

"She said it was no more than you should have done sooner," he said. "She also gave me this for you."

He held out my Eye of Horus pendant, watching me with

curiosity as he waited for my reaction. The cord that should have fastened it to my wrist was gone.

I took the Eye from him, marvelling at the strange warmth it always held. I had quite forgotten I lost it. How did Abar facilitate that? Another spell? Or did the cord merely fray and finally break without me noticing? Perhaps Abar found it and took the opportunity to seek her revenge while I was unprotected.

The return of the Eye soothed my irritation at Abar's final message. I hardly expected anything else from her, and whether she was grateful or not, she *was* going home. I had given her the one thing I myself couldn't have, not as long as the alliance between Babylon and Egypt remained in place.

"Did she tell you who the magician was?" I asked.

It had to be Amanitore. There was no other woman at the Palace with the skill for such a thing, and surely Abar didn't have access to any other magician.

"I asked," Panouk said. "But she refused to give me any detail. With enough time, she would have been persuaded to reveal everything, but I thought it more expedient to act on her sentence than to delay in the hope of getting information."

"Very well." I wished I had thought to tell him to find out the magician's identity, but it was too late now.

It had to be Amanitore. If there were other magicians within the Palace, I knew none of them personally, which the healer said was required to enact such a spell. How Abar had paid for her services, I couldn't begin to imagine. But they were from the same country, so perhaps there was some kind of allegiance or loyalty between them, especially if Amanitore was also brought here against her will as so many Ornaments were.

"If you don't require anything else?" Panouk already edged back towards the door.

"You may go," I said.

CHAPTER 31

The door closed behind Panouk, and Sehener had only just let Tall and Half out again, when another knock came. I gave an exasperated sigh as they hurried back to their bedchamber. This was no way for them to live, but it wouldn't be for much longer. Once Tiye's plan was enacted, I would find a way to ensure all my companions were released with me.

It was a runner boy this time, and one I thought I recognised. Maybe he had delivered a message to me previously.

"The Lady Tiye is holding an urgent gathering in her chambers," he said, very seriously. "She asks the Lady Kassaya to attend at noon."

I blinked in surprise. We never met during the day. Something must have happened, or maybe this was the final meeting. The one in which we decided exactly when and how the plan would be enacted.

My heart already pounded harder than it should. It would all be over within the next few days. I would leave this place, and my babe with me. I couldn't imagine Tiye's son would have any reason to require Pharaoh's children remain behind without their mothers. I prayed to Marduk he wouldn't.

"You can advise her my lady will attend," Ettu said.

At least I was suitably attired. Ettu would never let me hear the end of it had I begged her to send away my maids today and then such a summons came.

"How unusual," Sehener said, following the men back out to the sitting chamber. She flashed me a bright smile. "It will be a pleasant diversion for you, my lady. I am sure you are still fatigued from yesterday, but this will help take your mind off it."

Merytre frowned and seemed more worried than curious. She didn't offer to share her thoughts, though, and I didn't ask. Marduk knew I had enough of opinionated maids with Ettu.

I barely had time to eat a slice of bread before I left. My stomach still felt empty as Ettu and Merytre accompanied me to Tiye's chambers. As we were almost there, I spotted Neferu approaching from the other direction. She gave me a nod, her face serious.

"Kassaya," was all she said.

A little surprised at her brevity, I nodded back. Our maids waited at the end of the hallway while Neferu and I continued on.

"Do you know what is happening?" I asked quietly.

"No more than you," she said.

Footsteps from behind us signalled someone else's approach and I turned to find Henutmire hurrying up behind us. She greeted us both with a quick smile and I was relieved that she, at least, seemed her usual self. Perhaps Neferu was just nervous.

Tiye's face was tight as she admitted us to her chambers.

Ineni was already there and Gilukhipa arrived before Tiye had time to close the door. To my disappointment, there was no sign of refreshments, not even wine to wet our mouths. At least I had eaten that slice of bread, although my stomach growled as loudly as if it was empty. If anyone noticed, they didn't comment. We arranged ourselves on the couches.

"Our plans are ready," Tiye said with no introduction. "We act tomorrow night."

Everyone else nodded and it seemed I was the only one surprised.

"Tomorrow?" I asked. "That is very... soon."

"You committed," Tiye said, giving me a stern look. "This is not the time for cowardice, and our plans are too advanced at this point for anyone to pull out."

"I am no coward," I said, rather indignant she would even suggest such a thing. "Nor did I intend to pull out. I was merely surprised."

"I have been saying we will make our move very soon," Tiye said. "I can't see how it could come as a surprise."

"To be fair to Kassaya," Henutmire said. "You did say it would be within the next week or two. You didn't exactly indicate it would be quite so imminent."

That made me feel a little less stupid. I had wondered how I was the only one to misunderstand how quickly the plan would be put into motion. Tiye shared her glare equally between Henutmire and me.

"I have told you over and over we were almost ready," she said. "If you feel unprepared, that is not my problem."

"Not unprepared," Henutmire said. "But I am upset at learning you kept information from me and I want to know why."

The chill Tiye exuded should have warned her to say

nothing further, but if Henutmire noticed, she ignored it. Perhaps she had spent too long preparing herself for this confrontation to stop now. I had been surprised she didn't say anything at our last gathering, but maybe she wasn't ready then.

"Why did nobody tell me what happened to Nebtu?" Henutmire's eyes filled with tears and she hastily wiped them away. "You knew what she meant to me, and you knew what happened to her, but nobody told me."

Tiye's glare seemed to soften a little and she made a small noise that might have seemed apologetic from anyone else.

"Henutmire," she said. "We didn't want to distress you any more than you already were."

"But I should have known," Henutmire wailed. "You should have told me. How could you keep such a thing from me? My own friends."

Gilukhipa reached over to put her hand on Henutmire's.

"You are too tender," she said. "We didn't think you could handle it."

"But I wanted to know what happened to her," Henutmire said. "You know I did. You knew how it bothered me to not know."

"Perhaps we were wrong," Gilukhipa said. She darted a glance at Tiye as if expecting to be contradicted, but Tiye studied the ceiling as if it was suddenly the most fascinating thing in the world. "How did you find out anyway?"

Henutmire's chin trembled and she darted a glance at me. Tiye must have caught it because she let out an exasperated noise.

"Kassaya told you," she said. "Of course."

"Why shouldn't I?" My voice was more defensive than I

would have liked. "They were friends. She deserves to know the truth."

"It was not up to you to tell her," Tiye said. "We would have told her when the time was right."

"Why is that your decision?" I countered. "Henutmire is my friend, too. I haven't known her as long as you, but that doesn't mean I shouldn't tell her something I think she would want to know."

"So it's true then?" Henutmire burst out. "What Kassaya told me, it's really true?"

I tried not to look offended. Given it was me who told her, and not the women she had known long enough to call friends, I could hardly blame her if she didn't believe me.

"I suppose that depends on exactly what Kassaya told you," Tiye said.

Henutmire darted a look at me, as if hoping I would answer for her. I kept my mouth shut. I wasn't going to get involved with this conversation any more than necessary. This was between Henutmire and the others. It was them who kept it from her, not me.

"She said Pharaoh…" Henutmire's voice broke and she paused to compose herself. "That Pharaoh… Nebtu."

"Yes," Gilukhipa said, as if wanting to spare her from having to say it. "It's true."

Henutmire buried her face in her hands and burst into tears.

"I can't believe you didn't tell me," she said between sobs. "All this time, I have waited and wondered what happened to her, and you knew. You knew all along."

They were silent as they waited for Henutmire to compose herself. What struck me about the moment was that nobody apologised. It seemed they all accepted it had been necessary to keep the truth from her, and although some of them might feel bad — Gilukhipa did, at any rate — they were unapologetic.

"Henutmire, you need to deal with this, and quickly," Tiye said. "We cannot afford to let anything interfere with our plans and right now you are too emotional."

Despite how Tiye's words must have stung, Henutmire wiped her eyes and made an obvious effort to compose herself.

"This doesn't change anything," she said. "In fact, it only makes me more determined to see him removed from the throne."

"Good," Tiye said with an approving nod. "Back to business then. My son has spoken with the librarians. Pharaoh's protective spells will be revoked tomorrow afternoon. Pentaweret has arranged to meet with Pharaoh under the guise of requesting more military responsibility. His men will be waiting near the palace, ready to enter once proceedings begin."

"Clever," Ineni said. "We originally planned for him to go in with his men."

"It was his idea," Tiye said. "He thought it best if he was already with Pharaoh so he couldn't be accused of entering the palace with force. Now then, the butler will put a puff adder as close to Pharaoh's person as possible. If he is wearing a shirt, the snake will be dropped down the back. Otherwise, he will find a way to slip it under his *shendyt*, or if all else fails, drop it at his feet. Once Pharaoh notices the snake, he will become agitated, which will draw it to him. He should be bitten quite quickly. If not, our man in Pharaoh's personal squad will be ready with his knife."

She paused as if waiting for comment.

"And Ramses?" Gilukhipa asked. "The heir. Where is he?"

"Aah, that is something that makes the timing so perfect," Tiye said with a smug smile. "He is actually on his way back to Thebes and is expected to arrive tonight. We will be able to deal with him at the same time. I expect he will be in Pentaweret's meeting with Pharaoh tomorrow. Our man will take care of him while everyone else is distracted with the snake."

"Why a puff adder?" I asked. "I don't remember that species being mentioned before."

I also wanted to ask why Bebi would be the one to do everything. If things went wrong, it would be he who took the blame. But, of course, that was probably part of her plan.

"It's what the butler has easiest access to," Tiye said. "And he assures me it will be the best option. Now then, Bonemwese will be ready with his archers. As soon as he receives the signal that Pharaoh has been bitten, they will create a distraction to allow Pasai's men to enter the palace. The local folk will be waiting, and once Pasai and his squads are inside, they will follow. The guards will be quickly overwhelmed. Then my son's men will enter, Pentaweret will claim the throne, and it will be done. A new era of peace and prosperity will begin."

Her voice rang out at the end as if she expected us to burst into cheers. Nobody did, though. Although I knew it had to be done, I had underestimated the number of people who would be involved. Folk would die tomorrow night, and not just Pharaoh. There would be armed clashes and innocent folk would lose their lives in the battle. It will be worth it, I reminded myself. We must do whatever it takes to stop him.

Tiye looked around the circle, meeting the eyes of each woman. "Tomorrow night. Be ready."

She gave us a nod and sat back. The meeting, it seemed,

was concluded. I started to get up, but hesitated when nobody else moved. Tiye waved me on.

"It's all right, Kassaya," she said. "Go if you must. I hear you had a rather eventful day yesterday. You probably need a nap. The rest of us might sit and have a mug of wine."

I hesitated, wondering if I was being rude, but Henutmire gave me a little smile, which I took as encouragement, so I left. At the end of the hallway, the maids started getting up until they realised I was the only one to emerge from Tiye's chambers. They sat back down again and resumed their conversations.

"My lady, are you well?" Ettu asked as we made our way back to my chambers. "Did the pain start again?"

"No, we had finished talking and I thought I might as well leave. The others were staying for wine."

I knew I'd said the wrong thing as soon as the words left my mouth.

"So Lady Tiye had something specific to say?" Ettu asked.

"Nothing particularly interesting," I mumbled, hoping she would let the matter drop.

She likely would have had more to say except we turned down the hallway to my chambers and discovered Khensa waiting there. She gave me a nervous smile.

"Khensa, what are you doing here?" I asked as we stopped at my door.

"My lady, I must speak with you," she said. "It's most urgent."

CHAPTER 32

"Why didn't you wait inside?" I asked Khensa.

Sehener would have surely have offered for Khensa to sit with her. She would have already locked the men away before answering the door anyway, and she would hardly let them back out to the sitting chamber while Khensa was in the hallway.

"I didn't want to intrude," Khensa said.

As I expected, Sehener was alone in the sitting chamber, her needlework draped over her knee. She tucked her needle into the linen and set it aside.

"Welcome back, my lady," she said, already getting to her feet. "Let me pour you some melon juice."

She brought a mug for me and also one for Khensa. Khensa gave her a startled look as she took the mug.

"Oh, you don't need to bring refreshments for me," she said.

"You were waiting out there for such a long time," Sehener said. "My lady, she arrived not long after you left. I said she could sit in here with me, but she insisted on standing in the hallway."

"A maid doesn't need to sit and be entertained," Khensa mumbled, although she was swift to drink her melon juice. "You surely had other tasks to do while my lady was gone."

"Not really." Sehener went back to the couch and took up her needlework again.

I hesitated, wondering whether I should ask Khensa if she wanted to sit down. Her visit was highly unusual — none of my lady's maids had ever come to see me like this before.

"Is Baby Ishtar ill?" I couldn't imagine why else she would have come.

"Oh, no," she said quickly. "You need not fear for her. I received a message from my friend only yesterday and she said your babe was healthy and well. She is growing at a tremendous rate and she smiles at everyone all day."

Her words made my heart hurt. I had already missed out on so much. How much bigger was she? Would I even recognise my own babe? When would I see her smile at me? I had never seen her smile. I sat and gestured to a nearby couch.

"Sit, Khensa," I said. "Then you can tell me what was so important that you waited so long to see me."

"Oh." She gave me a startled look, but she sat down. I thought I saw her hands tremble as she smoothed her skirt over her knees.

My heart pounded harder as I waited for Khensa to find the words to tell me whatever it was. If it wasn't my babe, I couldn't imagine what else it could be. Had she guessed we hid someone in my chambers? Was she here to tell me that even now the administrators were on their way to arrest me? No, she would have blurted it out to Sehener when she first arrived if it was something like that. She wouldn't wait for me to get back, then take her time and arrange her skirt. But still, I couldn't imagine her news was anything good.

"My lady," Khensa started.

I gave her an encouraging smile and tried not to show how much I dreaded whatever it was she had come to say.

"Go on," I said.

"There are rumours." Now she had decided to speak, the words came out in a rush. "We have all heard them. We decided it would be me who came to tell you. But maybe you already know. I hope I'm not wasting your time."

I assumed the "we" must be the rest of my maids, but I couldn't guess what the rumours were. Perhaps something about Abar's departure. Maybe they were still worried I intended to dismiss them after all.

"There are men gathering in the city," Khensa continued. "Armed men."

"Soldiers?" So, it was about Tiye's plan. Tall and Half were still safe. I couldn't imagine why folk would be gathering already, though. Did they intend to spend the night in the streets?

"Some are soldiers," she said. "But many are common folk. They are trying to be inconspicuous, but there are many more people on the streets than usual, and they all bear weapons of some sort."

Sehener made a soft noise, and when I glanced over to see how the women took Khensa's news, she and Ettu were leaning forward to listen. Merytre studied her hands. If Sutem was involved, as I suspected, Merytre probably knew some-thing of the plan. I doubted she knew about my involvement, though. Surely she would have said something if she did.

"There is nothing to fear," I said. "This place is well

guarded. They won't get past the guards at the gates and nor will they get over the walls."

"I have lived in Thebes my whole life," Khensa said. "And I have never seen anything like this. I fear the city is about to break out in civil war."

Her guess was closer than she knew, but she mustn't have heard any whispers of an impending attack on Pharaoh's person. She wouldn't hold back that information, not after she had already told me so much.

"Civil war would be a terrible thing to live through," Ettu said. "Even if we are safe here, supplies would be disrupted. How long would it take before food ran low in a place the size of this?"

"Deliveries usually arrive many times a day," Sehener said. "Food, wine, linens. All sorts of things. The Palace couldn't function in the way we are used to if the deliveries stopped."

Merytre still said nothing. I would wait until Khensa left before I asked what she knew. Ettu had no such reluctance.

"Why do you have that look on your face, Merytre?" she asked.

"Me?" Merytre glanced up at Ettu. Her gaze flicked over to me, then dropped to her hands again.

"What do you know?" Ettu asked.

"Oh, nothing more than what Khensa already said," Merytre mumbled.

"My lady, if you want to flee, we will help you," Khensa said in a rush. "Your ladies are loyal to you. I have already sent a message to my friend to be ready to secret your babe away. We will get her out of Pharaoh's palace for you."

"She would do that?" I tried to hide my surprise, but I couldn't imagine what kind of penalty the maid might suffer if she was caught smuggling out a child of Pharaoh. Surely there was no benefit to her to do such a thing.

"But of course," Khensa said. "And the rest of us will do what we can. Do you need a diversion to get out the gates? Or perhaps we should smuggle you out. I have access to some carts and the rest of your lady's maids will help. We could hide you in one and get you out that way. Do you have something you might need transported away from the Palace?"

"Gowns," Ettu said promptly. "My lady has more gowns than she could ever wear. What if she decided to donate some of them to the poor women of Thebes?"

"Oh, what a marvellous idea." Sehener was so excited, she actually clapped her hands. "My lady's generosity is well known. Nobody who has met her would question such a thing."

I couldn't think of when I had done something that might be called generous. It was an excellent idea, though, to give away my excess gowns. I wished somebody had thought of it earlier. Actually, I wished *I* had thought of it.

"Why would you do something like that?" I asked. "You must know you will all lose your positions if you are discovered."

"You gave us a picnic," Khensa said. "Nobody has ever treated us as fine ladies before, but you gave us food and wine and blankets on the grass. We would do anything you ask."

It had seemed such an insignificant thing at the time, and even now I couldn't quite understand why they so treasured the memory, but it pleased me I had done something nice for them. I only wished I'd treated them to more picnics.

"I have been very pleased to have you serve me," I said, including all the women in my gaze. "Every last one of you. Please make sure they all know."

"Oh, I will," Khensa said. "But in the meantime, do you wish for me to make arrangements for you to sneak out tonight?"

I made a swift decision. Khensa, I was certain, could be trusted.

"I am not leaving. Not tonight, at any rate." Tiye said we would be allowed to go. I had to trust she was telling the truth, and the whole truth, for once. "But could you get two other people out for me?"

"Of course." Her voice was eager. "Anything you need."

"My lady," Ettu started, obviously guessing what I intended.

I waved away her comment.

"Sehener, would you let the men out?"

"The… men?" Khensa's voice was faint.

I watched her carefully, hoping I hadn't made a grave error of judgement. A hurried conversation down the hallway must be Sehener relaying what had happened to Tall and Half. They entered the chamber slowly. Tall kept his gaze fixed straight ahead and looked as if he would flinch if anyone noticed him, while Half held his shoulders back and seemed to try to appear unconcerned.

Khensa's mouth dropped open. It was the usual reaction to anyone who saw the pair, but it must be even more startling for her, given they shouldn't be here.

"My lady," she said, gathering herself at last. "Do you… I mean… Have they…"

"They have lived in my chambers for some months now," I said. Khensa's eyes boggled. "They travelled with me from Babylon, but the administrators wouldn't let them stay. They went to Pharaoh's palace for a while, but certain events occurred which meant it wasn't safe for them there.

We smuggled them inside and they have been here ever since."

"Oh, my." Khensa's hand fluttered between her mouth and her chest, as if she didn't know what to do with it. "No wonder you always had so much food brought for you. We thought you were just very hungry."

I snorted, finding myself amused despite the gravity of our situation. The truth was that even with the men, whose appetites were far bigger than my own, the kitchen still sent so much food that we never managed to eat it all before they brought more.

"This is Tall and Half," I said to her, before turning to the men. "Khensa is one of the maids who attends me every morning."

"I recognise your voice," Half said with a little bow in Khensa's direction. "I'm sure we would know all my lady's maids, even though we have never seen your faces."

Khensa went bright red and set her hand firmly over her mouth, as if to stop herself from saying whatever it was she wanted to.

"Can you get them out tonight?" I asked.

Khensa folded her hands in her lap and seemed to make an obvious effort to compose herself, then gave a decided nod.

"Since my lady wants to give away her old gowns before she orders new ones, I will arrange for two carts," she said. "I'm sure you have a great many gowns to be disposed of."

"That sounds perfect," I said to her. "Ettu, would you—"

"I already have." Ettu held up a silver finger ring set with a pretty pink gem. I never noticed her leave the chamber, but she must have slipped away while I introduced the men to Khensa. "Is this what you had in mind?"

I nodded and she pressed the finger ring into Khensa's hand.

"Oh, my." Khensa gaped at it, then shook her head. She held it out to me. "My lady, I cannot accept this."

"Keep it," I said.

Marduk knew I had more jewels than I could use in several lifetimes. I would take some with me, of course, but there were a great many more than we would ever need.

Ettu dropped a handful of jewels on top of the one Khensa already held.

"For the others," she said.

She looked at me, obviously waiting for my approval.

"Whatever you think is appropriate." In truth, I was grateful she had thought of such a thing. It pleased me that although my maids would probably lose their positions when I left, they wouldn't be destitute.

"I should go and make arrangements." Khensa's voice was faint and she stared at the jewels in her hand as if she didn't know what to do with them.

"Best put those in your pouch," Ettu advised her. "You don't want anyone seeing them."

"Oh, yes." Khensa quickly hid the jewels away, all except for her silver finger ring. That she slipped on her finger, then held her hand up to admire it. "I never imagined I would possess something so beautiful and expensive."

"You deserve it," I said. "Now, go. Make your arrangements and be as careful as if it was me you are smuggling out tonight."

"I will return a couple of hours before sunset." Khensa gave me a bright smile and hurried out. The door closed behind her and we were all silent for a few moments.

"I think you can trust her," Ettu said at last.

"I hope so," I said.

"And I think you should go with the men," she added.

"I cannot." I could hardly tell her why. "But I will release from my service anyone who wants to leave tonight." I met the eyes of Ettu, Merytre and Sehener in turn. "Take whatever jewels you want and go."

"I don't understand," Sehener said. "I heard what Khensa said about the military and everything, but how does this affect us here? We are safe, regardless of what happens in the city. We might go hungry if supplies are interrupted for a while, but we will be safe."

"Sehener, please," I said. "Just go. Make arrangements with Tall to meet him somewhere and go tonight. I can't say any more than that."

"Because you are involved in whatever it is," Ettu said.

There seemed little point in denying it anymore, so I just shrugged.

"Ettu is right." Merytre spoke quickly, as if wanting to get the words out before she changed her mind. "My lady, you should leave tonight. Go out in the carts with Tall and Half."

I settled myself on the couch and tried to look unconcerned.

"I can't," I said. "There is something I need to do tomorrow."

I had committed, after all. I had helped make the plans. Even if I had no specific role to play in what was to occur, I should be here. And once Pharaoh was dead, I would be allowed to take my babe and leave. There was no need for me to flee in secret. If I left with Pentaweret's permission, I might even be able to go home. I didn't know where I would go otherwise.

"It's a revolt, isn't it?" Ettu asked. "They intend to overthrow Pharaoh."

Sehener gave an audible gasp.

"But that would be treason," she whispered. "My lady would never be involved in such a thing."

"I can't tell you anything," I said. "But this might not be a safe place for any of you by tomorrow night. Go now while you can."

After all, if something went wrong — if there was civil war as they said — it was possible that nowhere in Thebes would be safe. Tomorrow might be too late to get out of the city. I could only pray to Marduk it wouldn't be too late for me to get to Baby Ishtar and get us both to a safe place.

Ettu sat down and smoothed out her skirt.

"I, for one, will be staying," she said. "I promised to serve you until you bore a son, and you have not yet done so."

"I release you," I said. "There will be no son."

She only shrugged at me. "I will not leave you alone, whatever is about to happen."

"Well, I can hardly leave then," Half said. He used the little stool we left out for him to climb up beside Ettu. "I won't go without you."

"You must." She patted his hand and gave him a fond look. "This might be our only chance to get you and Tall out safely. Go while you can."

He gave her a sorrowful look. "You never did love me as much as I love you," he said.

"I love you well enough," she replied. "But I have told you time and again, I will tie myself to no man. Once my lady is finished with her business here, I will leave, but I won't be following you."

Half gave a heavy sigh. "How did I have the misfortune to

fall for a woman who is so determined to make her own way in the world?"

She patted his hand, then withdrew hers and set it on her lap. "That, my dear, is why you fell for me. You always knew it would end. It just came a little sooner than either of us thought."

Half leaned forward, resting his arms on his thighs as he sighed again.

"What of you, Sehener?" I asked. "Will you leave tonight while you can?"

Her gaze went straight to Tall. He reached for her hand.

"Me!" he said.

"Yes," she said fondly. "I will tie myself to you. Wherever you want to go, I will follow you."

CHAPTER 33

A knock at the door sent Tall and Half hurrying away to their bedchamber again.

"A message for the maid Merytre," a runner said. "From her husband."

Merytre gave him a wide-eyed look. Sutem had never sent a messenger to my chambers before and I could feel her anxiety.

"Go on, then," she urged him.

"Sutem asks that his wife meet him by the gates immediately," the boy said. "The matter is most urgent."

He gave a little bow and raced off. Merytre closed the door and darted a look at me, as if wondering whether she would be allowed to go to Sutem.

"Go," I said. "Whatever it is, it must be dire."

"I will return as soon as I can," she said.

Maybe Sutem thought they should leave. If he was involved, he knew there would be violence to come. He might want to get his pregnant wife away before there was any danger.

"Merytre," I said. "You should leave while you can. Go choose something from my jewellery chests before you go."

She shook her head. "I am coming back," she said. "I will just see what Sutem needs and then I will return."

She edged towards the door and I guessed she probably didn't want to waste time arguing with me when she could be on her way to her husband. She had the ring I had given her as a wedding gift, anyway, and the one I gave Sutem as her bride price. It wasn't like she would leave with nothing. Not like Belet-ili. I hadn't seen her for weeks and didn't know why she came to my mind just then. All my other maids would have something to live on, but not her.

"Before you go," Ettu said, as if she knew exactly what I was thinking. "I kept a jewel aside for Belet-ili."

"I can send a runner to her." Merytre held out her hand and Ettu dropped the gem into it.

Perhaps I didn't owe Belet-ili anything, but she did come with me from Babylon, and it pleased me she would have something to fund her new life if she chose to leave once this was all over.

After Merytre left, the men came back out to the sitting chamber. We sat and looked at each other. There was none of the usual chatter and conversation. I supposed they, like me, were all too aware this might be our final moments together.

"Do you have things to pack?" I asked. "Khensa will be back very soon."

"I already have my knife." Half patted the little wood-carving knife in the waistband of his *shendyt*. "Neither of us has much other than a couple of changes of clothes. It will take but a moment to toss them in a bag. The only other thing I want to take with me is this."

He showed me a little figure he had poked into his waistband. It was a woman, small enough to fit in the palm of my hand. Her face reminded me of Ahmose.

"I made this for Teacher," Half said. "I'm not particularly skilled at carving people, but it was meant to represent her daughter. Just something she could carry with her."

Ettu made a little sound, as if restraining a sob. I carefully avoided looking at her. It wasn't like her to be sentimental and if Half's words had brought her to tears, she wouldn't thank me for noticing.

"She's very fine," I said, taking the little figure from him. I marvelled at how he had managed to make her look so much like Ahmose that I recognised her before he told me. I had chanced on Ahmose late one evening with something in her hand. I never saw what it was, but perhaps it was Half's little figurine. I handed her back to him. "You should go pack your clothes. We need to be ready as soon as Khensa returns."

Half slipped away down the hall and Ettu trailed behind him. Tall watched them go, but made no move to follow. I guessed he meant to give them some privacy. Sehener sat on the couch and patted the space beside her. They put their heads together and spoke quietly, or more likely, Sehener did the talking.

Feeling like I intruded on what should be a private moment, I went to the window. I couldn't see the front gates from here, but I pretended I watched Merytre hurrying to them. Did she wonder if this might be the last time she ever went to the gates? Despite her promise to return, if Sutem thought they should leave immediately, would she go with him? I could hardly blame her if she did, although I would be sorry I missed the chance to properly farewell her.

Things were moving too fast. I wasn't ready to say goodbye to all my companions. I had imagined we would have this last night together, then I would calmly tell them what was about to happen and send them away. If things went wrong, I wanted none of my companions left behind to share my punishment. I hadn't yet come up with a plan for how we would get Tall and Half out of the palace, though, so Khensa's intervention was invaluable.

Irritation welled within me when yet another knock came. Surely there couldn't possibly be any more messages that needed to be brought to my chambers today. Tall hurried out and Sehener opened the door.

"A message for the Lady Kassaya." It was a different runner this time, a young one I had never seen before. "The Lady Amanitore asks you to meet her at the place where the walls bear a painting of Sekhmet, the Lady of Pestilence. She says you owe her a favour and she intends to collect. Also, she says you should go to her alone."

"And when does Lady Amanitore expect my lady to meet her?" Sehener asked.

The boy seemed to shrink beneath her glare. I felt sorry for him. He was obviously new to the job and hadn't yet learned how to deal with precocious lady's maids.

"Right now," the boy said. "I apologise if I forgot to say that bit."

Sehener closed the door and his swift footsteps retreated down the hallway. Ettu had returned in time to hear the boy's words.

"Surely you don't intend to go," she said. "Not when we suspect she is the magician who cursed you."

"I must," I said. "This was how I paid for her help to speak with my sister. I agreed to give her a favour of her choice."

"I cannot help wondering at the timing," Ettu said, "given everything else that seems to be at play right now."

But Amanitore wasn't involved with the plan. Maybe she wanted to explain why she helped Abar. She might intend to apologise, perhaps even release me from my promise.

"I will go now," I said. "I think I know the mural she means."

Indeed, I wondered at the significance of Amanitore choosing that particular location. The hallways were lined with images of the gods and yet she chose one of the very few that depicted the lioness, Sekhmet.

"It's a rather long walk," Ettu said. "Perhaps I should come with you."

It was indeed some distance from my chambers, almost all the way to the other side of the Palace and near the chamber Pharaoh dined in when he visited.

"She said for me to go alone," I said.

Amanitore would want privacy for whatever it was she intended to say or to ask of me. I did wonder that she didn't call me to her chambers. Surely that would be more private. Or even come to mine.

"I could accompany you as far as the last hallway," Ettu said. "I will wait out of sight. She won't even know I'm there unless she happens to come the same way, and she won't because her chambers are in the opposite direction."

For a moment, I considered it. Ettu's presence would be reassuring since I didn't know what Amanitore wanted of me. But Khensa might return while we were gone and I could hardly ask Ettu to potentially miss her last moments with Half.

"Stay here," I said. "Make sure Tall and Half are ready to go, and that they have gems sufficient for anything they might need."

She nodded, although she didn't look happy about it.

I walked swiftly to the place where I was supposed to meet Amanitore. My mind whirled and I didn't know how worried I should be. Was this really about calling in her favour, or did she mean to finish what she had started with the little spell woman? Maybe Abar had asked her to do something else to me if the first spell didn't work. Perhaps I should have brought Ettu after all. She could at least scream and draw attention to us if Amanitore attempted some harm on me.

But this might be about nothing more than the favour I owed her, although I couldn't even begin to guess what she might ask from me. Did she want me to talk to someone for her? Carry out some task? Please Marduk, don't let it be something designed to humiliate me.

But when I arrived at the designated place, it wasn't Amanitore who awaited me, but another runner. He straightened his shoulders when he saw me approaching.

"Are you the Lady Kassaya?" he asked when I reached him.

"I am."

"This is from the Lady Amanitore," he said. "She asks that you wait here until she arrives, and she wishes to remind you that you owe her a favour."

He handed me a small linen-wrapped package, gave me a jaunty little bow, and skipped away. I didn't know whether Amanitore meant for me to open the package, but the messenger didn't say I wasn't to. Inside was a dagger no longer than the distance from my wrist to the end of my thumb. The handle was exquisitely carved and made of what looked like bone, or maybe tusk. Was it a gift? Or did this have something to do with whatever favour she intended to request? Maybe she meant for me to take it to someone.

My feet grew sore as I waited, and I would have sat on the

floor, except I didn't want Amanitore to catch me in such an inelegant seat. So I leaned against the wall and waited.

It was Merytre who found me. She came running and skid to a halt in front of me.

"Merytre, whatever is wrong?" I asked.

"My lady, it's a trap," she managed between gasps. "You must flee."

"What?" My muscles were already tensed for flight at the seriousness on Merytre's face. I couldn't imagine any scenario in which she might be joking or playing some game with me, and I had never seen her run before.

"Sutem heard it from Khaemmalu who heard from Bebi." She doubled over, her hands on her knees as she tried to catch her breath. "Pharaoh is coming here. He intends to summon one or two of the Ornaments to dine with him. He is expected within the hour."

And I would be found loitering in the hallway with a dagger. I needed to hide it somewhere. Maybe I could drop it behind a potted plant. I didn't want it on my person if we encountered Pharaoh and his entourage in the hallway.

"Go on," I said even as I looked around for a suitable place to stash the dagger.

"Bebi heard Lady Tiye telling Pharaoh he should call for you tonight, but that he should wait until he arrived and surprise you with the summons. She said you were still distressed about how your game of *senet* with him ended, and you might get nervous if you had too much notice."

Where in Marduk's name did Tiye get such an idea from? I hadn't even mentioned the *senet* game to her again. Why would she think I was upset about it?

"I'm confused," I said. "What makes you think this is a trap?"

Tiye was obviously playing some game, and I couldn't guess her motive, but it hardly sounded sinister. Merytre stood up, having finally caught her breath.

"Because Bebi also heard her remind Pharaoh of how angry he was with you that day and that he hadn't yet chastised you for it," she said.

"She... What?" I was so surprised, I didn't have the words to express myself.

"She also told him you came here expecting to be queen."

That much was true, at any rate.

"And that you have not given up on it," she added. "She told Pharaoh you intend to be queen sooner or later, and he should be careful of you."

Dumbfounded, I could only shake my head. How could I even reply to such a thing? It was true I had once said that if the only way to be near my babe was to be queen, then that was what I wanted. But I had said that only to Ahmose, and Tiye couldn't possibly know.

Except she could, I realised with a sinking feeling. If Ahmose told Henuttawy, the woman would have surely told Tiye. She had told her mistress everything else.

Ettu had warned me not to trust Tiye. *Never forget what she told you she did to the woman who was Top Ornament,* she said to me, but I had been lulled into complacency.

"Khaemmalu thinks she is setting you up," Merytre continued. "He said you must avoid Pharaoh tonight at all costs. Quickly, you can't be found here if he comes."

We set off to my chambers and made it there in half the time it took me to get to where I was supposed to meet Amanitore. Ettu was waiting with the door cracked open. She ushered us in and barred the door behind us. Her gaze went straight to the linen package in my hand.

"What do you have there?" she asked.

I showed them the knife. Ettu understood immediately.

"So you were waiting near where Pharaoh dines when he visits, and with a dagger in your hand?" she observed.

"It's a very strange kind of favour," I said. "I can't figure out what Amanitore was thinking."

"I would guess she is in on whatever it is Lady Tiye has been plotting," Ettu said. "And my other guess is that whatever you are involved in, the plan is probably not what you think it is."

Pounding on the door interrupted whatever else she had been about to say.

"Kassaya," came Henutmire's voice. "Are you there? Quickly, open up."

She must have been leaning on the door as Ettu unbarred it, because she came tumbling into the chamber.

"Amun," she gasped. "I was so afraid I would miss you."

"What is it?" Could this day get any more dramatic?

"It is happening tonight," she said. "Not tomorrow."

"The plan changed?" I asked.

"No." Her face bore an ominous expression. "But Tiye wants you to think it's not until tomorrow."

"I don't understand."

"She intends to make it look like it is you who planned to attack Pharaoh. You and you alone. Do you understand me?"

So, this was how Tiye intended to ensure the blame didn't fall on herself. She was setting me up for it. *You are naive,* she once said to me. *That, I think, is what will be your downfall.* And that was what she counted on now: that I would be naive enough to believe I was really a part of her plan.

"She deceived me," I said.

"Yes." Henutmire seemed relieved I understood so quickly.

"While the guards are distracted at discovering you with a knife, the butler will release his snake. You will be arrested, Pharaoh will be bitten, and nobody will think it anything other than a coincidence that the two things happened together. We are all ready to leave tonight if the plan fails."

"And I would be the only one left here tomorrow. The only one to take the blame."

"You must flee," she said. "Go now, before it is too late."

"I..." What could I even say? I can't? I shouldn't? I don't know where to go? There were too many questions, too many things to consider, but it seemed there was no time for any of it.

"I'm sorry I didn't come sooner," Henutmire said. "We were all sworn to secrecy before Tiye went to Pharaoh's palace. I've spent all afternoon trying to decide whether to tell you. But you have shown yourself to be a friend to me and I had to warn you."

"Your brother," I said. "If the plan fails, what will happen to him?"

"I will get him out," she said. "It seems chaos is about to descend on us. What better time for a lone prisoner to disappear? Nobody will think to look for him until after this is all over, one way or another."

"I wish you well," I said. "You and your brother. I hope you both make it home."

She gave me a twisted little smile that looked more sad than anything else.

"You, too. You have been a true friend to me here." She darted forward and hugged me tightly. "Fare you well. I am very pleased to have met you, and I will not forget your kindnesses to me."

She cast her gaze around the chamber, nodded at my

maids, then left. The open door let us hear the rumble of approaching carts.

"Here comes Khensa," Ettu said. "Quickly, get anything you need to take with you. I have put some jewels in this bag for you." She pointed to a linen bag on a chair. "There was no time to think about what would be most suitable, so I just threw in everything I could. If there is anything else you can't bear to leave behind, you should get it now."

I looked at her, open-mouthed. She seemed to know what I wanted to ask.

"We will all go with you." Ettu's voice was determined. "That is…" She paused and looked at Merytre.

"Sutem and I will go," Merytre said. "We have already discussed it."

The carts drew to a halt at my door, then Khensa's face appeared over the top of the first.

"Are you ready?" she asked.

"Bring them in," Ettu said. "Go," she said to me.

I raced to my bedchamber. There was little I couldn't leave without, just my favourite necklace, the yellow heart-shaped gem I had had since I was a girl. The rest of the special things I brought from Babylon were long gone. My hairbrush went to Tiye to pay for information about Abar's sister. The shell my father brought back from Syria was used as an offering to Ishtar when Amanitore helped me speak with her. I gave the scarf Ishtar embroidered for me to Gautseshen for stitching Half back together. The necklace was the only thing left that mattered to me.

Inside the crate with my necklace was the little box of jewels I had taken from Ishtar's chambers. My fingers lingered on it, but I didn't know how far I would be travelling tonight, and speed would be necessary. I couldn't afford to carry anything that might slow me down. *Farewell sister*, I thought, and snatched up my necklace.

There was one other thing I needed to do. I took the little lioness from my pouch and studied her. Ineni's offering to Kia. I had carried it with me ever since I found it in the mud beside the pleasure lake. It felt like something that should stay here. A thing that belonged to this place. I set it on my dresser, turning the lioness so she looked out over the chamber. Perhaps she was a guardian of some sort. I would leave her to watch over the next inhabitant.

As I left my bedchamber for the last time, my gaze fell on the wallhanging Merytre stitched for me. The narcissus gleamed, despite the dimness in my chamber, and I snatched it from the wall. That, too, I would take. A reminder I once had a friend who cared enough to spend so much time making such a thing for me.

There was another wallhanging Merytre had made, the one of Sekhmet which still hung in her old bedchamber. That one I would leave here. Another guardian to watch over the next residents of these chambers.

I raced back out to the sitting chamber. My maids were all there, each adorned with some jewel or other from my collection. They gave me nervous smiles, but nobody spoke. Two large wheeled carts stood in the middle of the sitting chamber. Someone had pushed the couches aside to make room for them.

"Here," I said, breathlessly, holding up my necklace and the wallhanging. "This is all I need."

Merytre gave a little gasp when she saw what I had.

"Oh, my," she said and burst into tears.

"Give it to me," Ettu said. She quickly rolled up the wallhanging and tucked it into the bag of jewels.

I fastened the necklace around my neck. The pendant settled into the hollow at my throat, its familiar weight a comfort.

"Get in," Ettu said, gesturing towards the cart. "There are only two carts, so I'm afraid you and Half will have to share. Since Tall is the largest, he will go in the second cart alone."

"My babe," I said. My eyes met Khensa's.

"Ettu has already explained you need to flee with your men," she said. "As soon as we get you out of the Palace, I will send a runner to my friend so she can get your babe and be ready. Then I will take you to her. Quickly now."

"Gowns," Ettu said. "Ladies, come help me. Half, Tall, get out here."

There were gasps from various maids as the men entered the sitting chamber, but nobody asked any questions. Khensa must have prepared them for this. She had positioned one of the carts beside a couch.

"I suppose you will need to climb up on the couch and jump in," she said to me, a little doubtfully. "I don't know how else we can get you in. The sides are too high for you to climb."

"Lift!" came Tall's voice behind me. He swooped me up and put me in the cart. Half appeared beside me, also deposited by Tall.

"Please get as comfortable as you can, my lady," Khensa said. "You may be in there for a while."

Half and I hunkered down on the bare wooden floor. There wasn't really room to sit comfortably, nor to have our own space, so we huddled together. He sat on his behind with his legs pulled up to his chest. I crouched and quickly realised I wouldn't be able to stay like that for long. I managed to manoeuvre myself onto my knees with Half pressed up against my side.

Someone passed the bag of jewels down to me, followed by a linen bag that I assumed held Half's spare clothes. A second bag was probably some clothes someone had packed for me.

"Are you ready?" came Ettu's voice before an armful of gowns dropped on top of us. "Get down as low as you can. If somebody decides to paw through the gowns, we want to have plenty for them to look at without getting all the way down to you."

Half and I huddled down further. The weight on top of us increased as several more loads of gowns were added.

"Marduk be with you," came Ettu's voice.

The lid was set on top of the cart, then somebody tapped the side. The cart shifted, the wheels creaked. The women groaned with the effort of pushing it.

My head spun and I suddenly felt like I couldn't breathe. If they found us in here, we would be trapped. It would be better to run away than to sneak out like this. At least if I was running, I would see them when they came for me.

Then Half's hand found mine, and I found I was somehow able to breathe again.

CHAPTER 34

The lingering scent of perfumes and lotions filled the cart. My ladies always applied them so liberally that the smell never quite came out of the fabrics, no matter how many times the gowns were laundered. My nose already tingled from the mix of aromas.

I knew we had reached the first flight of stairs when the cart paused, then tilted on an alarming angle. I managed to catch my gasp just before it came out. Half's hand in mine tightened, and I guessed he, like me, feared we were about to go hurtling down the stairs. My spare hand clutched the bag of jewels to my chest. My nose ran, but I didn't dare move.

The cart bumped down each step, then levelled out again. We trundled along another hallway, then came the next flight of stairs. I sneezed and prayed to Marduk nobody heard it over the sound of the cart.

By the time we reached the bottom of the third flight, my legs were cramped, my stomach wobbled the way it had that first day onboard the ship, and I felt faint from lack of air.

We rolled along for a very long time, then the cart halted

and I heard a muffled conversation. I couldn't make out the words, but I recognised Panouk's voice. Time stretched interminably as I imagined what he must be asking my maids. Where were they going? What was in the carts? Why were they taking my discarded gowns out so late in the day?

Another sneeze built and I prayed to Marduk Panouk would let us move on quickly. Half squeezed my hand, although I didn't know whether it was intended as a reassurance or if he sensed something was wrong. My nose tingled, my throat closed, and I knew I couldn't hold the sneeze in for much longer.

Then it came out.

Please Marduk, let the gowns have muffled the sound. Don't let Panouk have heard.

A long pause, then the lid of the cart was raised. I could finally hear what was being said.

"I assure you," Ettu said. "I heard nothing other than the squeak of a wheel."

"They are very squeaky," Sehener added. "And I suppose one could mistake the noise for a sneeze."

Panouk made no reply, but the fabric above us shifted. Its weight lessened as someone removed the gowns. Then light and fresh air flowed in as the last one was pulled aside. Panouk studied both me and Half.

Half clutched my hand so tightly, I couldn't feel my fingers anymore. This was it. We were caught.

Panouk would check the other cart, and then he would arrest all of us, including my maids who were obviously complicit in smuggling out two men who should never have been in the Palace to start with.

My heart pounded so loudly, I surely wouldn't hear whatever Panouk said when he arrested us.

He looked at us for what seemed like a very long time. Then from somewhere out of my sight came Amankhau's voice.

"What do you have there?" he asked.

My heart felt like it would burst right through my chest. My vision went black and if I hadn't already been sitting down, I probably would have fainted. Panouk pulled the gowns back into place over us.

"Merely a load of old gowns," he said. "Apparently Lady Kassaya has decided she needs a new wardrobe and is donating her old gowns. Very charitable of her."

"Let me see," Amankhau said.

"There is no need," Panouk said. "I have already inspected the contents and I am satisfied all is in order."

"It's very unusual," Amankhau said.

"Yes, but as we have discovered, Lady Kassaya is an unusual woman," Panouk replied. "Help me put this lid back in place. Tell the gate guards I have approved your departure —" this I assumed was directed at my maids "—and that you are expected to return within two hours of sunset. And do see to it that those wheels are oiled as soon as you have made your deliveries. The noise is very disruptive."

"We will," Ettu said, sounding for possibly the first time since I met her like she was lost for words.

The lid was replaced and we were moving again. I should have trusted Panouk earlier, and I had no doubt now he had indeed intervened in Hydna and Weren's sentence.

Despite the very loud pounding of my heart, I made out a change to the surface over which we travelled. We must have left the tiles of the Palace and were now outside on the path that led to the gates. Some time later, the cart stopped.

Another muffled conversation, probably with the gate guards, and then we were off again.

When the cart next halted and the gowns on top of us were removed again, it was Khaemmalu's face which peered down at us. His hands reached for me.

My legs spasmed when I tried to move and all I could do was cry as I clung to him.

"Come now," he said. "We have to be quick. I'm sorry, but there is no time for tears. Things are happening as we speak, and we need to move fast."

He hauled me out of the cart, then turned back to help Half. Arms reached for me and I let them hold me while I tried to make my cramping legs function.

"Can you walk?" Khaemmalu asked.

"I will manage," Half said. "It is my lady who needs you, not I."

But Khaemmalu didn't come to me. Instead he went to the other cart to help Tall out. It was only then I realised the arms holding me up were Sutem and Merytre's.

"This is where we leave you, my lady," Tuya said as the others tossed the gowns back into the carts and replaced the lids. "Except for Khensa, who will take you to her friend."

I looked at each of the women who had served me for the last year since I arrived in Babylon. Other than Ettu, Merytre and Sehener, I had never taken the time to get to know any of them well, but they had risked their lives for me today.

"Mutnofret, Hemetre, Ipu, Nebetah, Tuya," I said. "And Khensa. I can't tell you how grateful I am for your help."

The women drew themselves up proudly and more than one wiped a tear from her eyes. Hemetre reached up to touch her ears, each of which was graced with a pale blue gem, and Nebetah studied the silver bracelet on her wrist.

"You do not need to thank us, my lady," Ipu said, her hand at her throat where a pendant bearing a purple gem sat. "We are in your service. Our positions require we do whatever our mistress wants of us. That is all we have done today."

"I won't forget your extraordinary kindness when I needed you," I said.

Khaemmalu finally returned to me.

"We need to move," he said. "Whatever the situation is like in Pharaoh's palace, it's only going to get worse."

"Thank you." I met the eyes of each woman for the last time, then I let Khaemmalu take my arm and lead me away.

CHAPTER 35

"I suppose they can't go back to the Palace," I said as we walked away.

"No," Khaemmalu said. "Once it is discovered that you have disappeared, anyone close to you will be questioned. They have been warned not to risk going back."

"Except for me," Khensa said. "I have no family and nowhere else to go."

"You can go anywhere you want," Ettu said. "Make a new life for yourself."

Khensa shrugged and seemed to sniffle. "This is the only life I know. I don't even know anyone who doesn't work in one of the palaces. I wouldn't know where to go if I don't go back."

"Then come with us," I said.

"My lady?" She gave me a wide-eyed look.

"We wouldn't have gotten out without you. Once we get my babe, we are leaving Egypt. I don't know where we will go, but wherever it is, you can come with us."

"Oh." She seemed momentarily lost for words, before she straightened her shoulders and looked me right in the eyes. "Yes, I will come with you."

We had only been walking for a short time when I spotted a familiar figure. She stood beside a dom palm, one hand on its trunk, and I had the wild thought that she communicated with the tree. The shawl on her head fell low over her face, hiding the scales. I didn't need to see them to know her, though, and I wasn't surprised we had encountered her as I left the Palace for the last time.

"Do you need to speak with her?" Khaemmalu asked, obviously noting my gaze on the woman.

"I will be quick," I said.

"Go on, then," he said, and he only sighed a little.

The others were silent as I approached the seer. When I stopped in front of her, I still didn't know what I would say.

"I told you to leave." Her tone was mild and if she was angry or upset I didn't take her advice, I got no sense of it. I truly couldn't tell what she thought.

"Why?" I asked.

It wasn't what I meant to say, but once it was out of my mouth, I realised it was exactly the right question.

"Because you must," she said. "You and your child both."

"Why me? Why us?"

"Because you, both of you, must live."

We eyed each other. Her face was as implacable as ever. Why had I thought she might finally tell me something I could comprehend this last time we would ever speak?

"Why is that important?" I asked.

She gave me one last look, then turned away.

"Wait," I said. "Tell me. Please. I want to understand."

But I blinked, and then she was gone.

"Come," Khaemmalu said. "We need to go."

The walk between the palaces was just as long as I remembered from the night we arrived. I had made this journey a number of times since then, but not on foot. That first night, I had been confused about why I wasn't allowed into Pharaoh's palace. I was tired from the walk from the river port, and my sandal had rubbed a patch of skin away. This time, I was afraid, rather than confused, and my body felt like it was tangled up in knots after being huddled in the cart for so long.

Khaemmalu walked beside me. When I stumbled, he was quick to grab my arm, but he released me just as fast. Every now and then, his hand briefly touched the small of my back. I supposed it was his way of letting me know he was nearby. I longed to take his hand, as Merytre had with Sutem, but it still felt too dangerous to be seen touching him. Until we knew Pharaoh was dead, he was forbidden to me.

Behind us, Sutem walked with Merytre, and Tall with Sehener. Tall seemed to limp a little, but he made no sound of complaint. Sehener was pale, her face fixed in a mask of determination.

Ettu walked beside Half, although I never saw them touch each other. There was a distance between them, and I supposed he was still hurt by the knowledge she intended to leave him.

On Ettu's other side was Khensa. Her face was thoughtful, as if she still processed her decision to join us.

We said little on the way to Pharaoh's palace. I glanced up at Khaemmalu from time to time, and his face was always so serious, it frightened me. Whatever involvement he did or didn't have with Tiye's plan, he definitely wasn't happy about what was happening. Did he know yet she meant to betray me? Tiye would be fortunate if she never saw him again.

Runners dashed past, most heading towards the Palace of the Ornaments, although two overtook us, heading to Pharaoh's palace. They ran as if their lives depended on the swift delivery of their news. Several guards thundered past in chariots, whipping the horses that pulled them. I averted my face and prayed nobody would recognise me. What had happened to cause such a number of urgent messages to be sent this afternoon?

As the palace came into view, Khaemmalu gestured for Khensa to come walk beside him.

"Where is the meeting place?" he asked.

"There is a shaded grassy spot on the west side of the grounds," she said. "It is circular and surrounded by beds of narcissus."

My babe would be surrounded by narcissus and the lion would retrieve her for me. I was hardly surprised. This was what the seer had meant for me to understand all along. It had never been about the lion taking my babe. He was supposed to rescue her from amongst the narcissus. She meant for me to know that all would be well. That when the time came, the lion would get my babe for me.

"I know where you mean," Khaemmalu said. "The rest of you wait here. I will go get the babe."

"I'm coming with you," I said.

"No." His voice was curt and he didn't even look at me. "I need to know you are safe, and I don't want to be distracted with watching over you. Let me get her and I'll be right back."

"I'll have to come," Khensa said. She looked rather pale, but her voice never wavered. "My friend won't hand the babe over to a stranger, even one who claims to have been sent by my lady."

"Very well." Khaemmalu gestured for her to keep up with him. "The others will stay here."

They strode off, with Khensa taking two steps for every one of Khaemmalu's. They were a dozen paces away when I realised I couldn't let them go without me. I hurried after them.

"Kassaya, go back." Khaemmalu must have heard me coming up behind them. He didn't even look at me.

"I'm coming with you," I said. "She is my babe and I will not let you make such a decision."

He sighed and I didn't have to see his face to know he rolled his eyes.

"Fine then," he said. "Keep up and be quiet."

He led us around the perimeter of the gardens. At one point, a guard stepped out. He and Khaemmalu spoke in low voices, before the guard continued on his rounds.

"What did he say?" I asked.

Khaemmalu gave a brief shake of his head. "Nothing we need be concerned about right now."

"Tell me," I said.

"Not now," he replied. "We need to focus on locating your babe and then getting both of you away from here. Be quiet and let me do my job."

I couldn't see how it would have hurt for him to tell us what the guard said as we walked, but he was not in a mood to tolerate being argued with. He was right, anyway. Our priority was getting Baby Ishtar.

Khaemmalu paused behind a tree and peered between its branches. I leaned out to peek around the trunk and he shoved me back behind him. I glimpsed no more than a swathe of grass bordered by narcissus.

"That's the meeting place?" he asked Khensa.

She nodded.

"The babe will start crying and my friend will take her away from the others to settle her," she said.

She had barely finished before a babe squealed, then burst into noisy sobs.

"Is that her?" I whispered. "Why is she crying like that? Is she in pain?"

"Hush," Khaemmalu said. "The maid with the crying babe is walking away. Is that your friend?"

Khensa peered through a gap and nodded.

"If we circle around behind these bushes, we will meet her on the other side of the clearing," Khaemmalu said, already in motion.

Khensa and I hurried after him.

We came face-to-face with the young woman as she slipped between the bushes.

"It's you," I said with a gasp.

She met my gaze and nodded. "It's me."

"I remember you. I saw you at the parade for Min."

"Yes," she said. "You rode past in your palanquin and met my gaze. I couldn't believe such a fine lady would bother to look at me."

"You had a bruise around your eye," I said. "And a newborn in your arms."

"My babe went to the West only a few days later, and my husband would have sent me with her if he could." She looked fondly down at the babe in her arms. My babe. She had stopped crying now and seemed content to be held. "Your daughter is a treasure. She reminds me much of my own, but I'm very pleased she is going back to her mother where she should have been all along."

She held my babe out to me and I took Ishtar with shaking hands. What if I dropped her? What if she started crying again?

"How did you stop her cries?" I knew nothing about my own babe. I felt so inadequate compared to this woman who held her so competently.

"I'm sorry about that," she said. "I jabbed her with a pin. I needed a reason to take her away from the others and she doesn't usually cry. I hope you don't think me a terrible person, but it was the only way I could ensure she would make enough noise to justify leaving."

"That was very clever," I said. "I'm sure I wouldn't have thought of such a thing."

"Thank you for the earrings," she said. "I keep them in my pouch. My husband doesn't know about them. I thought that maybe one day…" Her voice trailed away.

"One day you might finally leave him?" Khensa asked.

The woman nodded.

"Why can't that day be today?" I asked.

She gave me a startled look. "My lady?"

"We are leaving Thebes right now," I said. "Come with us."

"Yes, come," Khensa said.

"You're going too?" her friend asked.

"My lady asked me to go with her." Khensa's voice was proud. "And I thought, why not? I'm going to sail across the seas and have an adventure. Come with me."

The two women looked each other in the eyes for a long moment.

"The babe still needs a wet nurse," Khensa said.

I hadn't even considered how I would feed her. My milk was long dried up.

"Come with us," I said. "For my babe's sake, if you won't do it for your own."

Khensa reached for her friend's hand and squeezed it.

"I will come," her friend said.

Khaemmalu gave the tiniest sigh.

"We should keep moving," he said. "Things are about to get bad here."

CHAPTER 36

*B*aby Ishtar made not a sound as we hurried back to the others. I had no time to marvel at how she was finally in my arms as I concentrated on keeping up with Khaemmalu without either dropping her or falling on my face. Just as we reached the place where we entered the gardens, the hooting call of a bird brought Khaemmalu to a halt.

"Wait," he said. "That's Bebi's signal. Look casual."

We all stopped and tried to appear as if we merely paused to rest. I gazed down at the babe in my arms. She looked back up at me, her eyes serious and far too knowing.

"She likes to be jiggled," Khensa's friend said, somewhat hesitantly. "Just bounce her a little. Yes, like that."

I bobbed the babe up and down. She continued to eye me seriously, but then she gave me the tiniest smile.

"Oh," I said. "She smiled at me."

"She smiles a lot," Khensa's friend said. "She is one of the happiest babes I've ever looked after."

"I don't even know your name."

"Minefer," she replied. "And if there is anything else I can do for Ishtar, or for you, my lady, you only have to say it."

"They called her Ishtar?" I wasn't sure they would let her have the name I gave her.

"No, my lady," Minefer said. "They gave her a different name, but Khensa said that was what you named her."

I didn't bother to ask what they had called her. It didn't matter. Nobody would ever call her by that name again.

"You should call me Kassaya." I couldn't make myself look away from my babe while I spoke. "I'm hardly a lady any more, and I'd appreciate any advice you can give me. I know nothing about looking after her."

"It would be my pleasure to help you," Minefer said.

Bebi slipped out from the depths of some shrubbery. His gaze darted around as he approached us, studying our surroundings. He and Khaemmalu gave each other a nod of greeting.

"It's done," Bebi said. "The hawk has gone to the West."

"He is dead?" I asked over the gasps of Khensa and Minefer.

"I saw his body with my own eyes," Bebi said. "There can be no doubt."

"How did it happen?" I asked.

He gave me a guarded look. "Are you sure you want to know? It is quite gruesome."

"I was there when they talked about how to do it," I said. "I already know the possibilities."

"A blade," Bebi said, rather briefly. "Across the throat."

It was only then I noticed the blood splatters on his tunic. I tried to picture the scene. Bebi sneaking up behind Pharaoh, perhaps as he ate or drank or fondled some unwilling maid. His arm slipping around Pharaoh's neck as he drew the dagger across his throat. Blood spurting, Pharaoh crying out, then slumping to the ground.

"That wasn't the plan," Khaemmalu said.

"Pentaweret," Bebi replied with a shrug that implied it explained everything.

"He took a blade to Pharaoh?" Khaemmalu's voice was incredulous. "What a fool. He only had to wait another few hours."

"I don't know why he acted," Bebi said. "But he suddenly charged at Pharaoh. His aim was off, though. I had to finish the job while the rest of the squad managed Pentaweret. He knew he'd made a mistake and he fought them hard."

"Nobody saw you?" Khaemmalu asked.

Bebi shook his head. "There was too much chaos, and given they already saw Pentaweret with his blade to Pharaoh's throat, I doubt anyone will question whether I might have aided the hawk's departure. I made a show of checking on Pharaoh and crying out that he had gone to the West. Nobody would wonder why I had his blood on me after that."

"Regardless, you shouldn't be here," Khaemmalu said. "If Pentaweret says he didn't make the killing strike, they will look to you."

"I knew you would come," Bebi said, glancing at Baby Ishtar. "I couldn't leave without warning you. They will be out for blood after this. Pentaweret is talking and there have already been a number of arrests. Some of them women you know, my lady," he said with a nod at me. "The ladies Tiye, Ineni, Neferu and Gilukhipa. Some of their maids also. They are charged with treason and conspiracy to murder."

"Lady Tiye will try to strike a deal," Khaemmalu said. "She will give us all up to save herself. You can't afford to be here when they come looking for you."

"At least Pentaweret never knew of my involvement," Bebe said. "He would have already given them my name."

"What about Henutmire?" I asked.

I could barely get the words out. That could have been me. If Henutmire hadn't come to warn me, I would have been arrested with them.

"She is with her brother," Bebi said. "A friend is helping them. They should be almost out of the city by now."

"And the maids?" I asked. "Do you know who?"

Bebi rattled off several names. There was only one I recognised: Nammu. So, Tiye must have involved her in the plan. She once told me a maid like Nammu might be useful. As much as I could take no joy in knowing the women who had been arrested would likely be executed, I found a grim satisfaction that Nammu would finally face punishment, even if it wasn't for what she had done to me.

"Your disappearance disrupted their plans," Bebi said to me. "They intended for Pharaoh to dine tonight at the Palace of the Ornaments where a snake would be set on him."

"Or at least that was the plan as we understood it." Khaemmalu's tone was grim as he and Bebi exchanged looks. "It was Bebi who discovered they intended for you to be found waiting for Pharaoh with a blade. The snake was to be released in the chaos of your arrest."

"When they realised you weren't where they expected you to be, Lady Tiye and the others tried to flee," Bebi continued. "Maybe they thought you would turn on them and expose their plan. The gate guards wouldn't let them out, though, since they had no authorisation from Panouk. Then, of course, the first runner arrived with word of an attack on Pharaoh, and Panouk detained them. When more messages arrived about Pentaweret taking a blade to Pharaoh, Panouk had the women arrested. He must have realised they were involved as soon as it became clear Lady Tiye's son was part of it."

And yet Panouk let me leave. There was a point where I wondered whether he might have been involved in Tiye's plan, but perhaps not. Perhaps he was just an honourable man trying to do the best he could.

"I would have still been there if Henutmire hadn't warned me," I said.

"She is an admirable woman," Bebi said with what might have been a wistful smile. "If things had been different... Well, there's no point thinking like that now."

Khaemmalu clapped him on the back.

"I know you intended to stay, but come with us," he said. "You're a dead man here. It won't be long before the whole story comes out. Those women will willingly name anyone they must to save themselves."

Bebi gave a decided nod. "There is nothing left for me here, other than the certainty of execution. I believed in the cause, but it's over."

"Let's go, then," Khaemmalu said. "We need to be out of the city before anyone comes looking. There is a boat waiting for us at the port."

Most of the rest of our party had sat down while they waited for us, but they got up when they saw us coming. Although they must have been curious about Minefer and Bebi, nobody asked who the strangers were.

"Oh," Half said as we set off. He pointed to a boy of about twelve years who hurried past. "That's the runner who helped me when I came to search for evidence about Lady Ishtar."

"The one who brought you food and information?" Ettu asked.

"I promised him a reward." Half looked to me. "My lady…"

"Of course," I said. "Where are the jewels?"

I had a bag of them in the cart, but someone must have taken it from me as I got out.

"I have some." Ettu was already reaching into her bag. She withdrew a magnificent gold necklace. "This?" she asked me.

I shrugged and she handed it to Half. He hurried after the boy and I could feel the way Khaemmalu reigned in his frustration at the delay. It would only be a few moments and it would be worth it for the boy to receive his reward.

We watched as Half caught up to the boy and gave him the necklace. Their conversation was brief. As Half hurried back to us, the boy just stood there, the necklace dangling from his fingers and tears streaming down his face.

"Come on, then." Khaemmalu's voice was terse. "We have dallied too long."

But before we could move, a strident voice called for us to halt. A man strode towards us, his gaze locked on Half and his face already turning red with fury.

"Oh no," Half breathed.

CHAPTER 37

Khaemmalu stepped forward to stop the man before he reached Half. From the corner of my eye, I saw how Tall edged in front of Half, shielding the little man with his own body.

"Userhet," Khaemmalu said amicably. "I have not seen you for some months."

"You." Userhet stabbed his finger in Half's direction as he tried to push past Khaemmalu. "You're supposed to be dead."

"As you can see," Half said, "I am not."

"I knifed you in the belly," Userhet said. "Your guts should have been on the floor."

"What can I tell you?" Half asked. "I am very much alive."

Userhet let out a cry and reached for the dagger which poked from the waistband of his *shendyt*. Khaemmalu and Bebi both moved before he even had time to touch it.

"Walk away, man," Bebi said, his hand on Userhet's arm. "It's not worth it. You won't see him again."

"He knows too much," Userhet said. "He is supposed to be in the West."

"What does it matter anymore?" Half asked with a nonchalant nod as if he had not the slightest fear of Userhet. I supposed he didn't need to be afraid this time, not with Khaemmalu and Bebi and Tall here to protect him. "He's dead now. There will be no more bodies to be removed for him."

"That is irrelevant," Userhet yelled as he tried to pull himself from Bebi's grasp. "I never fail, ever, and I will finish the job."

"Not today you won't," Khaemmalu said.

Userhet spat at the ground, then lunged forward. Khaemmalu and Bebi moved so fast, I never saw whose blade it was that went into his belly. He cried out and they released him as he slumped to the ground. Khaemmalu and Bebi shared a look, but neither commented.

"Let's go," was all Khaemmalu said.

As we hurried away, he stopped to wipe his blade on the grass. He kept the dagger in his hand after that.

Khaemmalu went in front of us and Bebi followed behind. I walked beside Minefer, and spent almost as much time looking at Baby Ishtar's precious face as I did watching where I put my feet.

By the time we reached the Great River, my breath came in gasps and my legs wobbled. We had walked a long way and Ishtar was much heavier than I expected. The boat waiting at the dock was a flat-bottomed vessel with a single mast, like we had sailed to Thebes on. A familiar figure was already on board, a babe in her arms, and a man I didn't recognise beside her.

"Gautseshen." Merytre greeted Khaemmalu's sister with a hug. "I'm so pleased you changed your mind."

"The plan has gone awry," the stranger said. Gautseshen's husband, I assumed. "Arrests are already being made. We decided not to wait to learn whether we would be incriminated."

Bebi untied the rope securing the boat to the dock and the others started boarding. Khaemmalu offered me his hand and I had just taken it when someone sidled up beside me. Khaemmalu shoved me behind himself.

"At ease," said a voice with a familiar accent. "I mean her no harm. I bear a message from her father."

I peered around Khaemmalu to find myself face-to-face with a man of Babylonian appearance. After being surrounded by Egyptian men for so long, he looked like a foreigner, with his dark hair and neatly trimmed beard. He wore a tunic in the Babylonian fashion, its bright blue almost absurd amongst so many white *shendyts*. His face was vaguely familiar. One of my father's attendants at court, perhaps. He certainly recognised me even if I couldn't place him.

"Princess," he said. "I bring a message from your father, the great and mighty Marduk-apla-iddina."

"Go on," I said, trying to hide my surprise.

"Your father sends his sincere regrets at the news of your sister Ishtar's demise. He greatly regrets the circumstances that led to both his daughters being sent so far from home, and he desires you to know that should you ever want to return, you are welcome."

"What about the alliance?" I asked. "If I go back to Babylon, the alliance will be broken."

"Your father's exact words on that subject were Marduk damn Pharaoh," the messenger said.

Stunned, I couldn't think of a reply. Tears filled my eyes, and with the babe in my arms, I had no spare hand with which to wipe them. Baby Ishtar gave a little gurgle as a tear landed on her face.

"I see you have been delivered of your child," the messenger said.

"I did send word to my father."

"It would have been after I left. I have been here several weeks, waiting for a chance to speak with you."

"Why didn't you send a message to the Palace?" I asked.

"Your father believed such a message wouldn't get to you," he said. "He instructed me to wait until such time as I could deliver his message in person, no matter how long it took. He was very precise about it. I was under no circumstances to trust his words to someone else."

My father loved me. He put more importance on me than on the alliance. For a few moments, all I could do was sob. Minefer's gentle hands took Ishtar from me, allowing me to wipe my eyes. I turned to my companions who watched us curiously. Of course, most of them wouldn't have understood our conversation, conducted as it was in Babylonian.

"It seems we have a destination," I said. "How do you all feel about Babylon?"

Half gave a hooting cheer, Tall clapped his hands, and everyone else smiled and laughed. Khaemmalu invited my father's messenger to travel with us and the man agreed without hesitation. I supposed he, like me, must be pleased at knowing he now travelled towards home.

We crowded onto the boat and Gautseshen's husband, who it seemed would be our captain, pushed the vessel away from the dock, then took up an oar. Khaemmalu and Bebi grabbed the other oars, and Ettu reached for the last one. After a brief tussle between her and Tall, she relinquished it to him, although she didn't look happy about it. The men rowed us out into the middle of the river where the boat caught the current and shot off.

As we sailed past Thebes, evidence of the revolt was everywhere. Men armed with bows and spears, swords, and even farming implements. Buildings burned, leaving the air thick with smoke and ash. Women and children loaded with linen bundles hurried through the streets. Men herded their families into boats and the river grew crowded.

"Is that Lady Hilde?" Ettu asked, shading her hand as she looked into the setting sun.

On a boat not far ahead of us, I recognised Hilde's profile. Beside her was her cousin who had come to Egypt as her lady's maid. So, either someone had warned Hilde, or her father had sent for her after all. It pleased me to know she had gotten out safely.

Then we were past the city. Our surroundings became lush riverbanks, cows grazing peacefully, water fowls, and even a family of brown ducks. I settled myself on the bare wooden deck, my babe in my lap, and thought I had never been happier. Khaemmalu came to sit beside me. When he draped his arm over my shoulders, I stiffened and he leaned over to murmur into my ear.

"Relax," he said. "We don't have to worry anymore. There is nobody left alive who cares whether we are together."

He was right. Pharaoh was dead, so it mattered not whether anyone saw us. I let myself lean against him and rested my head on his shoulder. Baby Ishtar gurgled and reached one tiny hand towards him. He offered her his finger and she grabbed hold of it. I glanced up in time to see the look of wonder on his face.

"You told me that one day, whoever was responsible for the women who disappeared would take the wrong one." Khaemmalu's voice was low, intended for my ears alone. "You were right. Lady Ishtar was the wrong woman. You wouldn't have gotten involved if it wasn't for her."

The same could be said for him. Would he have aided Tiye's plot if it wasn't for Tabiry?

"Nothing went the way I expected." I hadn't yet fully comprehended Tiye's betrayal. There would be time for that later. "I'm not sure I was of any help in the end."

"Whether the plan went the way we intended or not is irrelevant. He will never harm another woman again. That is the only thing that is important."

Ettu had said the plan probably wasn't what I thought it was, and she was right. I may not have played the part they intended for me, but it was done. The hawk had gone to the West, as Bebi said. Pentaweret would never be Pharaoh, and Tiye would never be queen, but perhaps Ramses would be a better pharaoh than his father.

Around us, all my companions had found places to sit. Ettu and Half, still with a distance between them, although the way he looked at her told me he hadn't yet given up hope. Tall and Sehener. Merytre and Sutem. Khensa, Bebi, Minefer, and Gautseshen.

It was well over a year since I left Babylon. I never expected to return there again, and yet here I was, on my way home and bringing with me folk who had proved themselves to be my friends.

You wish to be a queen, the narcissus had said in one of my dreams. *This place has corrupted you. You seek power and glory, but it will be your ruin.* They were wrong, though. I only ever sought power in order to remove Pharaoh from the throne. I never wanted either power or glory for myself. If that dream was from the seer, she was wrong about that much.

I might have been only the youngest daughter, and not expected to amount to anything, but I had helped change this place for the better. The Palace would be a safer place for the women who came after me. And that was far more important than power or glory.

ALSO BY KYLIE QUILLINAN

The Amarna Age Series

Book One: *Queen of Egypt*

Book Two: *Son of the Hittites*

Book Three: *Eye of Horus*

Book Four: *Gates of Anubis*

Book Five: *Lady of the Two Lands*

Book Six: *Guardian of the Underworld*

The Amarna Princesses Series

Book One: *Outcast*

Book Two: *Catalyst*

Book Three: *Warrior*

Palace of the Ornaments Series

Book One: *Princess of Babylon*

Book Two: *Ornament of Pharaoh*

Book Three: *Child of the Alliance*

Book Four: *A Game of Senet*

Book Five: *Secrets of Pharaoh*

Book Six: *Hawk of the West*

See kyliequillinan.com for more books, including exclusive
collections, and newsletter sign up.

ABOUT THE AUTHOR

Kylie writes about women who defy society's expectations. Her novels are for readers who like fantasy with a basis in history or mythology. Her interests include Dr Who, jellyfish and cocktails. She needs to get fit before the zombies come.

Swan – the epilogue to the Tales of Silver Downs series – is available exclusively to her newsletter subscribers. Sign up at kyliequillinan.com.